Praise for Susan Meissner's novels
viewers everywhere...

Why the Sky Is Blue

Tracy Farnsworth, reviewer for roundtablereviews.com, says, "Bring out the Kleenex—you are certain to need them....an impressive debut and one that leaves me hungry for more."

A book group leader in Tennessee reports, "It was one of [our] favorites out of all the books we have read...We discussed the characters in depth, and how you made them so real. One woman said you had a gift for allowing the reader to identify with each one, rather than with just one or two. A few shared how they had cried as certain parts of your story touched their hearts in various personal ways...We are a diverse group of readers with quite a range in ages and in tastes. Only a few books have been as well received by this bunch as *Why the Sky Is Blue.*"

Roxanne Henke, author of *After Anne, Becoming Olivia*, and *Always, Jan* says, "*Why the Sky Is Blue* was so real it broke my heart, then, somehow, mended it. I loved this book!"

A Minnesotan says, "Wow! What a brutally honest, beautifully expressed, compelling book! I simply could not put it down. I will definitely recommend it to many, since I work in my local public library. This book is so personal that I thought I was reading a diary or personal letter."

Jill Elizabeth Nelson, Romantictimes.com reviewer, says, "Meissner crafts a gripping novel of lives torn apart by tragedy but healed by the light of sacrificial love."

A Window to the World

A high-school teacher in Minnesota writes, "I just finished *A Window to the World*—it was amazing! I could hardly put it down and snuck it to school to finish the last couple chapters because I just couldn't wait...There is so much in this novel! You really made each character come to life and filled the events with meaning at every turn...Thank you for writing one of the most entertaining and thought-provoking books I have ever read."

A teenager in cyberspace says, "I am only fourteen years old but I bought your book, and I couldn't put it down...I just wanted to tell you that your book doesn't only have an impact on grown-ups but also on teens. It really made me understand how bad things that happen to us are also a way God is shaping us, even though we may not realize it till later."

Sara Mills, reviewer at www.christianfictionreviewer.com, says, "POWERFUL. I can sum this book in a single word...When I finished the last page, all I could think was, WOW. The book was beautiful...The threads of happiness and joy blend with the threads of sorrow to make something that is stronger than either could be alone...I highly recommend this book, and applaud Susan Meissner for writing so eloquently what is almost impossible to put into words."

The Remedy for Regret

Kelli Standish, reviewer at focusonfiction.net, comments, "This timeless story, and Susan Meissner's lilting, lyrical prose, entranced me from the first page... The plot moves well, and climaxes with a scene that is so powerful and laden with such an unmistakable sense of the Divine it had me in tears. And the message of the story is so poignant and gentle, you feel as though you've been hugged. Bottom line? Meissner's incredible gift with words has never shone truer than in *Remedy for Regret*, and this book is a must for any discerning reader's library."

Marilyn in Iowa declares, "You did it again! I have read all three of your books—just finished *The Remedy for Regret* and love it! Can't wait for number four!!

In All Deep Places

Susan Meissner

HARVEST HOUSE PUBLISHERS

EUGENE, OREGON

Cover by Left Coast Design, Portland, Oregon

Cover photos © Peter Dazeley/The Image Bank/Getty Images; Steve Cole/Photodisc Green/Getty Images; Lloyd Ziff/Nonstock Photography/Veer

IN ALL DEEP PLACES
Copyright © 2006 by Susan Meissner
Published by Harvest House Publishers
Eugene, Oregon 97402
www.harvesthousepublishers.com

Library of Congress Cataloging-in-Publication Data
Meissner, Susan, 1961–
 In all deep places / Susan Meissner
  p. cm.
 ISBN-13: 978-0-7369-1665-3 (pbk.)
 ISBN-10: 0-7369-1665-2 (pbk.)
 1. Detective and mystery stories—Authorship—Fiction.   2. Newspaper publishing—
Fiction.   3. Fathers and sons—Fiction.   4. First loves—Fiction.   5. Iowa—Fiction.   I. Title.
 PS3613.E435I5   2006
 813'.6—dc22

                                                          2005018227

Printed in the United States of America

06 07 08 09 10 11 12 /BC-CF/ 10 9 8 7 6 5 4 3 2 1

For Bob,
who would follow me to the deep
and back again if love required it

Special thanks to...

Rand Kuhl
encourager, educator, endearing egghead

Judy Horning
parent, pal, proficient proofreader

Mary Cross Horning
grandmother, gentle guide, good to me

Linda Emmert, Tanya Siebert,
and Marlene Emmert
fantastic, fabulous forever friends

Nick Harrison, Kimberly Shumate, and
Carolyn McCready
expert, exceptional, enabling editors

God
coach, counselor, compassionate companion

"Earth, I think, will not be found by anyone to be in the end a very distinct place. I think earth, if chosen instead of Heaven, will turn out to have been, all along, only a region in Hell: and earth, if put second to Heaven, to have been from the beginning a part of Heaven itself."

C.S. LEWIS
The Great Divorce

"Whatever the LORD pleases He does—in heaven and in earth, in the seas and in all deep places."

PSALM 135:6

PART 1

1

The young woman in green, silent and attentive, nevertheless spoiled Luke Foxbourne's favorite speech as surely as if she had climbed atop the table where she sat and shouted the Gettysburg Address. Though she barely moved any part of her body and made no sound, she was Luke's sole distraction all the same. He stammered through his folksy lecture entitled "Finding Your Writing Voice" like someone with a sudden case of stage fright, though he had given the speech to countless other audiences flawlessly. It wasn't the dimmed lights, the clinking of dessert forks on china plates, or the occasional, obligatory cough from somewhere in the back of the ballroom that shattered his concentration. Every badly timed pause in his delivery was caused by the sight of the young woman seated off to his left, and he knew it.

Luke's eyes were drawn to her as if she were the only person there, though the dining room was filled to capacity. The elegantly attired, assembled members of the New England Mystery Writers Association seemed to collectively pity him as he stood there at the podium, alternately prefacing every other sentence with "um" or "ah." His colleagues—some known to him and some not—blinked and nodded, leaning forward in their chairs as if this would aid him: him, the award-winning murder-mystery writer who surely must seem to have been stricken with sudden short-term memory loss.

But Luke could not help it. The woman looked just like he imagined his character Eden Damaris looked, right down to the shape of her long, graceful fingers and the soft gray hue of her eyes. It was startling, to say the least, how much the young woman resembled the lady who lived only in his mind. The only apparent difference was that the woman in the green dress was most certainly not deaf.

She leaned forward on an elbow and rested her left cheek in her hand. Her slender fingers were slightly curled as if in frozen caress, and her neck was delicately bent as she gave the weight of her head fully to her upheld arm. She seemed quite at ease; she gave him her full attention, turning her head only once during his bumpy oratory to listen to a whispered comment from the gentleman who sat next to her. Luke wondered as he fumbled if she was the writer or the guest. Had the man brought her to the annual banquet or was it the other way around? Was she the wife, girlfriend, or mistress of the man who leaned toward her and spoke into her ear? Was he saying something like, "Can you believe this guy has actually been on the *New York Times* bestseller list?" Or, "Thanks for coming tonight, darling. I know how boring this must be for you." Or, "Promise me when you get rich and famous you won't forget how to talk to people."

Luke forced his eyes away and sought the familiar, comfortable image of his wife, Téa, seated at a table just below the podium. She was leaning forward, too, on both elbows, her arms making a triangle over her nearly finished slice of chocolate cherry cheesecake. His own chair was next to hers—his napkin over the back of it—as was his untouched dessert. He had planned on eating it after he gave his speech. "Don't let the waiter take it," he had whispered to Téa twenty minutes earlier when he had stood to resounding applause. "Or my coffee cup." He wasn't sure now he would want to eat it after all.

Téa's eyes met his, sought his. She cocked her head and smiled at him. Her eyes said, "You're doing great, honey." He grinned in spite of himself at the absurdity of such a kind, silent—and clearly fallacious—message. And remarkably, grinning seemed to improve his overall delivery, at least the last five minutes of it.

With effort, Luke kept his eyes off the woman in the green dress, staring instead at his notes, then at the clock at the back of the room, and then at the line of waiters waiting for their cue to retrieve the dessert plates. He felt the end of his speech coming and he relished it, finishing his remarks with the Françoise Sagan quote—"I shall live bad if I do not write and I shall write bad if I do not live"—that he had always thought made for a nice close. As the people in the room began to politely clap their hands, he murmured his thanks and grabbed his single page of notes. He willingly stole one last look at the woman in green. He wasn't sure if he would ever see her again, and that thought oddly unnerved him.

Taking one last glance he was aware of a ridiculous urge to run up to her and say, "Eden! What on *earth* are we going to do about Bowles?" He looked away again, quickly, forcefully, eyeing the steps that led off the stage. He silently scolded himself as he made his way to them. *That woman is not Eden Damaris. Eden Damaris does not exist! Eden Damaris is a fictional deaf character employed by a fictional detective agency who lives in a fictional brownstone in New York with other fictional employees of the fictional Red Herring Detective Agency. Murder suspect Randolph Bowles is fictional too, for that matter!*

Then, in the midst of his silent reprimand, while he descended the three stairs to the ballroom floor, Luke had a revelation. It suddenly made sense why seeing this woman had unsettled him so. She was simply a vivid reminder he had hit a wall. Seeing the very personification of Eden Damaris had awkwardly reminded him of the one thing he daily tried to minimize: He was desperately behind schedule with his new book. The July 1 deadline loomed in front of him like an invitation to oral surgery without anesthesia.

It was late May. He was stuck squarely in chapter ten—the halfway mark—and had been for three weeks. That was surely the reason.

He took his chair next to Téa, who rewarded him—to his chagrin—with a motherly smile full of I'm-so-proud-of-you sentiment. The president of the association reappeared at the podium and began to thank Mr. Luke Foxbourne for his inspirational and timely message. Luke pushed his dessert plate away.

The president's closing comments fell about him unheard as he folded the page of notes and slipped it into Téa's purse, on the floor in between their chairs.

"It's really yummy," Téa whispered to him, motioning with her head to the slice of cheesecake resting atop an elaborate drizzle of dark chocolate.

Luke shrugged. "Guess I'm not hungry for it after all," he whispered back.

More applause followed as the president wished everyone a safe journey home as well as a year of unmatched creativity and success. The applause died away and was replaced with dozens of conversations as people rose from their chairs and began to chat with those near them.

The other officers of the association, who had shared the dinner table with Luke and Téa, rose, too, and began to thank him for speaking.

"It was my pleasure," he lied. Well, actually, accepting the invitation to speak at the banquet had been pleasurable. Practicing his favorite speech the past week had been pleasurable. The lamb in mint sauce had been pleasurable. The first few seconds of delivering his favorite speech had been pleasurable. Then he had seen the alarming apparition and pleasure had gone out the window.

Time to go.

"It was very kind of you to ask me," Luke said to a board member of the association as he reached for Téa's arm. It was the move of a man about to escort his date to the door, to the car, to home.

"Lovely to see you again, Téa!" one of the wives was saying.

"Yes, it was. Hope to see you again soon!" Téa replied even as Luke began to propel her away.

"You have another pressing engagement?" she said under her breath, but maintaining a smile as she placed the strap of her purse over her shoulder.

"I just want to go home," he replied, smiling also and moving her forward.

But Luke was stopped every few seconds as they made their way to the doors by fans, well-wishers, and hopeful agents who handed him their business cards.

He spent several minutes in polite but strained conversations, answering questions, accepting praise, and offering advice.

Then he was aware that the image of Eden Damaris was just a few yards away. He had caught a glimmer of green as he listened to the woes of the unpublished man in front of him. He looked toward the flash of emerald and there she was, in conversation just like he was—but she was laughing and enjoying herself. She was explaining or describing something to the little cluster of people she was near, and her hands were a part of her story as they moved to the beat of her voice. He could not hear what she was saying but he was transfixed nonetheless. Those hands he knew so well mesmerized him: They were the same hands Eden Damaris used to give meaning to her thoughts. Those were the hands Eden used to speak to the other characters in his books. The ones she used to speak to him.

"I said, do you think I should send a registered letter telling them I'm withdrawing my manuscript?" the man was saying.

Téa nudged him. Apparently the man had asked this once already.

"Yes...yes, by all means," Luke said. "Six months is a long time to wait. If they were really interested I think you would have at least had some kind of response."

"Well, that's what I'm thinking. You know, they haven't answered one e-mail from me since that first one. Not one."

"Yeah," Luke said, trying to pull his eyes away from the ballet of hands. A man stepped in front of the woman in green, obscuring his vision, making it easier. "Not a good sign. I think I would look for another agent."

"Well, I think I just might. You know, I'm not getting any younger."

"Nice to have chatted with you," Luke said absently, wanting more than ever to get home. He started to move away.

"Good luck to you," Téa said to the man as she followed, and Luke winced. That was usually his line. He knew what it was like to *feel* like a writer, to have already written a complete manuscript and be unable to find anyone in the industry willing to read it. He had told Téa once he would always give whatever encouragement he could to undiscovered writers.

Definitely time to go.

Luke wove his way through the crowd, avoiding eye contact, especially with people he knew. He and Téa emerged from the ballroom, and he led her down the carpeted steps to the hotel's glistening lobby. He walked over to the valet parking counter and handed the man his receipt.

"Let's wait outside for the car," he said to Téa as he walked back to her. She took her shawl off her arm and draped it across her shoulders, saying nothing.

They stepped outside. The late May sunshine had given way to a warm, starry night with only a slight chill in the air. Luke wrapped his arm around Téa's waist as they waited, and he felt her snuggle into his one-armed embrace.

At least I've managed to do one thing right tonight, he thought, grateful he had suddenly considered Téa might be cold standing there next to him.

The silver Jaguar he had bought three years ago—when he finally came to terms with being a rich man—appeared at the curb, and a smiling young driver hopped out, beaming like he had the best job in the world.

"Thanks," Luke said, handing the young man a ten-dollar bill and then helping his wife get in. He walked quickly over to the driver's side and slid in.

Neither one said anything as he negotiated the heavy downtown Boston traffic. When they were at cruising speed on the freeway, headed home toward Connecticut, Téa spoke.

"So, you want to tell me what's bothering you?"

Luke thought for a moment. Did he? He wasn't entirely sure he knew. He decided he would just mention the result, not the cause.

"That was the lousiest speech I have ever given," he said.

"It wasn't that bad," Téa said, laughing just a little.

"It was still the lousiest speech I've ever given. You know it was."

She slid her hand over to his knee and rubbed it gently. "Maybe you're just getting bored with that one. Maybe it's time to come up with something new."

"People like that one," Luke replied, not really knowing why he was defending his speech. It almost seemed like he was lying to her. Keeping something from her.

"Yes, they do, but maybe *you* don't like it anymore. Maybe you need a fresh topic to work with."

Luke sighed and reached down to hold his wife's hand as it rested on his knee. He had given Eden Damaris his wife's hands. They were delicate, small-boned, and artistically beautiful. They were the first thing he had noticed about Téa when he saw her playing the violin at his college roommate's wedding reception at Cape Cod nine years ago. He was not dating anyone at the time and had instead been engrossed in the wonder of having the first book published in his Red Herring Detective Agency series. Téa had been sitting in a half-circle of unbelievable talent; one-fifth of a string quintet all dressed in black velvet. It was her instrument that seemed to sing above all the others. She had told him later that it was because she had the melody line. But he never did think that was the reason. Luke didn't know enough about classical music then to know what tunes the quintet was playing. He only knew he was fascinated by the golden-haired violinist with the amazing hands, because everything she played seemed to be the music of heaven itself. He hovered nearby, waiting for the musicians to take a break, waiting to speak to her. Within minutes of introducing himself he found himself asking her for a date.

She was hesitant to accept an invitation to dinner, first telling him she was too busy and then making it seem like her responsibilities with the Boston Philharmonic were too difficult to work around. But Luke had persisted, and he'd taken her to dinner the next week and the week after that and the week after that. By autumn, they were seeing each other exclusively, and his first book, *Slight Imperfections,* had found a place on the *New York Times* bestseller list. Six months later, on a breezy day in June 1997, they married and set up housekeeping in an apartment just outside of Boston. After the release of his second book, which hit the *Times* bestseller list in its fourth week, they bought a fashionable townhouse. A year later, when the third one hit the list in its first week, Luke and Téa moved with their then infant daughter, Noelle, to a beautifully restored manor home in rural Connecticut. Téa began giving violin lessons to keep her fingers limber and to have something to do, but Luke's royalties soon elevated them to a financial state neither one had dreamed possible. Then a year after Noelle was born, Téa gave birth to another daughter, Marissa.

Book four, published last year, earned him the celebrated title of Mystery Writer of the Year and his first contract for screenplay rights. It was book five that awaited him, unfinished, at home.

He'd never stumbled onto a writer's block before and was daily surprised that he was masterfully unskilled at how to maneuver past it. Or jackhammer his way through it. Or scale it with grace. His characters had always driven the story, not him. They controlled it. It was a quirky arrangement with his characters he had never been able to adequately explain at writer's conferences and workshops. Aaron Spaulding, the afflicted owner of the Red Herring Detective Agency and also the main character, usually directed the plot, "telling" Luke where to go with the story, followed by Eden, both speaking to him without words. He usually wrote as the ideas flowed out of the characters' encounters with each other. He had always felt like a spectator, narrating the actions as they took place. He had always been comfortable not knowing how the story was going to end until he got there, because his characters always came through for him.

But those imaginary people had seemed to fall silent three weeks ago for no apparent reason. It had been wildly frustrating. He now inwardly smirked at the thought of Eden Damaris, the deaf woman who does not speak, falling silent.

Eden actually wasn't a character in his first novel, though she'd appeared in every one after that. Luke rewrote much of *Dinner with Enemies,* his second book, just after his honeymoon and only weeks before deadline, after his editor told him his fictional agency needed a strong female character. He fashioned Eden to have Téa's beautiful hands, but the resemblance stopped there. The rest of Eden's persona—though he had never confessed this to his wife— was crafted from the enigmatic pull of a peculiar girl from his childhood named Norah—the first girl he'd ever kissed. Luke had given Eden honey-blonde hair and pewter-gray eyes like Norah's, and he layered Eden's character with Norah's uncanny intuition into human character.

Eden's deafness, however, was like Aaron Spaulding's allergy to the sun—a characteristic he felt would lend itself to creativity. It also made her adept at espionage when lip-reading was required and allowed her and Aaron to communicate with each other in a room full of suspects without making a sound. And it allowed Eden to turn off the world if she wanted to by simply turning her head. This came from Norah, too. Norah was not deaf and had never been able to turn off the world, but Luke was certain there were many times she had probably wished she could.

Luke now stroked the hand that lay under his. To not tell Téa the real reason he had been so distracted on stage tonight seemed somehow like being unfaithful to a small degree.

He kept his eyes on the road but continued to caress her hand.

"It wasn't the speech. I mean, it's not because I'm bored with it that I botched the speech," he said.

"What was it, then?"

He looked over at her, wondering for a moment if she would think he was nuts when he told her. Or would she be offended? Would she be mad? Jealous? It suddenly seemed like a dangerous thing to admit having been rendered nearly speechless by a woman other than your wife.

But not telling her was starting to needle him. Better to just get it out in the open. Surely Téa would understand that he had *not* been attracted to another woman. He had been *distracted* by one. He hoped there was an obvious difference.

"There was a woman at the banquet that looked just like Eden Damaris," he said as casually as he could. "I mean, she looked just like I imagine Eden Damaris looks. Face, hair color, build—even the way her hands move. It totally distracted me from my speech."

"Really?"

She didn't sound mad. She sounded interested. So far, so good.

"Yeah. She was, like, seated just off to my left. So she was in my line of vision for the whole speech. It was very unnerving. It was like seeing a ghost."

"Who was she? Which woman was it?" Téa said, smiling.

Luke got the distinct impression his wife thought this news was remarkable.

"I don't know who she is. I haven't seen her at these gatherings before. I don't know if she was someone's date or if she is a writer or a new agent."

"Wow, that's...that's kind of cool, don't you think?" Téa said. "I mean, I feel bad that seeing her threw you off, but, wow...how bizarre!"

Bizarre, yes. Cool, no.

"I finally had to just avoid looking at her table completely until I finished," he said, glad they seemed close to being done with this conversation. For some reason he wanted it to be over.

"I wonder who she is."

"Well, it doesn't really matter. There are probably a lot of people who look like my characters. I just happened to be unfortunate enough to run into one while at the microphone and in front of three hundred people."

"Really? You think there really are lots of people who look like your characters?"

"Well, I guess so. I don't know. I've never really thought about it before."

"I wish you'd pointed her out to me," Téa said, squeezing his hand. "I would have liked to have seen her. You know, to see if she matches how *I* imagine her."

Luke wondered for the first time why he hadn't pointed her out to Téa. Why hadn't he?

"Sorry," he said, like it was no big deal. *It wasn't.*

A few seconds of silence passed between them.

"Funny, isn't it, how characters in books can seem like real people," Téa finally said.

Luke stroked her hand. "It's essential," he said with a smile.

They fell into an easy silence. Luke reached to a console in front of him to slip in a CD of Spanish guitar music.

"You don't have to stay awake to keep me awake. I'm too keyed up to feel drowsy."

"I don't mind," she replied. "I like this CD. I can almost imagine a violinist playing some of this stuff."

They both smiled.

Sometime later they passed through the outskirts of Hartford. The rolling countryside of rural Connecticut looked welcoming in the violet starlight.

As they neared their house, Luke realized that talking about his characters had soothed him somehow, had taken the edge off the frustrations of the evening, and had reconnected him to that place in his mind where his characters lived.

Perhaps it was a sign that tomorrow they would start speaking to him again.

2

Luke sat back in his chair, his hands clasped around his coffee mug as he saw Noelle and Marissa through the window playing with the family cat in the morning sunlight. Before him on a wide desk sat his laptop, open to an e-mail inbox. Displayed there were several unopened messages. Two, several days old, were from his agent, Carmen Templer. Another one, from the day before, was from his editor, Alan Porterman. Near the keyboard was half a toasted bagel, already cold. The room where he sat was spacious, the ceiling high, and the wooden floors and walls glistened as sunny rays filtered in through paned windows. Built-in bookcases lined the walls, and Ansel Adams prints dotted the spaces between the shelves. Luke called the room The Lab. Téa called it the carriage house because that's what it had been back when the well-to-do banker who built it and their house had filled it with a fleet of personal carriages. Noelle and Marissa simply called it Daddy's office.

It was the perfect working environment, much more conducive to writing than the crowded coffee shops he'd haunted when he wrote *Slight Imperfections*. The comfortable townhouse in Boston had been a nice step up, but even it paled in comparison to The Lab. When he and Téa had bought the manor house and its outbuildings, she had assumed he would want the guest cottage for an office. But Luke had grimaced at that suggestion.

"Cottages are for tea and naps," he had said. "The carriage house is perfect. It's got style. Intrigue. Character."

"It smells," she had commented.

"I like the smell. Besides, after I fix it up, you won't recognize it."

Within a few months of moving in, the carriage house had been scrubbed, insulated, painted, re-wired, and plumbed. Luke installed a wood-burning stove for chilly mornings and a kitchenette to make strong coffee and simple things like tomato soup when he was on a writing roll and didn't want to come to the house to eat. He also installed an intercom to the main house so Téa could reach him in an instant. But she still called it the carriage house. And insisted it had a peculiar smell.

When The Lab was finished and he was spending his first morning in it with his laptop, a mug of Sumatran coffee, and a CD of Ottmar Liebert playing in the background, he had casually mentioned to God that it didn't get much better than this. The calendar-page-perfect New England countryside met his view from the new French doors, rewarding him with vistas of birch trees and grassy knolls. It was so unlike his Iowa beginnings. There were no cornfields or grain elevators or flat horizons to remind him he once only dreamed of writing books in a room like this.

He knew he wasn't a true New Englander, never would be. He was a transplant. But the graft had been wonderfully complete for years. He would never go back to Iowa. Sometimes, even now and without any apparent provocation, he felt like calling Bart Newell, his college roommate at the University of Iowa, to thank him for getting him out of the Midwest. When Luke had graduated in 1992 with a degree in creative writing and no job offers, he had dreaded the thought of returning home to Halcyon, Iowa, where he knew a job was always available for him at his father's newspaper. It wasn't the thought of working alongside his dad that bothered him. His father was a gifted writer and every kid's dream of a dad. But Halcyon had no pull for him. If anything, the pull of his hometown felt like strangling vines that sought to hold him prisoner—a captive of his past. There was no future for him in Halcyon, only a double-sided history that was as heartrending as it was wonderful. When Bart convinced him to move with him from Iowa City to Boston, it had truly been the beginning of the rest of his life.

"We have to be as close to New York as we can get," Bart, also a writing major, had told him. "We'll never get anywhere if we stay here."

"We can't afford to live in New York!" Luke had protested. "Where are we going to live? Who's going to hire us?"

"We start out in Boston, okay? I've got this uncle who owns a swanky restaurant. You can make a hundred bucks a night easy *just in tips!* A hundred bucks a night! Just in tips! We can sleep in late and then write all afternoon. It will be great!"

"A restaurant. I spent four years and thousands of dollars on a degree to wait on tables," Luke remembered saying and shaking his head.

"You got it all wrong, man," Bart had said. "You'll wait on tables to get the money to write classy stuff with that degree you bought. I am telling you, it will be perfect, Luke. Boston is less than two hundred miles from New York. We can meet agents and editors, go to conferences, get some freelance work. It'll be great. And a hundred bucks a night in *tips!*"

It actually hadn't taken him very long to agree to Bart's plan. Luke had just broken up with Amy Frendle, the girl he had dated for two years in college and who, as an interpreter for the deaf at their church, had taught him sign language—and who had suddenly decided she was in love with someone else. He didn't want to go back to Iowa where only an old life awaited. And it wasn't just the thought of writing obituaries for the Halcyon newspaper that bothered him. It was also the thought of being reminded on a daily basis of the final two years he'd spent at home, trying to be a knight in shining armor to Norah and her little brother, Kieran. Having them and their grandmother for next-door neighbors had been very complicated, for all kinds of reasons. He never really liked thinking about those last days of his senior year in high school.

He didn't even enjoy remembering the kiss he and Norah shared, though it had been magical, because the rest of those last few days was the stuff of nightmares. He knew he avoided going back to Halcyon to visit his parents because it meant seeing that house next door—no matter that different people had lived in it since then. It was always easier to invite his parents to come to New England to see him. He hadn't been home to Iowa in four years, not since his high-school reunion. His brother, Ethan, and his wife, Pamela, had been home on furlough from a mission school in Burkina Faso at that time, too, so it was almost like killing two birds with one stone. One visit to Halcyon, two reasons for going. This past summer when Ethan, Pamela, and their new baby, Charlotte, were again home for a visit, Luke invited them to stay a month with them. In New England.

Noelle and Marissa shrieking with delight outside the French doors roused him from these thoughts. Then his daughters scampered off, following Arthur the cat, who was chasing a butterfly. He looked at the clock on his desk. It was a little after ten, and he was off to an incredibly late start. He usually worked from 8 AM to noon on Saturdays since he took Mondays off completely, but it had been after midnight when he and Téa had arrived home from the banquet last night. And when he'd finally slipped into bed after taking the babysitter home, he hadn't slept well.

He had done what he always did when sleep eluded him—he had prayed. Tried to, anyway. But his thoughts were as unfocused as they had been hours before when he had stood at the podium and slaughtered his favorite speech. He could not keep his mind centered on one thought at a time. He began by praying for his children, for their safety and happiness, but before he had barely whispered their names in his mind, he was thinking about the oddest things: the cheesecake he didn't eat, the young valet who had beamed with pleasure at being inside a Jag for three whole minutes, the balding man at the banquet who'd begged him for advice.

I'm not getting any younger, you know!

And mingled with these random thoughts was the image of the woman in the green dress.

Noelle and Marissa burst into the room, disrupting his thoughts.

"Daddy, Arthur really wants to come in here!" five-year-old Noelle said.

"He does!" chirped Marissa.

Arthur, sleek and lean in a shade of gray like a November sky, ambled into The Lab between the girls' legs.

"All right, he can come," Luke said, pretending to be slightly annoyed at the intrusion. Fact is, he nearly welcomed it. "And what are you girls up to this morning?"

"Ballet class, Daddy!" Noelle said, fixing him a perturbed look. "It's Saturday!"

"I have a new leotard!" Marissa chimed in. "It's pink!"

The intercom squeaked to life on the wall near Luke's head.

"Luke, are the girls with you?" Téa's voice said.

He winked at his girls as he stood to press the intercom. "They are," he said.

"Tell them to get in the car or we'll be late. I'm coming out."

The intercom went silent.

"Guess you ballerinas better go," he said.

Noelle and Marissa skipped out through the French doors.

"Don't forget about Arthur when you come out!" Noelle called as she and her sister began to sprint down the brick walkway to the house.

"I won't," he replied, walking to the door with his girls and closing it after them. He watched them disappear into the garage. Then the garage door rose and Téa's red Mini Cooper began to back out of it. Luke watched it drive away.

Luke sat down again, letting Arthur jump onto his lap. He

stroked the cat and stared at his open laptop. Several minutes later, he clicked on "My Documents" and moved the cursor to the document simply titled "Five." He opened it.

Scrolling down to chapter ten, he stopped at the beginning of the chapter to read up to where he had left off. He had done this same thing several times already in the past three weeks, sometimes writing nothing new, sometimes finishing the chapter but then reading it back to himself and erasing everything he'd just written.

Arthur began to purr in his lap.

Luke read the text, pictured Aaron, the owner of the Red Herring Detective Agency, sitting in his darkened office away from the shaded windows. He could see Eden, knees drawn up, sitting in the windowsill, where she had been peeking out of the slivered opening in the blinds. Aaron and Eden arguing about a case, arguing about which of them is headed in the right direction. The main office of the Red Herring Detective Agency silent, except for the whispers of sound their sleeves make as they trade words with their hands.

> *How can you be so sure of all this?* Aaron signed to Eden.
> She looked out the window, resting her head on the oak window frame behind her for a moment. Then she slowly turned her head toward him and raised her hands to speak.
> *Because a woman like Clarice Wilburt doesn't kill for money,* she noted. *She kills for love.*

Luke stared at the blank whiteness following. There was nothing but a yawning space after the words "She kills for love."

He sat there unmoving for several long minutes. Then he closed the document, powered down his laptop, and shut the lid.

He looked at the clock on his desk.

Not yet noon. The ticking of the clock began to mesmerize him, lulling him into a stupor—then suddenly the same gentle ticking jarred him to attention. The ticking clock. Marking off the hours. The hours of his life. The hours of his full but meaningless life. Something clicked in his mind as these thoughts tumbled within him.

"God, I don't know what I'm doing," he said spontaneously, and it was very much a prayer. Arthur looked up from Luke's lap and murmured a cat-like greeting.

"I don't know what any of this is for. I don't know why I do what I do," Luke whispered to the heavens. "I mean, why do I write these books? Why do I write books about people killing other people? Why do people buy books like that? What is it all *for*?"

The room was quiet except for the clock's ticking.

His restlessness was not about the book he couldn't seem to finish. It was not about seeing Eden in the flesh, though seeing her had certainly sent this newfound discontent rushing to the surface of his soul.

Something was missing from his life. He felt it. And his reason for writing was mixed up with it. He had lost his passion for writing. For writing anything. He knew now why the woman in the green dress had unnerved him. Eden Damaris was not real. The Red Herring Detective Agency was a charade. None of it was real. None of it. And *that* was what bothered him.

He suddenly wanted to be anywhere but in that room. He scooped up the cat from his lap, grabbed his laptop, and headed out of The Lab. He set Arthur down on the stone pathway, closed the door behind him, and headed to the house, anxious to find a quiet place where he could think. Maybe he would go for a drive. Maybe he'd call up his friend Mike and they could go out for coffee. He wished Téa wasn't at ballet with the girls.

Stepping inside the house, he made for the fridge, opened it, pulled out a Coke, and shut the door, wondering all the while what to do next. At that moment he noticed his cell phone, resting on the kitchen counter, was blinking. He had missed a call. It was probably Alan, his editor, wondering how the manuscript was coming along. Or wondering why Luke hadn't returned any of his calls. He picked up the phone and called up the ID screen. It wasn't Alan. It was his mother. He pressed the button for voice mail to see if she'd left a message.

She had.

> *Luke, it's Mom. Dad has had a stroke and he's...he's...in the emergency room at the hospital in Cedar Falls. I...I'm not supposed to use my cell phone in the ER. I'll try calling again in a little while. Maybe you can call the hospital and see if they'll let me talk to you. I...I have to go. I don't know where they're taking him.*

The message ended. Luke stood motionless for only a second. Then he frantically pressed the speed dial for Information. Minutes later he finally connected with the right hospital and the right floor. Finally after being placed on hold for several more agonizing minutes, he found out his father was at Sartori Memorial Hospital and had been moved to Intensive Care. A few seconds later, a woman's voice greeted him on the other end of his phone.

"ICU."

"My name is Luke Foxbourne. My father is Jack Foxbourne. He...someone told me he's in the ICU. I need to talk to my mother, MaryAnn Foxbourne. Is she there?"

"Can you hold a moment, please?" the voice said. So calm. Luke wondered for one crazy second what it would be like to work in a place where you saw lives changing in horrible ways every minute...and for you it would be just a normal day on the job.

Then a voice came over the line.

"Luke?"

His mother.

"Mom! What happened? Is Dad okay?"

She began to cry.

"He...they're doing some kind of test right now. The doctor in the ER said he's probably out of the woods but, Luke, he can't talk and he can't...he just has this blank look on his face like he doesn't know who I am!"

Her voice broke into sobs.

"Mom! Tell me what happened!"

He heard her sniffling on the other end.

"I don't know when it happened, Luke! I was at a ladies retreat and I got home after our own sunrise service at about ten-thirty. He was lying in the living room when I came in. I don't know how long he'd been lying there!"

Luke was now wildly pacing the kitchen. His own eyes were hot with tears. His dad was only sixty-two. Too young. Too young to be lying in a hospital bed in that condition. His mom was too young to have this happen to her husband. He had to get there. Fast.

"I'm coming, Mom. I'll get on the first flight I can, okay?"

"Yes, yes. I don't know how to get you here to the hospital. I don't know where—"

"Mom, I'll rent a car," he said, cutting her off. "I'll get there. Don't worry about that. Do you want me to call Ethan?"

"Oh, yes. I don't have his number with me!"

"I'll take care of it. And I'll get there as soon as I can. What's Dad's room number?"

"Oh, it's two…thirty-six. But he doesn't have a phone in his room!"

"I'll call you at the nurses' station just before I get on the plane, okay?"

His mother was sobbing again.

"Mom?"

"Okay, yes…yes."

"See you soon."

He clicked off the phone and wiped the tears from his cheeks.

"God," he said aloud, but nothing else came. His hands were shaking, and he couldn't think. He needed to call a travel agent or an airline or something. But he didn't know where to start. Just then he heard a car pull up in the driveway. He glanced out the side door window. Téa and the girls were home.

He stepped into the dining room, hiding from his girls and mentally focusing on steadying his breathing. He knew Téa would send them upstairs to change into play clothes. He needed to talk to his wife alone. And he wanted to be calm when he did. The door opened and voices filled the silence.

"Okay, you two," he heard Téa say. "Put those leotards in your dresser, not on the floor."

He heard the sound of his daughters scampering upstairs. He came around the corner, startling his wife.

"Luke!" she yelled playfully, at first thinking he had hidden to play a trick on her. But then she saw his face and her playful shock turned to concern. "What is it?"

"My mom called. Dad has had a stroke. Mom says he can't talk or move. She wasn't there when it happened, so no one knows when it happened, if it was this morning or last night before he went to bed…"

His voice choked up. He reached for Téa and she came to him, laying her head on his chest.

"I have to go to him," he whispered. He felt her head nod.

"Of course," she whispered back "Of course you do."

He held her tighter. "I don't know how long…I'll be gone," he said when he was able.

She looked up. "We'll just take one day at a time, okay?"

Luke sighed. "I'll miss Noelle's graduation from kindergarten on Friday. I might miss her birthday next week, too."

Téa reached up and touched his cheek. "She'll understand. She loves her Grampa Jack. And the girls and I can join you after school gets out if you're still there, okay?"

He wrapped his hand around hers. "Maybe."

She broke away. "You go pack. I'll call the travel agency. Then we'll tell the girls together."

He nodded, grabbed the address book from a basket near the phone, and punched in the number for Ethan's school in Burkina Faso.

While he waited for the call to go through, he began to climb the stairs to the bedroom. The sound of a faraway phone rang in his ear, followed by the sound of his brother's sleepy voice.

Luke began to speak, without so much as a stray thought about the startling revelation he had less than an hour before while he sat in his Lab with a cat on his lap.

3

*L*uke sat with his mother in a room off the nurse's station as dawn peeked through nearly closed miniblinds behind them. She was asleep, leaning into him on a borrowed pillow. He had dozed off, too, sometime in the middle of the night. They had been encouraged by the night nurse to get a decent night's rest at a nearby hotel. She had even recommended one, but neither Luke nor his mother wanted to leave the hospital. They had both felt compelled to stay close by, as if they expected Jack Foxbourne to suddenly awaken from his strange stupor and ask where his family was.

Luke yawned and stretched, and then felt his mother's small frame stir beside him. She lifted her head.

"What time is it?" she asked groggily.

Luke raised an arm and looked at his watch. "A little after six."

She was silent for a moment.

"I can't believe this has happened," she said softly. "I keep thinking I'll wake up. But I *am* awake. And this is real."

Luke involuntarily flinched when she said the word "real," remembering for the first time since he'd learned of his father's stroke that he had his own set of hurdles looming ahead.

"I've always known life can change in an instant," she continued.

"I've seen it happen to other people. I see it happen to people in Halcyon all the time. I saw it happen to the little Janvik boy in front of my very eyes. But I just never considered it might happen to us."

Luke put an arm around his mother's shoulder and she let her head fall into the place on his chest his movement created.

"I'm afraid he's gone, Luke," she whispered.

"Don't…" he replied. But he could say nothing else.

When Luke had finally arrived at the hospital the evening before, it was nearly six-thirty. Jack Foxbourne's face had been expressionless when Luke first saw him lying on layers of white, but his father's eyes seemed to glisten with fear as Luke made eye contact with him, as if his dad knew exactly what was happening and it scared him to death. A thick, bright-white bandage was taped above his right eye, evidence he had hit something hard and unforgiving when the stroke had felled him.

The emergency-room doctor had told them the stroke had occurred on the left side of Jack Foxbourne's brain, disabling the speech center and paralyzing his right side.

"But he will recover, right?" his mother had asked.

The doctor had paused before telling Luke's mother she really needed to talk with the stroke-rehabilitation doctor, whom Jack would see for the first time later today, about her husband's recovery.

"Why can't *you* tell me?" she had said, sounding very young and afraid.

"Recovering from a stroke is sometimes very slow and difficult, Mrs. Foxbourne. And it can be different for everybody. The most significant recovery will happen in these next thirty days. And most stroke victims continue to recover for several months. Usually by six months, though, whatever recovery is going to take place will have taken place. Some of the skills he has lost he will recover, some he probably won't. He will need to learn to adapt to his new limitations.

And you need to know it takes time to learn to compensate for skill deficits."

"What deficits? What do you mean?"

"Well, your husband may need to learn how to hold a fork differently, or walk with a cane or a walker, or button a shirt with one hand. He may need to relearn how to read and write. When the brain is damaged, we enter into a whole new realm of unknowns, I'm afraid."

I'm afraid, too, Luke had wanted to say.

The doctor had said nothing else, and Luke and his mother had spent the rest of the evening and night wondering what awaited them. For Luke's mother, it was a fresh set of troubles. For Luke, it seemed like his dilemma had just been magnified three times over. And another long day was just beginning.

By nine o'clock that evening, Luke had convinced his mother to leave the hospital for a night of rest at a nearby hotel. He had offered to drive her home to Halcyon for the night but she refused to make the forty-five-minute trip. He got her situated in a hotel three blocks from the hospital, taking care of the arrangements and escorting her to her room. As he got ready to leave the hotel, his mother looked at him, a question poised on her lips.

"Luke, I need to ask something of you…something I would never ask if there was any other way…" She stopped.

Luke knew what it was she wanted to ask him but was struggling to say. He had known all day, ever since his mother had called Lucie at the newspaper to tell her his father had had a stroke. His father's paper was currently without an editor. He was the most likely and qualified person to step in for a while.

"I know what you're going to ask me, Mom," he said quietly. "It's all right. I'll do it. At least until we can make other arrangements."

"I hate to have to ask you," she said. "I know you never wanted to go back to the paper. But Lucie can't do it all. And Gretchen and Todd don't even *know* how to write. Cubby can only write sports stories. You should have seen the last story he did on the city council. It sounded like a play-by-play of a wrestling match."

She was crying again but her sudden humor was welcome—the first he had seen of it since he arrived.

"It's not that I hate it, Mom, it just wasn't the career for me," he said, trying to reassure her. "It's not what I wanted to do with the rest of my life. I don't hate it, okay? But I honestly can't stay indefinitely. We may need to think about selling the paper, Mom."

She looked up at him, her brief display of humor gone. "You're already giving up on him?" she said, with a slight edge in her voice.

"I'm not giving up," he said, surprised by her response. "I just think we need to be prepared for some unpleasant choices. Mom, he may not be able to—"

"We don't know anything yet! We don't have a crystal ball!" she said, standing at the little table. "Luke, don't give up on him. You can't! If you do, he'll see it. He needs to know he can get well!"

"Mom, maybe we should talk about this another time. You're tired, I'm tired." Luke said with regret.

"Luke, you must promise me you won't say a word to him about selling the paper!" his mother insisted. "And you can't mention it to me when I am with him. He hears everything just fine. He mustn't think his life won't wait for him!"

"Mom, let's just forget it for now, okay? I shouldn't have brought it up."

"But you're already thinking about it," she said, nearly pouting.

Luke wanted to collapse into a bed. He wanted sleep. "Mom, please," he said.

She was silent for a few seconds. "Promise me you won't give up on him."

Luke looked intently at his mother, trying to match her determination.

"Mom, I will not give up on *him*," he said.

But the newspaper was another matter. He could stay a month, maybe two. But that was it. He had a book to finish. He had a wife and kids back in Connecticut. He had a life. And it wasn't here in Iowa.

Although his mother wouldn't go back to Halcyon for the night, Luke would. He would need to stop by the newspaper in the morning anyway. Lucie would be eager to know how Jack was... and what the future held. The latter question was as hard for Luke to consider as his writer's block. Halcyon in the late spring moonlight looked as peaceful and serene as its name suggested. The tree-lined residential streets were dotted here and there with the warm hues of creamy yellow and fairy blue; colors cast by porch lights and glowing TV screens in living-room windows as Luke made his way through town. His hometown was home to three thousand with another eight hundred or so on nearby acreages. The true heart and soul of the community—the family farms—were visible on any road leading out of town; they were marked by grain silos, solitary clusters of trees, and two-storied, shuttered houses that all faced south.

Luke wove through the quiet streets, traveling past the lamplit town square, the silent band shell in Memorial Park, and the darkened storefronts without a great deal of interest. He purposely eased up on his speed as he drove past the offices of the *Halcyon Herald,* though. He supposed it had been crazy in there earlier today as the staff pulled the paper together for the printers tomorrow morning. He was glad the office was dark and that Lucie and Cubby were not still inside trying to put the paper to bed. He would have felt compelled to stop and help them.

Luke turned past the bank and the post office and cast a glance down the street that led to his old high school. It seemed odd to be driving these familiar streets in a strange vehicle without Téa and the girls. It seemed even more out of place to be headed toward his childhood home, knowing he'd be sleeping there tonight and would be alone.

He turned down a side street and followed it for several blocks, slowing down by the house where his best friend, Matt, had lived. He had no idea who lived there now. He had long since lost track of Matt. He turned left onto Seventh Avenue.

Luke's parents' house came into view, standing in a pearly splash of moonlight but wrapped in its own darkness, with not even a light in a bedroom window showing. As he pulled into the driveway, he noticed that the Janvik place next door looked the same—dark and unwelcoming. It was obvious no one was inside either house. He wondered if Norah's grandmother's old house— still painted the same nauseating shade of green—was empty again. He wouldn't be surprised if it was. That house was cursed. No one had ever truly been happy in it. Not before Nell Janvik had owned it and not after. And certainly not *while* she owned it.

Luke stopped the car in the driveway and got out. He took his suitcase out of the trunk and walked up the dark pathway to the front door, noticing that a *For Sale* sign was indeed poking out of the front lawn next door. Dandelions had sprouted all around the sign's legs, and even in the darkness, Luke could tell the sign had been there for a while. He pulled his mother's key ring out of his pocket, slipped the key into the lock, and stepped inside.

When he switched on a light in the living room he saw at once where his father had fallen. He saw the lamp on the floor, the small spot of blood on the carpet, the end table that was out of alignment with its twin on the other side of the sofa. His dad had no doubt fallen against the table, hitting his head on the corner. The lamp had crashed to the carpet with him. Three indentations in the carpet showed where the legs of the little table usually rested.

Luke closed the door behind him, stepped farther inside, and put his suitcase down by the sofa. His mother's overnight bag was there, too. He moved the end table back to its rightful spot and replaced the lamp. He'd tackle the little bloodstain tomorrow. What could one more day matter?

He sank down onto the sofa and rested his head in his hands for a moment. It was after ten but he needed to talk to Téa. He pulled his cell phone out of his pocket and pressed the speed dial for home.

"Hello?" Téa's voice at once began to soothe him.

"It's me," he said wearily.

"How's it going?"

"There wasn't a whole lot of change today. He's trying to talk but can hardly get one word out right. And it's driving him crazy. They're moving him to a regular room tomorrow. And he starts occupational and physical therapy tomorrow, too. The doctor said the first days of therapy are like hell. For everybody."

"I'm sorry, babe. I wish the girls and I could come."

"Actually, I think maybe it's best if you don't for a while. He wouldn't want you or the girls to see him like this."

A few seconds of silence passed between them.

"So, do you know how long you'll be staying, Luke? The girls are already asking."

Luke took a deep breath before continuing.

"He's going to be in recovery for several months, Téa. He may get some of his movement and speech back, but the doctors aren't even suggesting he'll fully recover."

"So...what does that mean?"

"Well, between you and me, I think it means my parents are going to have to sell the paper. Dad's going to have to retire a little early."

Téa was quiet for a moment. "That'll kill him," she said. "Sorry, I know it's a bad choice of words. But Luke, I can't imagine your dad not having that newspaper."

"Well, my mom can't either. She won't even discuss it with me. I'm thinking she's going to have to realize it on her own, and I'm betting these next thirty days will convince her of it. That's when the most recovery will be made."

"So you don't think he'll be able to go back?"

Luke sighed. "I suppose it's possible. But I really think it would take a miracle, Téa." He suddenly couldn't continue. He blinked back the hot tears that had formed so swiftly in the corners of his eyes.

"Luke, I'm sorry," Téa said, her voice also filled with sadness. "Is there anything I can do?"

"Just pray for him," he said gruffly, struggling for control.

"I already am," she said. Then she added after a momentary pause, "So, you'll be staying then. I suppose you're handling the paper for him? Do you know for how long?"

Luke rubbed his left temple with a free hand.

"I don't know," he answered, clearing his throat. "I didn't say anything to my mom, but I can't see how I can stay longer than a couple months."

"A couple months," she repeated tonelessly. "And you don't want the girls and me to come at all? The whole time?"

"No, that's not what I meant. I just don't want you to come right away. Dad would...I think it would devastate him to see No-elle and Marissa and not be able to hug them or talk to them. I don't think any of us could handle what that would do to him."

"Are *you* doing okay?" Téa said gently, after a moment's pause, and Luke could almost feel her caress.

"Yes and no," he answered honestly. "Mostly no."

"Is it more than just your dad, Luke?" she continued. "You've seemed a little preoccupied lately, even before his stroke."

Luke was at once grateful for his wife's intuition. It made it easier to tell her he was feeling more and more like a trapped an-imal—caught in a snare of his own making.

"It's the book mostly. I can't seem to move forward with it, no matter how hard I try. I seem to have lost my vision for what I do. I don't know. I feel like…I feel like I have everything but suddenly know it's not enough."

"I'm not sure what you mean," she replied warily.

He was quick to clarify. "It's not about you and the girls. You're the only one for me and you always will be. And I would give my life for our girls. It's not that. It's more like, there has to be more than just *this*. More than just what I have, what I have done with my life."

Téa was silent for a moment.

"I don't know if I understand what you're saying, Luke."

He knew he was not making a whole lot of sense. He wasn't even sure he could explain it to himself.

"I don't know how to describe it, Téa. I feel restless."

"Luke, do you want me to come? The girls could stay with Jeff and Dana for a few days. Should I come?"

"No, Téa. I just need some thinking time. Maybe it's better this way."

"I'm worried about you."

"I'll be all right. I'm not worried about me. It's this book hanging over my head that rankles me the most. I've got to finish it somehow."

"That won't be easy with trying to run a paper and helping your dad."

"No, but I think I'm going to hire some students from the high school to help me out at the paper. And there's not a whole lot I can do for Dad. Mom will probably stay in an apartment in Cedar Falls while he's in rehab. So I'll have the house to myself every night."

"I want you to call me if it feels like you have too much to deal with, Luke."

"I promise."

"Call me tomorrow, okay?"

"I will. I love you, Téa," he said, wishing he could say it to her face.

"I love you back. Good night."

Luke clicked the phone off and set it on the coffee table, very much aware of the silence and darkness all around him. He couldn't remember the last time he had been alone in this house at night. It probably was when he was a teenager. And that seemed like ages ago. He rose from the sofa and headed up the stairs to his old bedroom, turning on lights all the way and leaving them on.

His old room didn't look at all like it did when it belonged to him; it had been redecorated in shades of lavender the year he'd moved to Boston. But he instantly knew the view from the window would be the same. He walked over to the double-hung window on impulse to look at the ancient elm between his house and Nell's old house. Just outside the glass were the weathered boards of the tree house his father had built for him the summer he'd turned twelve. Beyond that, the limbs of the tree reached for the glass of the facing window in the Janvik house—Norah's window, when she lived there. The tree house looked more battered then it had the last time he had seen it, but he was still overcome with its vivid sameness. The room he stood in was not the same. He was not the same. But the tree on the other side of the window had not changed much, and the decaying structure that rested in its branches was still brimming with long-kept secrets and that one solitary kiss.

Luke stood there for a few more minutes, and then in one single motion, he picked up his suitcase and walked out of the room. He stepped into the hallway and into Ethan's old room. He'd sleep there tonight.

4

*L*uke arrived at the *Halcyon Herald* office half an hour before opening, hoping to quietly refamiliarize himself with his father's newspaper. He had worked there during his senior high school years, and there probably wasn't one thing about the business he hadn't been a part of. He had taken photos of accidents on the highway, and children kissing Santa Claus, and the yearly coronation of Miss Halcyon. He had attended school-board meetings, political rallies, and ribbon cuttings. He had interviewed WWII vets, cancer survivors, and inventors of farm implements. He had typed up obituaries, legal notices, and senior dining menus—even sold advertising. There wasn't much about the *Halcyon Herald* that was foreign to him except the flair for community journalism, which his dad had and he did not. But he had not worked for his father since the summer before his freshman year at the University of Iowa—seventeen years ago.

Right off the bat, Luke could see there had been some changes to the office since he had last visited. The 35mm cameras had been replaced with digitals. The computers looked new. The laser printer did, too. The layout tables in the back were gone since the paper was now assembled on-screen and sent not by vehicle to the printer in the next county but electronically. He wondered for a moment how his father had paid for all this new technology. But it didn't take him long to remember that Jack Foxbourne didn't hesitate to dip into the inheritance his mother had left him if that's what it took to keep the paper viable.

Despite the changes, some things were still the same. The hodgepodge of coffee cups in the break room. Cubby's collection of baseball caps. Lucie's impeccably kept front desk. His dad's numerous piles of manila folders, strewn about his desk in no apparent order and decorated with copious amounts of yellow sticky notes.

He had been in the office five minutes, taking it all in visually, when Lucie Hermann, the 58-year-old office manager and lifelong Halcyon resident, arrived carrying a basket of blueberry muffins.

"Oh my, Luke!" she exclaimed, setting the basket down on the front counter and wrapping her arms around Luke in a warm embrace. "We're so glad you're here. And we're all so hopeful your father will be as right as rain in no time!"

"Thanks, Lucie," Luke replied. "I hope he will be, too."

"Let's get some coffee going," she said, grabbing the muffins and making her way to the break area at the back of the main office, talking all the while. "Now, your mother called me this morning and said we're to do whatever you say," she said as she poured water into the coffeemaker from a battered plastic jug. "If you want to cut back two pages, we'll cut back two pages. If you want to put obits on the front, we'll put obits on the front."

Luke smiled. "We're not putting obituaries on the front—" he began, but Lucie cut him off.

"Well, I'm just saying we'll do whatever you say," she said, dumping bargain-brand coffee into a filter. Luke winced. He hadn't had a cup of bargain-brand coffee in years. By choice.

"Lucie, you know as well as I do that when my dad is gone, you're the brains behind this operation, so let's not mess with success," he replied, giving away nothing about his disdain for what was now brewing happily away in the coffeemaker.

"Oh, go on!" Lucie said gruffly, but her smile was broad.

"Between you and Cubby and the guys down at the coffee shop, I think the paper will pretty much write itself," he said, leaning back against the front counter and crossing his arms. "I'll just help it along a little."

"Give yourself more credit than that, Luke," Lucie said, turning to face him. "You'll probably turn this paper on its head and end up with a Pulitzer. Folks around here won't want you to leave when your dad comes back."

An uncomfortable silence arose between them as if they both knew the chances of Jack returning to his newspaper were slim. Lucie filled the silence quickly.

"We're just so happy to have you here, Luke," she said. "Even though the reason that brought you here isn't a good one. We're all so proud of you. There isn't à one of us who isn't bursting with pride over your success."

"Thanks, Lucie."

The front door opened and in walked Charles "Cubby" Vortberg, the *Herald's* sports editor. A retired football coach and high-school athletic director, there wasn't much about sports that Cubby Vortberg didn't know. But it was all he knew.

"Well, well, well!" Cubby boomed. "There he is! Mr. Bestseller!"

"How's it going, Cubby?" Luke extended his right hand, but Cubby pulled him close and wrapped him in a tight hug, slapping him on the back as if he were choking on something half-chewed.

Cubby broke away but kept his big, beefy arms on Luke's shoulders. "Now, I want you to know we got your dad on our prayer chain at church. We got Elsie Frommer on our prayer chain. *Elsie Frommer.* She's got an in with God. She's top-notch at praying. You know what I mean?"

Luke couldn't help but smile. "Thanks, Cubby, I appreciate that."

"No problem," the older man boomed.

Luke looked about the main office, unsure of what to do next. "So, has the paper been sent?"

"Cubby and I sent it last night around eight so you wouldn't have to worry about it first thing," Lucie said.

"Okay. Um, well, do you still have Tuesday-morning planning meetings?" Luke continued.

"Of course," Lucie said, smiling. "That's what the muffins are for."

"That's why I'm on time!" Cubby roared, heading to his glassed-in office at the back of the main room. He picked up a calendar, grabbed his swivel chair, and pushed it to the break area.

"Your dad's planner is in the top left drawer of his desk," Lucie said, grabbing a tablet and her own chair.

Luke stepped into his dad's office, opposite Cubby's on the far west wall, and tried not to hesitate as he opened a desk drawer and pulled out a black, spiral-bound planner. He didn't feel right about opening his dad's desk drawers, but he knew he had to shake that feeling pronto. He grabbed a mechanical pencil from a Halcyon Hornets coffee mug that was filled with pens, more pencils, and an X-acto knife. He started to walk out, but then walked over to his dad's desk and grabbed hold of the swivel captain's chair. It appeared this was how it was done: No one used a break-room chair to plan the next issue of the paper.

"Here you go," Lucie said, handing him a steaming mug when he reached the break area. "Black, like you like it."

Luke accepted the mug as graciously as he could. "Thanks, Lucie."

The three of them sat in a silent circle for a few seconds. It was clear they had been told to let him take the lead. His mother's idea, no doubt. He wished she had told them the exact opposite. *He's busy trying to finish a book! And he's worried about Jack! So just take the paper and run with it, okay?*

He had come up with a plan while he showered that morning, and it seemed like he was going to be able to present it after all.

While he had stood under the hot spray of water he had decided he desperately needed to concentrate on his own career, not his dad's. He didn't want the full burden of filling the *Halcyon Herald's* sixteen weekly pages. For Pete's sake, he *did* have a book to finish. He would get help. He'd pay for it himself.

He cleared his throat.

"Okay, guys. Here's the deal," he said. "I need to know exactly what everyone does so I can see where we need to get some extra help."

"Extra help?" Lucie asked gently.

"I want to hire a few extra people, on a temporary basis, to help us get through this. I'm afraid I'm way behind on my own writing schedule."

Lucie looked at Cubby and her bottom lip disappeared as she sucked it in. Cubby scratched his head.

"You don't think that's a good idea?" Luke asked.

"Well, no, it's not *that*," Lucie said, still looking at Cubby.

"See, it's like this," Cubby said. "We are like a nine-man football team, B-squad. We'd like to be a Class AA school with all-varsity players, but we have to play with the resources we have. We're skinny and short and we don't have special teams and we have to play both offense and defense. You know what I mean?"

Luke grinned at Cubby's explanation. So it was about money.

"Look, I'm going to take care of the financial arrangements," he said. "It's worth it to me to be able to have the time to write."

Cubby nodded. It sounded okay to him. No extra work would be headed his way.

"Well, if you think that's the way to go," Lucie said cautiously.

"I do," Luke said.

"Even though your dad will probably throw a full-blown fit when he comes back and learns you spent your own money to hire people?" Lucie added.

Luke's face softened. "Nothing would give me greater pleasure than to see my dad throw a full-blown fit."

Lucie nodded and looked down at her tablet. Then the phone rang, and Lucie answered it, took a message, and came back to her chair. The interruption had been well-timed.

"Now, Gretchen only does composition and ad design, right?" Luke said after Lucie had returned.

"That's right," she said, looking up again. "She only works four days a week. She has Tuesdays off. She won't answer the phone or type any notices. She likes to work in the corner there with her Walkman on and her headphones in her ears."

"And Dad is okay with that?"

Lucie shrugged. "She's the artist. No one can design anything like she can. He lets her have her way because she's so good at what she does."

Okay, no help there, Luke thought.

"And Todd only works after school?"

"Yes. He takes all the sports photos, all the school photos, Saturday events, accidents that happen after working hours. And he picks up the papers from the printer's Tuesdays after school and takes them to the post office. Oh, and school gets out next week and then he'll be available during the day, too."

"Can he write?" Luke asked.

"Ah, let's not go there," Cubby said.

Luke nodded. "Okay. This is what I want you to do. Lucie, you keep running the office, doing the books, payroll, all that. But I want you to hire a teenager to take over for you at the front desk every day after one o'clock so you can do legal notices, obits, announcements, press releases, and the like. I want you guys to find out which student is the top seller at the high school for fundraising, offer them a job, and tell them they can make a dollar more than minimum wage and twenty percent on every advertising sale they close."

"Twenty?" Lucie said, eyes wide.

"Twenty," Luke said. "Tell them it's temporary. Maybe just through the summer. Cubby, you have to fill those three sports pages. I don't care how you do it. Do surveys on the street, have Todd take pictures of little girls playing hopscotch, do a feature story on local fishing legends, I don't care. You just need to fill them, okay?"

"Will do," Cubby said.

"I will write three front page stories a week and my dad's column, but that's it," Luke said. "When Todd comes in today, we'll tell him he's in charge of getting the main photo for the paper each week and three or four other stand-alone photos. And Lucie, you need to find two noncritical stories that can go on the front if we have space to fill."

Lucie and Cubby nodded and waited.

"Okay, so what about this week's paper?" Lucie said.

"What about it?" Luke replied.

"What's going on the front page?"

Luke thought for a moment. "Get me a copy of last year's issue for the same week."

Lucie walked over to the former darkroom and opened a door. Inside were rows of filing cabinets. She opened a drawer, pulled out a folded newspaper from within a file folder and walked back, placing the paper in Luke's lap.

Luke unfolded it and read the front-page headlines.

"Okay. High school graduation preview. City Council meeting. Annual bloodmobile visit. Feature story on a lady that makes dolls. There's our front page."

Lucie looked at the year-old issue. "Well, I'm sure the graduation, city council meeting and bloodmobile are all on for next week, but we can't do the doll lady again."

"Of course we can't," Luke said, taking a sip of the coffee and trying not to grimace. "Just find me somebody who makes something else."

With the meeting over and Lucie and Cubby off to fulfill their duties, Luke headed back to his father's office. He surveyed the top of the desk with its array of scattered manila folders and sighed.

He would have to put them in some kind of order. He stood for a moment longer and then scooped them all up, putting them into one pile on one end of the desk, noting that at least they were all labeled. But he didn't feel like tackling any of it. He'd sort through them tomorrow one by one. Then he stepped out of the room. Half an hour of being emergency editor, and he had already had enough for one day.

"I'm going to be in Cedar Falls with my folks for the rest of the day," he said to Lucie, who looked up at him in surprise. "Let me know how you come out with those students, okay?"

"Yes, of course," she said, wide-eyed. "Give our love to your mom and dad."

He nodded and headed out the door, anxious to be away from his new responsibilities, anxious to see his father, and anxious for a real cup of coffee.

The house seemed even more lonely and unwelcoming when Luke returned to Halcyon that evening. He made a quick call to Téa and the girls, learning that Alan had called the house, wondering what he was up to. Téa had told Luke's editor the news about his dad, and Alan had responded, "Tell Luke to take all the time he needs." It was liberating to hear that, in ways Alan didn't even know about. Luke decided he would e-mail him and Carmen from the *Herald* tomorrow. He was oddly grateful that his current predicament would keep them both at a distance while he tried to recapture his writing edge.

Luke told his wife good night, clicked off the phone, and then grudgingly turned on his laptop, which was sitting on the bed next to him. He opened his current manuscript to chapter ten, the chapter that refused to be written. The house was quiet, and there was no reason to suspect he would have any distractions. But the words would not come.

After ten unproductive minutes, he was suddenly struck with an idea. He had a box somewhere in this house of his first stories and rough drafts, written when he was still in high school. In that box were three or four notebooks of stories and ideas as well as a large envelope full of newspaper articles he had read as a teenager that he had thought would inspire great stories. There was no way his mother would have thrown that box out. No way. He thought of calling her at the hotel to ask where it was, but he decided he would look first and then call her if he came up with nothing. Maybe in that box was a story idea that would break the spell, give him back his enthusiasm for writing. He could file this one away or pitch it altogether if he was able to start fresh with a new story.

Energized, Luke walked into his old room, opening the closet doors and scanning the floor and the shelves above the hangers that held his parents' winter clothes. No luck. He looked under the bed. No box. Next he tried Ethan's room. Not there, either. He descended the stairs to the kitchen and then went down into the basement, flipping on a light. The finished part of the basement hadn't changed a great deal in the seventeen years he had been gone. The Foosball table was gone. In its place was some sort of quilting frame. But the same tired-looking couch and TV set where he had watched scary movies with Ethan were still there, as was his grandmother's sewing machine and an antique wardrobe full of his mother's costumes. She had been retired from teaching drama at the high school for five years, but her favorite costumes were still in the wardrobe. Luke saw them when he opened the wooden doors, looking for his box.

He then went through the bi-fold doors into the unfinished part of the basement known as his mother's canning closet, stepping onto the cold concrete floor with bare feet. He winced at the chill. As he stood there letting his eyes adjust to the dim light, he remembered the time he and Ethan had fled to this room with Norah and Kieran when the tornado siren went off. The place looked the same as it did that day. Smelled the same. But the beating of his heart had been radically different. He had been scared to death that day.

Luke mentally moved past the memory as he poked his head into a few large boxes. He moved a few items as he searched for the box, like the rolled-up tent, a box that contained an artificial Christmas tree, the sleeping bags, and an old dehumidifier. He was about to go back upstairs and call his mother when he saw the box sitting atop a set of metal shelves. On the box's side, in his mother's handwriting, he saw the words, *Luke's Writings*. He walked over and stood on tiptoe to reach it. A plastic bag half full of Christmas paper plates fell on his head as he lowered the box—he closed his eyes as a little cloud of dust arose. He coughed and made his way out of the chilly room, closing the doors behind him.

He sat down on the old couch with the box and loosened the twine that held its flaps closed. Comic books, old essays from high school, and even a broken kazoo had found their way inside it, but he skipped past these to look for the spiral-bound notebooks—four of them, all blue. He found them at the bottom. He could not help but smile as he pulled them out. He had been so full of ambition and desire when these notebooks were a part of his daily life. He fingered the covers, remembering how he had dreamed of becoming an author, of getting published, of making it big. He slowly opened the first one, ready to feast on its contents, hoping, like he had back then, that there was a best-selling story idea inside it.

He scanned the first couple of pages, finding nothing of great interest. As he turned another page, he came across a folded piece of paper. It was pale blue, and when he saw it, it literally took his breath away. He knew in an instant what was written on the inside. He had not seen it or even thought about it in years...perhaps he had purposefully forgotten about it.

He carefully lifted it from the notebook. For a moment, he considered not unfolding it. Just slipping it back into the box—or better yet, balling it up and throwing it away. But it was only the

passing thought of a split second. He knew he would read it. And
he knew he would probably never be able to throw it away...be-
cause he had never forgotten how moved he had been the first time
he had read what was written there.

He had been fifteen then; Norah, just barely fourteen. They
were sitting in his tree house. Norah had snuck out of her house
while her grandmother, Nell, smoked and watched reruns of *Fantasy Island* on her downstairs TV. Kieran was already in bed. It was
early October, and there had been a twinge of frost in the night
air. He'd just read to her the first chapter of a story he was writing.
After she told him she'd liked what he'd read very much, she'd announced she'd written a poem.

"You did?" he had said.

"It's about the whales," she had replied.

And she'd given no other explanation, because Luke had already
known that Norah and Kieran's fascination with whales sprang
from the good memories they had of their mother—a woman who
adored whales, among a bevy of other odd things.

Norah had crawled back to her grandmother's house, re-entered
her bedroom window, and returned with a piece of blue stationery—
Nell's, no doubt, which Norah surely had had to steal from her.

"Would you like to read it?" she had said, handing it to him.

Luke unfolded the paper now in his parents' basement nine-
teen years later and read.

> *Underneath the rocking sea*
> *In the shadows of the deep*
> *The mighty kings in silent rule*
> *Swim the lengths of the salty pool*
> *Blast of steam, plume of spray*
> *Tails and fins like pennants wave*
> *But barely touch the world of man*
> *Content to stay where time began*
> *No show of force to change or scorn*
> *Nature's way, Earth's slow turn*

Unconcerned or unaware
That a world of light and air
Is not far; just there it lies
Just above their hooded eyes.

In his memory, Luke saw himself reading the poem in wonder. "This is really good," he had said to Norah when he was finished.

"You really think so?" she'd replied eagerly. "I have some others. Would you like to see them some time?"

Luke had said yes.

But she had never shown them to him. It wasn't too long after that that she and Kieran had been sent to live with Nell's sister in Minnesota. It was almost a year before they returned, and by that time, Norah had stopped writing poems.

Luke refolded the blue piece of paper and tucked it back inside the notebook. Memories, unbidden and unwelcome, washed over him—and though he tried, he could not stop them from coming. He didn't want to think about his unfinished book anymore at that moment. He slipped the notebooks under his arm, climbed the stairs to the kitchen, then to the bedrooms.

His head was swirling with events from his past, warm snippets of good times, sharp aches from the bad ones. He oddly felt like he did when a new story idea came to him, invading his brain and leaving him restless and unable to concentrate on anything else. Story ideas like that never gave him any peace until he began writing. It was how he had begun all his previous books—except the current one, the one that refused to be written. Or rather, the one he didn't want to write.

He made his way back to Ethan's old room and tossed the notebooks onto the bed. But he found himself staring at their covers. The pages in those notebooks held stories and ideas written during the most difficult times of his teenage years, and yet he had never written anything, not one word, about what he'd actually experienced. And he suddenly found that odd because he made sense of everything by writing about it. He always had. It was as if he wanted to pretend it had never happened.

He glanced at the open laptop on the bed beside the blue note-books—his new way of writing resting beside the old. He felt something like a shiver course through him as an idea slowly formed in his head. Maybe it had been no accident he'd found that poem today. Maybe it was no accident he was alone in his childhood home—and would be for many days—away from his comfortable life as Mystery Writer of the Year. Maybe it was no accident that now, when he found himself doubting his purpose and vision for his life, he was thrust back in time to the place where his hopes and dreams for his life had begun. And where some of them had ended.

For years he had thought the niggling voice that every so often called out, "Remember Norah?" was a hellish voice sent to taunt him with the garbage of the past. It was why he had pushed it away, kept his distance from Halcyon, refused to look back. Now, in the surreal quiet of his childhood home, he began to consider that the voice was not hellish after all, but quite the opposite. Perhaps it was not a taunting question meant to chain him to grief, but a command from heaven not to forget her. An instruction.

Not "Remember Norah?" but "Remember Norah."

Remember her.

He saw in his mind the woman in the green dress from the writer's conference, the silvery hue of her steel-gray eyes. Norah's eyes. No wonder he could not get the image of that woman out of his head. It wasn't seeing his fictional Eden that bewildered him. It was seeing Norah. He had been physically confronted with the part of his past he understood the least.

He was at once aware of a powerful urge to open the laptop and write. He had not felt this way in months. With the desire came the strangest notion that the story he simply *had* to write was his own. It would mean a departure from the Red Herring Detective Agency. It would mean a vacation for Aaron and Eden. It was quite possible that whatever he wrote would never see printer's ink. Alan might not approve. Might have a fit. He was a fiction editor, not a memoir editor. And Luke was certain his editor's words "Tell Luke to take all the time he needs" did not extend to starting a whole new book about himself and doing nothing with his current manuscript.

But Luke decided he didn't care. The story somersaulting in his head *was* a mystery. His genre. It was *his* mystery. But it was also real. It was real because the story had happened to him. As he envisioned journaling it, he began to sense that some kind of mental cleansing awaited him—that he was on the edge of finally understanding what it was that had suddenly made him feel like he had done nothing meaningful with his life.

Luke walked over to the bed, sat down, and pulled the laptop toward him. He felt energy churning within him, but he also sensed apprehension. He had never written about himself before. Even in college, he'd written very few nonfiction pieces. And this wouldn't be just an unimportant piece of nonfiction. It would be the written re-visitation of all the ugliness he'd left behind when Halcyon had ceased to be his home. It would stretch him, cleanse him. And, God willing, making peace with his past would hand him back his focus. If it didn't, he didn't know what he was going to do.

He called up a blank page on his laptop, took a deep breath, and whispered a prayer. As he positioned his fingers over the keyboard, he spontaneously looked across the hall to his old bedroom. He stared at its open doorway for a moment. A second later, he picked up his laptop. He walked into his old bedroom and sat down at the desk by the window that looked out onto his old tree house.

He whispered the prayer again as the first sentence formed itself in his mind: *Though I first met Norah when I was eight and she was six, it is the summer my dad built my tree house—the summer I turned twelve—that speaks "beginning" to me because so much happened within those four crooked walls...*

And as Luke began to write, he fell headlong into the tunnel of his past, into those forgotten days and nights that he had convinced himself—for the last seventeen years—he would never have to relive.

Part II

5

The nightly ballet of fireflies had just begun when Luke Foxbourne's father drove the last nail into the tree house of his son's dreams. It was early June, the summer of Luke's twelfth year, and despite his mother's dire predictions that a leg or two would soon be broken, his longed-for retreat was at last finished. It was made in two Saturdays—with scrap lumber and used nails—on the hefty limbs of the giant elm that stood outside Luke's upstairs bedroom window. It was lacking in engineering and design—there wasn't one 90-degree angle to be found anywhere in it—but it was not a bad effort by a small-town newspaper editor whose chief desire was to please his older son.

The elm itself was tall and robust, towering above the Foxbournes' house and the house next door, so that it kept the nearest side of both homes in perpetual shade. The tree was actually on Foxbourne property, but its stout branches reached across the little expanse of grass to the second-story windows of the green house next door, as if it begged to be shared. That detail about the elm bothered Luke. He didn't want to share the tree with the lady who lived in the green house next door. Penelope Janvik—everyone called her "Nell"—was perpetually in a sour mood. Her house was painted the color of green-goddess salad dressing, a kind of dressing Luke detested. To him, the house and the dressing looked like snot. It was an observation he had to keep to himself, as he was forbidden to say that audibly about either, especially at the dinner table.

The tree was one of the oldest and tallest in the quiet farming town of Halcyon, Iowa. Luke's mother, MaryAnn, who was admittedly melodramatic on occasion (and this partly because she was the local high school's drama teacher), panicked every time straight-line winds descended on the town, or worse, when the tornado siren began to wail. She always said a prayer for the elm tree when either of those things happened. She was not worried that the tree might get uprooted and then topple onto their house, crushing it like a pop can. She was just worried it would get uprooted. Period. Because that would mean the end of the tree.

"A house you can rebuild in a month or two," she had once said to Luke. "It takes a 120 years to grow a tree like this one."

When the tree house was finished, Jack told his son there would be two rules: One, Luke had to share it with Ethan, his little brother. Not all the time, but sometimes. Luke rolled his eyes at this. Eight-year-old Ethan asked too many questions. About everything. And Ethan hadn't been begging for the tree house the past year and a half. The tree house was Luke's idea, not Ethan's. But his dad pretended not to notice the eye-rolling and proceeded to announce Rule Two: There was to be no horseplay—no pushing or shoving, no dares, no show-off moves.

"You fall and break anything important, and out it comes," his dad said. "That's how I got your mom to agree to me building this at all."

"What if we break something *not* important?" asked Ethan, who was also listening to the rules. Luke gave his dad a look that said, *See what I have to live with?*

Jack looked at Ethan. "I suggest you break nothing at all," he said.

The tree house was accessible by a series of planks driven into the mighty trunk and also from Luke's bedroom window. It had taken Jack many hours of persuading before MaryAnn would let Luke access the tree house the second way. Luke had to first prove to her he could climb into the tree house by crawling—without the slightest jiggle—onto the thick branch just outside his window. It was a monstrous branch that had to be cut back every year so it wouldn't punch a hole in the yellow siding of the house. The first time Luke tried to show her—the day the tree house was finished—she wouldn't look.

"See, Mom?" he said from just inside the tree house after he'd made it across on the first try. His parents and Ethan were standing in his bedroom watching him. At least Ethan and his dad were watching. "It's easy."

But his mother hadn't seen anything because her eyes were closed. Luke had to do it again.

"See?" he said, when again he was speaking to her from within the safe confines of the tree house.

She shook her head and tapped her foot. Not usually a good sign.

"I can't believe I'm agreeing to this," she said between her teeth, surprising Luke.

He restrained himself from hooting, hollering, or doing anything that might be mistaken for horseplay.

"But Ethan, so help me," his mother continued, turning to her youngest, who was standing beside her in Luke's bedroom, "if you put so much as *one* finger on that branch outside that window, you will be grounded for the rest of your life. You use the little steps. Got it?"

Ethan pursed his lips together while he considered his mother's threat.

"How can you ground me when I'm an old man and you're already dead?" He was completely serious.

"The *little steps*," MaryAnn replied authoritatively and turned to descend to the kitchen, where supper dishes waited.

"I'm comin' up!" Ethan yelled to Luke, sprinting after his mother to head down the stairs and out the front door.

"You want to come in, too?" Luke said to his dad.

His dad smiled. "Thanks, anyway. Every bone is important when you're my age."

Luke smiled back. "Thanks for the tree house, Dad."

"My pleasure." His father turned away from the window and walked out of his bedroom.

Ethan began to climb up through the opening in the floor of the tree house. Luke scooted back, crawling on his hands and knees to the half he planned to claim as his own. He had a piece of chalk in his pocket, and he took it out and drew a wiggly line on the uneven floor.

Ethan poked his head through the opening.

"You're not allowed to cross this line," Luke said to his brother.

Ethan climbed in the rest of the way, looked at the part of the tree house that was left, calculated that it was certainly less than half, but shrugged. "Okay," he said as he sat down cross-legged and put his hands under his chin.

They sat in silence for a few minutes.

"So why do people say 'horseplay'?" his brother asked, furrowing his brow. "Horses don't play. Monkeys play. Puppies play. Why don't parents say 'no monkey-play'? Or 'no puppy-play'? Horses just stand around eating grass and swishing their tails."

Luke grimaced. "I don't have to answer your dumb questions when I'm on this side of the line," he said.

"Do I have to answer yours?" Ethan asked innocently.

Luke sighed, turned his back to him, and took a flashlight out of his pocket, shining it here and there until his mother called Ethan in to get ready for bed.

When his brother was gone, Luke stretched out on the floor of the tree house, peering at the stars that peeked through the slabs in the roof. He imagined he was alone in a great forest and there were elves hiding all around him, waiting to see if he would fall asleep there. Then they would sneak in and cut all his hair off, or steal his flashlight or paint his face with berry juice. He closed his eyes and listened to the sounds of crickets and bullfrogs serenading each other in the early June evening. He could almost forget there was a house on either side of him, one the color of lemon custard and the other the color of snot. He grinned. He could *think* that here. He could *say* it here. This was a magical place.

Halcyon sat on an expanse of prairie three hours northeast of Des Moines, two hours south of the Minnesota border and thousands of miles away from the mother country of the Dutch immigrants who settled the town in the late 1800s. Its founders initially chose a fine Dutch name for the town, but the railroad owners couldn't pronounce it—and since they owned more land than the settlers, the most educated of the railroad magnates changed it to Halcyon. The soothing name was supposed to attract newcomers so that the town would blossom and the railroad would make lots of money selling off its many parcels of land. But every child, and actually every adult, had to be told what "halcyon" meant. Youngsters who thought the town was named after Hal Somebody were set straight at Halcyon Elementary School as soon as they were old enough to understand that there are lots of complicated words that have simple meanings. Adults who didn't know that "halcyon" meant "peaceful and serene" found out as soon as they were brave enough to ask.

In its best days, Halcyon could meet every household need. It had at least one of everything essential to modern-day living. A bank. A hardware store. A factory. A hospital. A school. A library. A furniture store. A car dealership. A theater. Even a shoe-repair shop. There were half-a-dozen churches, four gas stations, three restaurants, two gift shops, and a drugstore. There were concerts in the park, community ice-cream socials where there was standing room only, and long lines to get theater tickets on Friday nights.

By 1982, however, the year Jack Foxbourne built Luke the tree house, times had changed for small Midwest towns like Halcyon. The ease with which a person could make the trip to Cedar Falls, about an hour's drive away, and even to Des Moines, changed the way Halcyon High School graduates chose a career. It changed the way their parents shopped. It even changed the way farmers farmed. The theater had long since closed, as had the furniture store, the shoe-repair shop, and two of the gas stations. The hospital had been downsized to a clinic. Typical headlines in the *Halcyon Herald,* Jack Foxbourne's newspaper, read, "School board discusses problem of declining enrollment" and "Corn prices fall again" and "Another downtown business closes its doors."

But there were also good things happening at that time in Halcyon. It wasn't all bad news. The town was still fiercely devoted to its high school's sports teams. Retired farmers still met for coffee at the downtown cafe every morning at nine o'clock. The churches were still full on Sundays. There were still old businesses on Main Street like Delft Delights, as well as new ones, like Denny's Movie Rentals. The paint factory was still hiring people. And the grain elevator at the edge of town had added a new metal storage bin that glistened like a mammoth tin can in the Iowa sunshine.

The town still had its newspaper, which was deemed by all as just as necessary to the town's survival as the school and the clinic. Jack wasn't the *Halcyon Herald*'s founder, and he wasn't a Halcyon native. He wasn't even Dutch. In fact, his last name was decidedly English. But he had slowly won the town's collective approval after ten long years of ownership. By then he was allowed to sip coffee with the Tante Anna's Cafe crowd, where all local news truly began and ended. The shrewd retirees who sipped cup after cup of black coffee and who liked to say to Jack, "If you ain't Dutch, you ain't much," nicknamed him "van der Foxbourne" that tenth year. And that's when he knew he was in the loop.

Jack and MaryAnn Foxbourne had moved to Halcyon from South Dakota in 1972 when Luke was two. Jack, who had been the editor, but not the owner, of a little newspaper in a town north of Sioux Falls, bought the *Halcyon Herald* from Abe DeGroot. The DeGroot family had owned the paper since its inception in 1902, and the passing of the torch had been tough for the older Halcyon generations. But Abe DeGroot's four children had all gone away to college and not come back, and no one else in town knew anything about running a newspaper. It was either welcome the newcomers or let the paper die. They opted to welcome Jack and MaryAnn Foxbourne simply because the other option was too frightening to consider. Besides, the newcomers had wisely kept Lucie Hermann, a Halcyon native, on staff, proving they weren't completely incompetent.

Two years after Jack Foxbourne took on the paper, he and MaryAnn had a second son, whom they named Ethan Abraham. The movers and shakers in town believed the infant's middle name was a sign that the Foxbournes were honoring Abe DeGroot and the newspaper's rich Dutch history. Jack wisely never let on that MaryAnn had picked Abraham as a middle name in honor of the great patriarch of Genesis.

The Foxbournes faithfully attended every community event, volunteered at the pancake booth at the Wooden Shoes Festival every July, taught Sunday school at the Christian Reformed Church on Tenth Street, and cheered at basketball games. MaryAnn became the new high school speech and drama teacher the year Ethan turned three, and the panache with which she helped Halcyon teenagers successfully pull off Broadway musicals earned her own fair share of admiration and respect. It had taken a decade, but the Foxbourne family had won Halcyon over.

Jack and MaryAnn were content with the way things had turned out, and inquisitive Ethan seemed comfortable with his birthplace, but as he'd grown, their older son, Luke had begun to feel slightly detached from his Iowa home. Though he'd been born in South

Dakota, and summer trips to see his grandparents had given him ample opportunity to see the state where his life began, he was familiar with no other life than this life. And because he knew no other life, he wasn't entirely sure why, as he grew, that he recognized a yearning to live in a big city, in a place far from Halcyon, and to do big things. Like write a book. Like write lots of books.

Luke knew from the first day he sat in it that the new tree house would be the beginning of leaving for him, though he did not say anything of this to his parents. He knew that whenever he would need to escape, whenever he'd need to travel somewhere faraway in his mind, all he'd have to do would be to climb out his bedroom window, scoot along the thick branch that beckoned him, and lose himself to his imagination within the crooked walls of the tree house. He knew he would look forward to those times. And then some day he really would escape.

6

Nell Janvik already lived in the house next door when Luke's parents moved to Halcyon in the early fall of 1972. She had lived there since 1948, the year she and her husband, Karl, and their son, Kenny, moved to town from the spare room at her parents' farmhouse. She had married Karl Janvik at the age of twenty, four months after they realized she was carrying his child. They had lived with Nell's parents for the first two years out of necessity since Karl seemed to have bad luck when it came to keeping a job. At least that's how he saw it.

When Nell's Grandmother Brooten died, she left her enough of an inheritance for a down payment on a small two-story house in town. It was common knowledge that Nell and Karl got a good deal on the house because it was in a mortgage foreclosure—the previous occupants had fled from their debts in the middle of a nameless night while Halcyon slept.

The following year, 1949, Nell and Karl had another son, whom they named Darrel, and the year after that the paint factory was built. Suddenly, there were jobs for everyone, even for unlucky people like Karl Janvik. Nell got a job there, too. But that was the last year friends and relatives remembered Nell Janvik being happy. By the time the Foxbournes became her neighbors, she had spent twenty-four years in the green house on Seventh Avenue, most of them as a single mother. She had lived there longer than anyone else on the block, which meant none of the neighbors had known her in better times.

The day the Foxbournes moved in, MaryAnn was given a pan of lasagna by the family across the street, a plate of brownies by the retired couple who lived on the other side of her new house, and a loaf of homemade bread by the widow who lived three doors down.

It was the widow, Ella Liekfisch, who warned MaryAnn not to expect much of a welcome from Nell Janvik.

"Nell's had a rough life," Ella said to MaryAnn in low tones, as if the walls in her new house were listening. "Her oldest son, Kenny, was killed in Vietnam last year."

"Oh, that's so sad!" MaryAnn replied, instantly feeling compassion for the woman named Nell she had not met yet.

"That's not all, either," Mrs. Liekfisch continued. "Her husband ran off on her when her boys were just kids. Never heard from him again. And the younger boy, Darrel, he's been in and out of trouble since the day his daddy left. He's living in California with some woman he's not even married to. I've heard there's a baby and everything. And usually one or the other is in jail for something."

MaryAnn must have shown on her face that she wondered how Mrs. Liekfisch knew all of this because the older woman suddenly told her.

"Nell bowls. She's in a league with a friend of mine. When Nell's drunk, she talks. Or so I've heard."

MaryAnn nodded, wondering how much of this she really needed to hear. "Sounds like she could use a friend," she said.

Mrs. Liekfisch studied her for a moment. "She could use a friend, but she doesn't want any more than the two or three she has, and she doesn't attract any others, I can tell you that," she finally said. "I've never seen her smile unless she's been drinking—and that's the honest-to-God truth."

"Well, thank you so much for the bread, Mrs. Liekfisch," MaryAnn replied. "It's wonderful to be welcomed so warmly."

"You just call me if you need anything, now," Mrs. Liekfisch said as she turned to go. "And I can sit for that sweet little one of yours anytime!"

MaryAnn stepped outside with her new neighbor and watched her walk past the green house, following her with her eyes and dodging the movers carrying in her sofa. Her eyes strayed from the retreating form of Mrs. Liekfisch and stayed on the green house for several moments before she went back inside.

The Foxbournes had been in the house for nearly three weeks before MaryAnn or Jack even saw Nell Janvik. Nell worked the swing shift at the paint factory and slept most mornings away. At 2 PM her TV would come on, and it would stay on until a few minutes before four when she left for work. When her windows were open, the smoke of her cigarettes would waft across the yards and drift into MaryAnn's kitchen. MaryAnn did not meet her face-to-face until they both happened to be on their porches at the same time one day, getting the day's mail.

MaryAnn had called out a cheery "hello!" And Nell seemed to become instantly irritated at having been noticed. She glanced up with a peeved look on her face.

Nell was a few inches shorter than her new neighbor but many pounds heavier. She had let her hair begin to turn gray any way it pleased. MaryAnn supposed she was in her early fifties, but the haunted expression on her face made her look older. She found out later Nell was only forty-six.

"I'm MaryAnn Foxbourne," she had said, as she closed the distance between them.

"Nell Janvik," Nell said without emotion, a cigarette dangling from one hand.

"Nell. That's a nice name. Is it short for something?"

"Penelope," Nell said gruffly, shoving her mail under her arm and starting to open her screen door.

"Nice to have met you!" MaryAnn said, hoping she sounded like she meant it.

Nell grunted a wordless reply and then disappeared inside her house.

Jack Foxbourne did not meet Nell until a week later, when he came home from a Saturday news event to see her struggling with a garage door that wouldn't open all the way. She was bent over on her driveway, pounding on the lower edge of her garage door with the flat of her hand—and cursing. He noticed for the first time the tattered remains of a net in a basketball hoop attached to the roof of her garage, a tiny reminder that the cantankerous Nell was someone's mother.

"Can I give you a hand?" he asked, walking toward her.

She whipped around to look at him. Jack noticed she had on a blue button-down shirt with her name embroidered on a patch. He figured she was on her way to the bowling alley. And was late.

"What?" she yelled back.

"I said, can I give you a hand with that?"

"Stupid thing won't open all the way!" she grumbled.

Jack took that for a yes.

He studied the door, checked the springs, and noticed a piece of rusted metal had wedged itself into the hinge on one side. He worked it loose and then raised the door the rest of the way.

"There you go," Jack said, grabbing his camera bag, waiting for her to say thanks. When she did not, he added, "I'm Jack Foxbourne, by the way."

"Nell Janvik," she said through her teeth, looking at her mischievous garage door.

"Nice to meet you, Nell," he said. She said nothing in return.

He turned to walk back to his own house and just as his back was fully to her, he heard Nell say, "Thanks."

Jack turned back around. "Anytime."

When he went into the kitchen, he put the camera bag down and walked over to MaryAnn, who was tearing up lettuce for a salad. He put his arms around her from behind and kissed her neck.

"I met Nell," he whispered.

She grinned. "I was right, wasn't I? Tell me I was right."

Jack grinned back. "You were right. She *does* make the Wicked Witch of the West seem as harmless as Auntie Em."

MaryAnn laughed and then shook her head. "Oh, I shouldn't say such things. She did lose her son last year, Jack. Ella Liekfisch told me his body was brought back in pieces. She must be hurting so bad to be so rude. It's probably her way of handling grief."

Jack tightened his embrace. "Maybe some day she'll come around and the two of you can have coffee together!"

MaryAnn leaned back into him. "Well, I seriously doubt that, but perhaps she'll get to the point where she doesn't scowl when she sees me coming."

Luke would spend his early childhood years in healthy fear of Nell Janvik. His parents knew he feared her, and they thought it was best that he continue to because then he would stay out of her yard and out of her way. As he grew, though, Luke's fear of Nell Janvik morphed into something more akin to disgust. And eventually, pity.

One late summer day, when Luke was eight and Ethan was four, while the two of them were making chalk drawings on their driveway, a van with a holed-out muffler drove down their street and turned into Nell Janvik's driveway. A man with stringy hair and a bandanna for a headband got out, followed by a woman with long, dark, curls. She was wearing very short cutoffs and a tank top that revealed too much. Even at eight, Luke knew enough to look away from her. The man opened the side door and a little girl with blonde braids jumped out. A baby was crying in the backseat.

"What do you think he wants?" the man was saying to the woman, but he appeared to be looking at the baby.

"He's probably hungry again," the lady said, opening a macramé purse and taking out a pack of cigarettes. "Here, I can take him."

Luke stole another look at the woman. She was wearing large hoop earrings and lots of makeup. Her nails were long and painted purple.

"Nah, I got him, Bel," the man said. "I want to show him to my mom."

"I have to go potty," the little girl said.

"Well, let's go inside and see Grandma," the man said, grabbing the crying infant out of the back of the van. "You can use her potty, Norah."

The man steadied the crying infant in one arm and slammed the van door shut. He walked to the front door, and the little girl trailed after him. The lady followed, stopping to cup her hand over the cigarette she was trying to light.

The man didn't knock on the door—he just opened it and yelled, "Ma! Are you home?" And then the four of them disappeared inside Nell's house.

Ethan went back to drawing looping circles on the cement. Luke noticed that the van had California plates. He pretended to draw, but really he was listening to see if the open windows in the Janvik house would reveal what kind of reception the man would get. The man had to be Darrel, Luke thought—the son Mrs. Liekfisch had said was born to break a mother's heart. Those little kids must be her grandchildren. He had heard Mrs. Liekfisch tell his mother that Darrel had two kids with that woman he lived with, so he knew Nell was somebody's grandma—but he'd never really thought of her as a grandmother until that moment. It didn't seem possible Nell Janvik would know how to act like a grandma.

He could hear noises inside the house, but he couldn't tell if they were happy noises or sad noises. Then the front door opened and Darrel stepped out. Nell was right behind him. She looked mad. Luke quickly looked down at the driveway and drew a large circle with his chalk, peering at the two of them with just his peripheral vision.

"Would it have killed you to call first?" Nell said. She had her hands on her hips.

"We wanted to surprise you, Ma," Darrel said, putting his hands in the front pockets of his jeans.

"I hear nothin' from you in two years—*two years*—and then you just show up on my doorstep! That's one heck of a surprise, Darrel. Are you in trouble? Is that why you came?"

"Come on, Ma! No, I'm not in trouble. Me and Belinda have been doin' really good."

"Congratulations."

"I mean it. I'm startin' a new job in two weeks, it's a good job. Benefits and everything. We're doin' great, Ma. I just wanted to see you before I start this new job. I won't get vacation time for a while. 'Sides, I thought you might want to see your new grandson. You know, we gave him Kenny's initials."

Luke heard Nell sigh.

"You could have at least called me, Darrel," she said, in as gentle a voice as Luke had ever heard her use.

Darrel stepped forward and put his arm around her. "But I wanted to surprise you! And I did!"

"Yeah, you did."

Out of the corner of his eye Luke could see Nell was smiling.

"I would have washed the sheets in the guestroom if I had known you were coming," she said, and Luke heard the van door open again. Darrel was pulling some cardboard boxes out.

"Ah, that's no big deal, Ma."

Nell was looking at the boxes. So was Luke. The boxes were full of clothes.

"Are those your clothes? Don't they use suitcases in California?"

Darrel laughed heartily. "Well, I'm sure they do in Hollywood! But we just make do with boxes from the grocery store. Look! They got handles!"

The two of them carried the boxes inside.

"I'm tired of drawing," Ethan said, getting to his feet and walking toward the front door. After a few minutes alone on the cement, Luke got up and followed him inside.

∽∞∾

That night, while Nell was at work, and while Luke tried to fall asleep in his bedroom, Darrel and the lady named Belinda sat on Nell's porch, drinking beer and smoking. They were laughing, too, and Luke could not fall asleep. He got up and went downstairs to announce his problem. His parents were sitting at the kitchen table having ice cream. He stood at the foot of the stairs. They did not see him.

"I bet you ten dollars *she's* not Dutch," his mother was saying, scraping up the last bit of ice cream from her bowl with her spoon.

"Well, I bet you ten bucks those aren't cigarettes they're smoking," Jack replied, pushing his empty bowl toward the center of the table.

"Jack! Are you serious? Should we call the police or something?"

"I think they'll be gone in a few days," he said, shaking his head. "That takes care of *that* problem. We still have to live next door to Nell when they go, you know."

"But Jack, what about those kids?" MaryAnn said. "When they go, they'll take their 'problem' with them *and* those kids. Don't you think maybe we should do something? Tell somebody?"

Jack sat back in his chair. "I don't know what kind of father

Darrel is, MaryAnn. I don't know if his legal troubles necessarily make him a bad one. And I don't know his wife, or whatever she is, at all. I don't want to jump to conclusions."

"Well, I think we should keep our eyes open while they are here," MaryAnn said, rising from her chair, grabbing the bowls, and walking to the sink with them.

"Always a good idea to keep your eyes open—unless you're sleeping," Jack said, and Luke heard his mother chuckle.

He decided then to make his way quietly back to his room without saying anything. As he climbed the stairs he wondered what it was his parents would be looking for.

He wondered why they would be keeping their eyes open when it came to those kids. And even though he didn't know why, he decided he would, too.

⁓

The following day began hot and humid and got worse as it wore on. At two o'clock, when Luke and Ethan began quarreling over who had the biggest scab, MaryAnn sent them outside to run through the sprinkler, promising them a Popsicle if they could manage to get along for twenty minutes without fighting.

After cooling down for a few minutes, Luke went dripping into the garage to get a box of plastic cars so he could sit in the spray of water and pretend the cars were being swept away in a hurricane. When he came back Ethan was standing on the edge of the wet grass talking to Nell's granddaughter. She was wearing green shorts with white dots and a purple shirt with blue stripes. She must've slept in her braids; wispy, blonde hairs were poking out of the twists every which way.

"I have to stay outside because Grandma and Kieran and my mommy are all sleeping," she was saying to Ethan. "Daddy went to see friends. He said if I bother them, I'll get it."

Ethan stuck his tongue out to catch a drop of sprinkler water falling off the tip of his nose. "What will you get?"

"A spanking, maybe," the little girl said, looking toward the house.

Luke was standing there holding his cars, and she turned to him.

"What's your name?" she said. Her unkempt hair and crazy fashion sense didn't hide her luminous gray eyes. Luke had never seen eyes that gray before. They were as gray as an old person's hair.

"Luke," he answered.

"My name is Norah Andromeda Janvik. I'm six. Are you six?"

"I'm eight," Luke replied, miffed she would think him a candidate for kindergarten. For Pete's sake. He was going into third grade in two weeks. And what kind of name was *Andromeda?*

"Are you six?" Norah said to Ethan.

"He's four," Luke said quickly.

"Oh."

"You want to run through the sprinklers with us?" Ethan said.

"Okay."

Before Luke could say or do anything else, Norah jumped into the arc of water waving back and forth on his front lawn. She didn't go inside to put on a bathing suit or to get a towel or to even ask if she could. She just did it. Ethan followed her. They started laughing and squealing. He was still standing there with his box of cars in his hands a few moments later when his mother came outside to see who had joined them. Luke thought his mom seemed pleased that Nell's granddaughter had come over.

"Hey, let's get the wading pool out!" MaryAnn said. "Luke, come help me."

Ethan started cheering, and Norah, watching him, started cheering, too.

Luke set his cars down, followed his mother into the garage, and steadied a ladder as she reached for a plastic wading pool resting on the rafters in the garage.

"Here it comes," MaryAnn said, and the yellow pool half floated, half fell to the garage floor.

"You grab one end and I'll grab the other," MaryAnn said, and Luke obeyed.

They set the pool down on the grass and MaryAnn walked over to the spigot and turned off the sprinkler.

"Take off the sprinkler and put the hose in the pool, would you, Luke?" she said. And again, Luke wordlessly obeyed. MaryAnn turned the spigot back on and the pool began to fill.

"Can I get the bath toys?" Ethan asked.

MaryAnn nodded. "Just dry off your feet first." Then she turned to Norah. "I'm Mrs. Foxbourne. I'm Luke and Ethan's mom."

"My name's Norah."

"Nice to meet you, Norah," MaryAnn said. "Would you like to go get your swimsuit on, Norah?"

Norah swung her head around to look at Nell's house.

"No," she said.

Luke thought his mother seemed surprised by Norah's answer.

"She can't go in or she might get spanked," he said suddenly. He wanted his mother to know he had kept his eyes open, too. Or maybe it was his ears.

MaryAnn looked from her son to the little girl.

"No problem. You can just get your clothes wet. It's so hot today, they'll probably dry in no time."

Ethan came back out of the house with a plastic container of bath toys and dumped the contents into the pool.

"Hey! A whale!" Norah said, stepping into the pool and plopping down into the water, not seeming to notice the chill. She picked up a plastic whale in a shade of cobalt blue. "I've seen a real whale. They don't look like this. They're gray."

"I've got a giant octopus, too," Ethan said, stepping into the pool but easing into the water slowly. He picked up a bright orange bath toy with sprawling, tentacled legs.

"That's a squid," Norah said, picking up a bucket with a sieve for a bottom and watching the water fall out of out it. "Look! Mermaid hair!"

Luke looked over at his mother. She, too, seemed amazed a six-year-old knew the difference between a squid and an octopus.

"You like sea animals, Norah?" MaryAnn said.

"Yup. So does my mom. She was born on the beach. She has a book about ocean animals her daddy gave her. Whales are her favorite. They're my favorite, too."

Norah picked up the hose and held it over her head, dousing her crooked braids.

"You going in, Luke?" his mother asked him.

He shook his head.

"I'll play on the porch with my cars."

She gave him a look that said, *The pool is plenty big enough for three,* and he gave her one that said, *But I don't want to go in.*

He played in the shade of the porch, lining up his cars on the top cement step and then sending them crashing off onto the middle and bottom steps. He pretended not to be interested in the deep-sea adventures taking place in the wading pool. He didn't care that Gumby rode the whale. Or that Pokey rode him next. He made crashing noises with his voice as his cars sailed to the cement walkway.

"Whales aren't fish," he heard Norah say. "They breathe air. They have to come to the top of the water like this." Norah was bringing the head of the plastic cobalt-blue whale to the choppy surface of the wading pool.

Luke found himself watching her, and when he realized it, he tore his eyes away. He didn't care what a six-year-old knew about whales. He scooped up his cars and sent them flying off the steps again.

After a while, his mom came out with a box of Popsicles in one hand, and a hairbrush and a towel for Norah in the other. While Norah sat drying in the sun and licking a Popsicle, his mother gently combed out her wet tangled hair and redid her braids.

Then they played Candy Land.

Then they watched cartoons.

All the while, Luke noticed that his mother kept an eye and ear to the front yard, no doubt ready to explain to Nell or Belinda that Norah was with them. But no one stepped outside the house to look for her or call for her.

At four-thirty the kids went back outside to play. Norah sat on Jack Foxbourne's old skateboard and scooted around in the driveway while Ethan puttered around her on a red tricycle. Luke pedaled back and forth up and down the sidewalk on his new two-wheel bike, waiting for his dad to come home from the newspaper office. At a quarter to five, Belinda opened the screen door of Nell Janvik's house. She had the baby on her shoulder and a cigarette in her other hand.

"Norah!" she called.

" 'Bye!" Norah said, scampering off the skateboard and running back to Nell's house without looking back. The skateboard rolled to a stop by a forsythia bush.

Luke and Ethan watched her go. She didn't glance back once.

"Hey, baby doll!" Belinda said when Norah reached her. "Did you have fun with the kids next door?"

They went inside, and Luke didn't hear Norah's answer. He wondered, though, how Norah's mom knew she had been with them. He didn't see how she could. She had to have just suddenly realized it and then been perfectly okay with it. Luke thought that was both odd and spectacular. His mother always had to know where he was. He wondered how long Darrel and his family were staying and if Norah would be coming over again. He couldn't decide if he liked that idea or not. She was a girl, after all.

But Norah did come over the next afternoon and the next. And apparently without having to check in with anybody. It was almost as if she was accountable to no one. As if she were older than he was. Knew more. Feared less.

All the while Nell's company stayed with her, the lights were always on in the house, and there always seemed to be some kind of yelling going on. Happy yelling, raucous yelling, and mad yelling. And in between the yelling were the intermittent wails of the baby.

And none of it seemed to faze Norah, who came and went without comment on any of it.

On the morning of the fourth day, the Janvik house was eerily quiet as Darrel began shoving cardboard boxes back in the van. A few minutes after nine, Norah got into the van, followed by Belinda, Darrel, and baby Kieran. The van's motor coughed to life, and Darrel backed out of the driveway, honking twice as he drove away. Luke saw that Nell was watching them drive away from just inside her screen door.

Luke watched, too, from just inside his.

He didn't see Norah again for four years. Not until he was twelve.

She came again the summer his father built the tree house.

7

A July day in Halcyon can be hot and sticky, breezy and cool, or cloudy with haze. It can begin sunny and pleasant and then end in blinding thunderstorms that make the grain farmers pace their kitchens in worry. It can distinguish an outdoor birthday party or ruin it. Summer days in Halcyon, contrary to its name, are defined by extreme weather that accompanies them, just like most winter days are.

Luke would always remember the day Norah came back to visit Halcyon as being breezy and sticky at the same time—an odd combination.

Luke and his family had just returned from a weeklong family vacation to South Dakota—all of the Foxbourne family vacations were seven days long because Jack Foxbourne would entrust the paper to his employees for one press day, and only one. Luke awoke a little after ten that first morning back, glad that his mother let him sleep in because at twelve he was already learning that sleeping in helped fill long, boring summer days. It was also the day before Halcyon's annual Wooden Shoes Festival. Jack Foxbourne usually took his summer vacation the week before the festival because there was so much preview information that the paper practically wrote itself the week he was away.

When Luke came downstairs that morning, Ethan was watching *The Price is Right* on TV, and his mom was scurrying about in the kitchen, obviously late for something.

"Oh, good. You're up," she said when he came in. "I'm running late. I was supposed to be at the gym at ten to help decorate for the coronation tonight." She pointed to a box on the kitchen table. "We got our mail from while we were gone, and there's an envelope in there that should have gone to Nell. It got put with our stuff by mistake. Can you take it over to her later this afternoon? And don't just put it in her mailbox, Luke. She'll wonder why it's so late, and it's not the carrier's fault. Just tell her whoever sorted at the post office that day just made a mistake, okay?"

Luke rolled his eyes. Why did he have to make excuses for the post office? "I don't see why I can't just put it in her mailbox," he said, grabbing a cereal bowl from the cupboard.

"Because, Luke, it'd be better for everybody if you just tell her what happened than for her to jump to conclusions," MaryAnn said, grabbing her car keys.

"It'd be better for everybody if she just jumped off a *cliff*," he mumbled.

MaryAnn ruffled his hair as she walked past him. "Nice comeback, dear, but you don't want to grow up to be like her, now, do you?"

He bristled at the unthinkable and then grabbed a spoon from the dish drainer.

"Oh," his mother said, popping her head back through the doorway. "Don't go over there until you know she's up. Oh, and if you and Matt go to the swimming hole today and there's no adult there, wading only. Don't go where you can't touch the bottom. And take Ethan with you."

"Mom!"

"I mean it, Luke. I mean 'em both. Wading only if there's no adult, and Ethan has to go with you. See you late this afternoon."

Then she was gone. Luke heard her yell a goodbye to Ethan in the other room.

As Luke ate his Lucky Charms he glowered at the envelope his mother had left leaning on a pitcher filled with plastic daisies.

Surprisingly, it was the envelope that annoyed him more than the thought of wading like a four-year-old in the swimming hole—even more than taking Ethan with him. He had long ago vowed to have as little to do with Nell Janvik as possible. His dad made him shovel her driveway every now and then in wintertime, but she was never awake when he did it, so thankfully he never had to talk to her. The only other times he ventured onto her property were to retrieve a ball or sometimes to play the tiniest of tricks on her. The tricks were mostly harmless, and he only did them when Matt, his best friend, was over and they were bored. And when Ethan wasn't around to tattle.

The two boys had once filled Nell's gardening shoes with water. They had been easy to get to because, like in most small Midwest towns, there were no fences between the houses and Nell always left her shoes on her back-door step. She had cursed something terrible when she slipped her feet into them, and Luke and Matt, who were hiding behind the giant forsythia bush between the two houses, nearly suffocated trying not to laugh out loud. And then one time while she was sleeping, he and Matt had twisted into an impossible mess the tiny strands on the wind chime that hung on her porch. She had cursed then, too, when she noticed it the next day. Matt hadn't been around to hear Nell call down curses on the wind, so Luke had to tell him how she'd mumbled obscenities and then finally grabbed the chimes and thrown them into her garbage can, sending a cacophony of nightmarish music, for a brief moment anyway, from out of the depths of her garage.

The most recent trick they'd played on her was just last month. It was actually sort of dangerous, and Luke had had the first serious pangs of guilt. Nell's car had been sitting outside her garage in her driveway. Luke and Matt had snuck over to it, released the parking brake, and then slipped the transmission out of park. They scrambled back to Luke's porch as the car slowly rolled down the driveway and came to a quiet stop in the middle of the street. Someone driving by had to pull over and get out, and come to the door to tell Nell her car was blocking traffic.

Matt had still been laughing when he'd gone home an hour later. But as the day wore on, Luke couldn't stop imagining how Nell's car could have caused an accident. Someone might have gotten hurt. His conscience had needled him the rest of the day.

As he sat at the kitchen table now, a month later, eating Lucky Charms and looking at Nell's mail, he still felt it: the shame of having wronged a person who hardly ever had anything good happen to her.

Ethan came into the kitchen and ambled over to the kitchen table, noticing the propped-up envelope.

"Penna…Penna…Penna-Loap. Penna-loap," he sounded out, looking at the envelope. "Who would name their kid 'Penna-loap'?"

"That's 'Penelope,' you dufus," Luke said, giving his younger brother a look of hearty irritation. "That's Nell's real name."

"*That's* 'Penelope'? Hmmm. Looks like Penna-loap to me."

Luke suddenly had an idea. "Mom wants you to take this over to Nell's later."

"Liar. I heard her tell you that *you* had to take something over to Nell's."

Luke pushed his chair back and stomped over to the sink with his bowl. "Well, why can't you do it?"

"She asked you. Besides, I don't like Nell."

"You think I do?"

Ethan grabbed the Lucky Charms box and walked back to the living room with it. "I'm not doing it."

"C'mon. I'll give you fifty cents," Luke called after him.

"I wouldn't do it for fifty dollars."

"You would so, you little twerp."

"I would not."

"Would so."

"Would not."

Luke fumed for a moment longer and then took the stairs, two at a time, up to his room. He stepped out of his pajama bottoms and pulled on a pair of swimming trunks and a T-shirt. He hoped Matt remembered they were going to the swimming hole later this afternoon. At least that had been their plan when Luke had left for South Dakota the previous week. He'd call Matt after lunch—after taking that stupid envelope to Nell. Until then, he'd go into the tree house with his notebook. He had a story idea about a brave young man with a dolt for a brother who had to live next door to an evil witch.

Luke had written a page-and-a-half, had read some of the comic books he kept in the tree house, and then was starting to write again when he heard the sound of a car in Nell's driveway. He peered out of a well-placed knothole. The car was silvery blue with a speckling of rust around every wheel rim. It made all kinds of noises when whoever was driving tried to shut it off. The engine finally died, and the driver's door opened. A skinny man, bald on top but with lots of hair on the sides, stepped out. Even with his limited view, Luke thought he knew him. Behind the man another car door opened, and a girl with honey-blonde hair climbed out. She turned and then leaned back inside. Luke couldn't see what she was doing. Then she stepped back and helped a little boy get out. The two children stretched and yawned like they had been asleep, though Luke figured it was after eleven by now. He moved to one of the window openings in the tree house and cautiously looked out. The car had California plates. The girl looked up then, and their eyes met. Luke scooted back.

He knew who these people were. He remembered their faces. At least the man and the little girl's faces. The baby was now a four-year-old boy.

Darrel. Norah. Kieran.

But where was Belinda?

He listened as he heard the door of the trunk open and close.

"I want my pillow," the little boy said.

"Let's just leave it in the car right now, bud," Darrel said. "C'mon. Let's see if Grandma is awake."

Luke heard Darrel and the kids walk up to the porch, heard Darrel try the knob, heard it stop in his hands. He began to knock. "Ma! Ma!" he called.

"MA!" Darrel repeated louder when there was no answer.

Finally, Luke heard the door open.

"Good Lord!" Nell's voice.

He had never heard Nell say anything about God that made it seem like she thought He was good. It was usually the other way around. But she said it today. *Good Lord.*

"Hey, Ma!" Darrel said. "Hope you don't mind us stoppin' through."

Nell let out a long sigh. "It wouldn't stop you from comin,' though, would it—if you thought I minded."

"Grandma's just foolin'!" Darrel said happily.

Luke heard the door open wide on squeaky hinges. Then it shut.

He frowned. He had to take that stupid envelope over, and now Nell had company. That weird Darrel. And those kids.

He scooted across the branch to the window and climbed back into his bedroom. He walked out and down the hall to his parents' room to call up Matt.

But Matt wasn't home.

"He's gone to his cousin's house for the day," his mother said.

"Oh. Okay."

Luke hung up. *Well, that's just wonderful,* he grumbled to himself. None of his other friends lived in town. That meant the only person to go with him to the swimming hole this afternoon was Ethan. He wasn't allowed to go there alone, and who could say if anyone else would be there today? And it didn't matter that he could swim circles around his brother. His parents wouldn't let him go to the swimming hole alone. Ever.

He trudged down the stairs. Ethan was still watching TV, but he had a jigsaw puzzle out and was sorting the pieces.

"So you want to come to Goose Pond with me?" Luke said, his voice flat.

Ethan whipped his head around. "Why?"

Luke gave him a look of exasperation. "Because it's hot and we've got nothing better to do."

"Yeah, but you called me a twerp," Ethan said, furrowing his brow and wondering perhaps if his brother might be planning to drown him.

"So?"

Ethan threw a puzzle piece into the box and stood up. "Okay."

"Let's take some sandwiches," Luke said, and Ethan followed him into the kitchen.

A few minutes later they carefully placed peanut-butter-and-jelly sandwiches into Luke's school bag, empty now since it was summer. A bag of Cheetos went into the bag next along with two cans of Orange Crush.

"Go get some towels and I'll put air in the bike tires," Luke said, heading out the front door to the garage at the back. The mile-long dirt road to the swimming hole was best traveled with firm tires. He had nearly finished when he heard Nell's back door open and shut. Then he heard voices.

"Bel and me are havin' a rough time right now, " Darrel said in a quiet voice. "She's living with one of her girlfriends. But she'll come back."

"You been sleepin' around on her?" Nell asked, and Luke felt his face color.

"Thanks a lot, Ma!"

"Well, have you?"

There was a moment of silence. Luke made not a sound as he listened.

"Hey, it's not like she hasn't been sleepin' around on me!"

"Did you learn *nothing* from the hell I went through with your father?" Nell snorted.

"She left *me*, Ma. It ain't the way it was with you and Dad. She left *me!*"

Seconds of silence.

"She left those kids, too? You telling me she left her kids?" Nell's voice again.

"She…I…I wouldn't let her take them. I took them to a friend's house. She didn't know where they were. She's doing drugs again, Ma. I don't want the kids getting mixed up with all that."

More seconds of silence.

"Does she know you're here? Does she know the kids are here?" Nell said.

"I'm not stayin' long, Ma. I'll go back and we'll work it out. I know we will. She'll realize she can't do drugs and have the kids, and then she'll come back and she'll be clean again."

"So why did you come?" Nell said after a pause.

"Because, Ma," Darrel said, "Norah and Kieran are your grand-kids. Don't you want to see them?"

"Darrel, did it ever occur to you I might want more than just a visit from you every three or four years? That a phone call that doesn't include a plea for money would be nice? That a note to tell me where you're living would sure be helpful? I sent those kids Christmas presents two years in a row and they came back unde-liverable both times because you didn't have an address and didn't even bother to tell me."

"Ma, I called you to tell you I lost my job. I told you we were living with friends."

"Yeah, you told me a year later!"

"Well, we had some rough times. I can't help that."

There was a long pause. Luke waited.

"I am through with getting hurt by people, Darrel," Nell finally said. "Through with it. It is a heck of a lot easier for me not to see those grandkids than to see them. Because who knows when or if I will ever see them again."

"Ma, what are you saying?" Darrel exclaimed. "Of course you'll see them again! They're *my* kids. You're *my* mother. What is with you?"

"What is with me? What is *with* me?" Nell said. Her voice sounded hard. "Nothing and no one is *with* me, Darrel. I am alone. I have learned to live this way because I've had to. My parents are dead, my sister ignores me, your daddy abandoned me, your brother lies dead and buried in the cemetery, and you're two thousand miles away in California and in and out of jail. There is *nothing* with me."

"Well, we're here with you now," Darrel said softly.

Nell said nothing. Luke heard her open the screen door and go back inside the kitchen. Darrel followed. Luke stood up and put the tire pump away. Listening to Nell and Darrel's conversation made him feel angry and ashamed. He didn't think he wanted to play any more tricks on Nell Janvik.

But he did have to get that envelope to her. Maybe Darrel would answer the door and he could just give it to him. He sighed. He just wanted it to be over with.

Ethan came out of the house with the backpack. Two towels were sticking out of it.

"I'll be right back," Luke said and he stepped back into his house, into the kitchen and grabbed the envelope. He came back out and Ethan looked at him. Something like compassion fell across Ethan's face.

"I'll come with you," he said, and the two brothers crossed the lawn to Nell's house.

Luke stepped onto the porch and couldn't help but notice the empty hook where wind chimes had once hung. He looked away and rang the doorbell.

Seconds later, Norah came to the door. Even through the screen, Luke could see she hadn't changed much in four years. She was taller, of course, and any traces of baby fat were gone. Her blonde hair had darkened some, but her eyes were still two circles of liquid pewter.

"This...this came to our house by mistake," he said, holding out the envelope. "It belongs to...to your grandmother."

Norah cocked her head, and it seemed to Luke she was surprised he knew who she was. Then a smile broke across her face.

"I remember you," she said slowly. "I played at your house the last time we came."

"Yeah, that's right. Well, here's the letter."

"Who's there, Norah?" Nell's voice rang out from somewhere in the house.

"It's, um...I can't remember your names," she said, looking at Ethan now too.

"Luke. I'm Luke. This is Ethan." His brother had a rather silly look on his face, Luke thought. But then it occurred to him that Ethan had only been four the last time Norah was here. He didn't remember her.

"It's the kids next door," Norah yelled over her shoulder. "They got some mail of yours by accident."

"Here," Luke said again, extending his hand.

Norah opened the door and took the envelope. Luke saw her eyes travel to the backpack Ethan was holding and the towels sticking out of it.

"You guys going swimming somewhere?"

"We're going to the swimming hole," Ethan happily volunteered.

"Oh? Where is it?"

"You gotta go past the water tower and then there's this dirt road that goes to it," he continued. Luke wanted him to shut up.

"Can I come with you?" she said.

Luke opened his mouth to say something—he didn't know what—but Ethan said, "Sure!" and Norah let the screen door fall closed and turned to head back into the house. Luke shot Ethan a look, but he was pushing the towels farther into the bag and wasn't looking at him.

"Can I go swimming with the kids next door?" Luke heard Norah ask.

"Where at?" Darrel's voice. "The pool? The swimming hole?"

"They said the swimming hole. Can I go?"

"Well, yeah, I guess. Take Kieran, though. And keep your eye on him. Grandma and I need to talk."

Luke closed his eyes and shook his head. A girl and a toddler. He hoped to heaven none of his other friends were there to see him arrive with a girl and a little kid. This whole day was turning out to be a disaster.

He turned to Ethan. "Why did you say yes?" he said through his teeth.

But his brother just gave him a blank look that said, *Why wouldn't I say yes?*

A few minutes later Norah appeared at the door wearing a turquoise-blue swimsuit and carrying two faded pink bath towels and a paper sack. Behind her was Kieran, a little boy with a head full of dark, curly hair. Luke wondered if the kid had ever had a hair-cut—ever. He looked like a little girl.

He said nothing as he turned and walked back to his own house, wondering if his mother would get after him for riding his bike and making Norah and Kieran run along behind him. He was aware of Ethan, Norah, and Kieran following him.

"Do you have an extra bike?" Norah said. "I can ride with Kieran sitting in front of me. I do it all the time at home."

Luke looked at her. And then he looked in the garage. Well, there was his mother's bike. His father's bike. And his own. He couldn't believe he was doing this.

"Take mine. I'll ride my dad's," he said, motioning to his three-speed Schwinn, only a month old, and then heading into the garage to get his dad's bike.

"Okay," Norah said, taking the handlebars and sitting down on the banana seat of the best birthday present he had ever gotten so far. She reached down for her little brother. "Here we go, Kieran," she said, scooping him up and placing him on the tip of the long seat. "Put your legs right here," she said, pointing to the horizontal bar that made his bike a boy's bike and not a girl's. She shoved the bath towels into the paper bag and started fiddling with how to carry it and steady her little brother.

"Here, I'll take it," Luke said, surprising himself with his spontaneous act of courtesy. She handed the paper bag to him wordlessly, and he tucked it under his arm.

They pedaled away. Luke kept as much distance between them as he dared. He knew if his mother saw how Norah and Kieran were riding, she would throw a fit. He wished for a second that she were driving home just then so she could see them. She wouldn't allow it. But then she would probably insist on driving them all out to Goose Pond.

Only sissies had their mothers drive them out to Goose Pond.

He took the shortest route to the street going toward the water tower.

8

Halcyon's swimming hole, also known as Goosen's Pond to the over-fifty crowd but simply as Goose Pond to the younger generations, was the only swimming hole in the county with a maintained beach of playground sand and side-by-side porta-potties. The swimming hole memorialized Halcyon pioneer and dairy farmer Hans Goosen, who willed the pond to the county's parks and recreation department when he died in 1950. The gift was partly because the farmland around the pond was untillable, and partly because scores of teenagers were already sneaking out to the pond on hot, humid evenings to splash away the summer heat, and had been for decades.

Shaped roughly like the state of Texas, the swimming hole was the size of two city blocks. It was home to several varieties of pan fish, a population of snapping turtles, and the occasional legendary lake monster; a tale spun every now and then to keep youngsters from visiting the swimming hole unattended.

It was surrounded on all sides but one with prairie grasses and gently rolling knolls. On the farthest edge, however, there was an outcropping of stone, perfect for jumping off of and for creating panic for mothers who liked to worry. The mile-long gravel road to the pond began at the back legs of the Halcyon water tower at the south end of Eleventh Street and across from Halcyon High School.

Luke now left the smooth asphalt and hit the uneven surface of the gravel road, adjusting his speed and tightening his hold on the handlebars of his dad's bike. He glanced back to make sure that little kid didn't go flying off the banana seat when Norah switched over to the gravel, and though the handlebars went every which way as she negotiated the transfer, she maintained control. Ethan was right behind her.

As Luke neared the pond he could see two cars parked on the pea-gravel parking lot next to the *Warning! No Lifeguard on Duty!* sign. Two large, pale-skinned women were lounging on the beach, talking and watching their children play in the water. Though the kids—there were five of them—were squealing and yelling and being otherwise annoying, he was actually glad those women were there with their noisy brats because it meant he could swim out as far as he wanted—though he had a hard time imagining either one of the hefty women coming to his rescue. Sometimes his mother's rules made no sense to him.

He parked his bike against a wooden parking-lot rail, and Norah and Ethan pedaled in behind him and did the same. It was hot, and he was sticky from riding and the rising humidity.

"It's so small!" Norah exclaimed as she lowered Kieran to the ground.

Luke looked across the blue surface of Goose Pond, thinking to himself that you could probably fit a dozen Olympic-size swimming pools in it. It was better than nothing. Wasn't it?

"Yeah, I guess," he said.

"Where I live you can't see the other side of the water," she said. "We live a block away from the ocean."

Luke had never seen the ocean. He had been to the shore of Lake Superior once with his grandparents, but he knew that was not the same.

He had nothing to say to Norah's comment, so he just stepped over the guardrail and walked across a grassy patch to the sand. He slipped off his sandals and pulled his T-shirt over his head. Ethan dropped the backpack on the sand and did the same.

"Are there jellyfish?" Kieran asked, looking across the strange water that had no tide.

"Nope. No jellyfish," Norah said, helping him take his T-shirt off.

Luke started to head to the water's edge but he turned back around. "Can you swim?" he said to Norah.

"Of course I can swim. I'm ten!"

"Well, you can jump off those rocks over there but you can't dive. Parents don't like it, and it's a park rule." Then he turned to Kieran. "Can he swim?"

"I can swim!" Kieran said.

"No, not really," Norah answered.

"I can so!"

"Kieran, don't be a liar."

"I'm not a liar!"

"Kids who can't swim have to stay at knee-deep water," Luke said.

"Is that a park rule, too?" Norah asked.

Luke didn't want to baby-sit Kieran Janvik. Nor did he want his mother to come down on him for not having been the responsible, oldest one in the group.

"It's *my* rule." He strode into the water and didn't look back.

He plunged through the water, the chill sending shock waves throughout his body. He took wide strokes, wanting to be far away from the beach, the big women, their noisy kids, and Nell's grandchildren. He swam out to the stone outcropping and arrived breathless several minutes later. He climbed out of the water and sat on the first ledge, his chest rising and falling heavily. The rock was warm from the sun, and the clammy breeze kissed his wet body. On the other side of the pond he could see Ethan standing in ankle-deep water, dashing about as if in pursuit of something—a frog perhaps. Norah was sitting in the water watching Kieran splash about. He had found an abandoned Frisbee and was scooping water with it while one of the other children watched him. Luke leaned back on the rock face behind him, letting the warming rays spread across his body.

He lost track of time. He didn't know how long he had been reclining there when he heard the sound of someone swimming toward him. He opened his eyes. It was Norah. He sat up quickly, looking past her to the beach across from them. Ethan had the Frisbee now and was playing with one of the other kids. Kieran was sitting at the shoreline, playing in the wet sand. Norah climbed onto the rock next to him.

"You left your little brother?" he asked.

Norah looked across the water. "He's okay." She turned back to him and then to the rocks above them. "I'm going to jump."

He moved aside, not wanting her to use his shoulder to climb to the jumping rock above him. But Norah climbed past him and past the jumping rock to the lip of the outcropping twenty feet above his head.

"You're jumping from *there?*" Luke asked.

She peered down at him. "Yeah. You said I could."

"I meant you could jump from the jumping rock," he said. "That one." And he pointed to the second ledge a few feet above him.

"What's wrong with jumping from here?"

"Well, that's not where people jump from."

"Why not?"

" 'Cause it's…it's high. I don't know how deep the water is."

"It looks deep to me."

"You can't tell how deep a swimming hole is by *looking* at it," he replied.

"Here I go!" Norah said, and before he could say anything else, Norah stepped off the top ledge, falling into the water at his feet and dousing him with spray. He sucked in his breath and waited for her to surface. It seemed like a long time before her head broke the churned surface of the water. He felt strangely relieved when she turned and looked at him with those steel-gray eyes.

"It's deep enough," she said. "I tried to touch the bottom but I couldn't see it. Too deep."

Luke was suddenly afraid she would challenge *him* to jump off the top of the rock and try to touch the deepest part of Goose Pond. He didn't want to do either, and it bothered him that it was fear that kept him from wanting to. She was a girl. She was two years younger than him. He shouldn't be afraid to do what she had just done, but he was—and there was nothing he could do about it.

Norah climbed back onto the rock beside him and as she did, Luke noticed movement on the other side of the pond. The women were gathering their things and their children. They were leaving.

"I have to go back to the other side," he said, slipping back into the water. "Not allowed to be this far out when there aren't any adults on the beach."

Norah followed his gaze to the other side of the pond. The women were getting into their cars. "Is that your rule, too?"

Luke pushed off the rock with his feet. "My mom's," he said, swimming away.

He didn't care if she followed him, but he had to admit he wanted her to. He didn't want to have to insist she keep to his mother's rules but he knew that since she was his so-called guest, his mother would expect him to insist on it.

He heard her swimming behind him, though. In fact, she overtook him halfway across the pond, arriving at the shore several seconds ahead of him.

"Take me swimming!" Kieran said to her when she arrived back at the water's edge.

"Okay, you can come out to me," Norah said, and Luke watched as Kieran dashed into deeper water into Norah's open arms.

Luke was inwardly glad he and Ethan had made two peanut-butter-and-jelly sandwiches apiece because they ended up having to share them with Norah and Kieran, who had brought nothing.

"You guys can have my pop," Ethan said, handing Norah his can of Orange Crush when the four of them finally came out of the water to eat. He ate only half of his one sandwich and then went back into the water. Kieran followed him.

Luke did not like being alone on the beach with Norah, but she didn't seem to mind in the least.

"Have you ever been to San Diego?" she asked him.

"No."

"I like it there," she continued. "There are no mosquitoes where I live. It never gets sticky like this either. My mom's dad lives on a boat. Sometimes he just sails away for a while. My mom was born right on the beach. Right by where we live. Her mom didn't want to go to the hospital. She wanted to have her baby on the beach, so she did. She got into trouble with the police, though, 'cause someone complained. My mom loves whales. They're her favorite animal."

I could tell you other things about your mother, Luke thought to himself. He wondered if Norah knew anything. He wondered if she knew her mother took drugs. He wondered if she knew what it meant to sleep around. He was pretty sure he knew what it meant, and it made him want to change the subject.

"Kieran thinks he can be a whale when he grows up! I told him he can't, but you can't tell a four-year-old anything," Norah continued. "That's what Grandma says."

Nell. When she said "Grandma" she meant Nell. That still seemed weird to him.

"I never met my other grandma, the one who had my mom on the beach, 'cause she died when I was a baby," Norah chattered on. "But I get to see my grandpa sometimes. His boat is kind of old and smelly, but he likes it. He loves the ocean, too. He gave my mom this book on ocean animals when she was little, and then she gave it to me. I am going to give it to Kieran when we get home. It's time."

She said it like it was time to go, and Luke looked over at her to see if that was what she really meant, but she was looking at her little brother, not at the sun or a watch or any other device that would give the hour.

"I wish I'd been born on the beach," she suddenly said. Her gray-flannel eyes had a faraway look. "And sometimes I wish I had a boat like my grandpa's that I could just sail away on. I haven't seen my grandpa in a long time. I'm starting to forget what his boat looks like."

She was silent for a moment. Luke didn't know what to say.

"Is it true your dad has been in jail?" he blurted out. Even as he said it he wished he hadn't. He couldn't believe he actually *had* said it.

But Norah didn't seem to be fazed by the question.

"He doesn't mean to do bad things," she said, wrinkling her brow and looking out over the water. "He just forgets stuff. He forgets to pay bills. And he forgets how to drive safe. Sometimes he forgets how to keep his temper. You know, when someone hauls off and slugs you, what are you gonna do? He has to slug 'em back. But then he forgets to turn and walk away." She turned to Luke. "That's what you're supposed to do, you know. Slug 'em once and turn and walk away."

Luke could hear in his head these words of advice coming from Darrel Janvik. He wondered what his parents would think of this bit of counsel.

"So have you visited him in jail? Did you go there?" he asked her.

"I went a couple times. It's not so bad. The food is pretty good. I had lunch with him once."

"So what does your mom do when your dad's in jail?"

Norah shrugged. "Oh, sometimes she gets mad and goes away for a while. She has some friends who live in Mexico. It's called Baja California, but it's really Mexico. I went with her once. We could see the whales from the beach where her friends live. The whales were migrating. We stayed there for a week. It was great 'cause I didn't have to go to school."

"Where was Kieran?"

"Oh, he stayed with these friends of my parents. They have a trailer. I stay with them, too, sometimes. Sometimes all four of us stay with them. They have three cats. The trailer kind of smells like cats but you get used to it. So, has your dad ever been in jail?"

"No!" he said. "I've never even *seen* the inside of a jail."

Norah looked at him, and it seemed she felt sorry for him. "The people there are a little scary. But they're just people who just...they just forgot to be nice...and then they got caught."

"Norah!" Kieran yelled from the water's edge. "Take me swimming!"

She stood up and walked to the water, the conversation abruptly over. She led her brother into the water and pulled him across by his arms to where he could no longer touch.

"Okay, kick your legs, Kieran, or you'll sink!" she said. "Keep kicking! Don't stop or you'll sink!"

A little after three o'clock, at Luke's direction, the foursome headed back to town. As they came back into city limits, Luke suddenly remembered it was the day before the Wooden Shoes Festival. On impulse he led the others down Main Street instead of Seventh Avenue. The city square would be bustling with preparations for tomorrow. Maybe they could stop by the newspaper office and get money from his dad for some funnel cakes. The funnel-cake guy always opened a day early. Maybe they could watch the Ferris wheel get put together, or maybe the petting-zoo people had arrived and maybe they would need help getting the goats and miniature horses and baby deer out of their trailers. Maybe the wood-carvers who made the wooden shoes would let them help them unload their truck for a few dollars.

He just didn't want to go home yet. He wanted to be somewhere where things were happening. Good things. He didn't want to go home and see the snot-colored house he lived next door to. He didn't want to hear Nell's voice or Darrel's voice or smell their cigarettes. He didn't want to think about scary men in jail or high rocks or deep places where you can't see the bottom.

And for some reason he couldn't quite make sense of, he didn't want Norah or Kieran to have to go back to that snot-colored house right then, and to whatever awaited them inside it.

❧

Later that evening, after his parents and Ethan had returned from the Miss Halcyon Pageant—Luke flat-out refused to go with them—and after Ethan had gone to bed and his parents had begun to watch the ten o'clock news, Luke slipped out his window and climbed into the tree house. He brought the little battery-powered camping lantern his dad had bought for him at the hardware store and his notebook. He wanted to write a story about a man who got sent to jail for something he didn't do but no one would believe him.

He scooted across the floor of the tree house to his favorite corner and set the lantern down. He opened the notebook and turned to a fresh page and started to write:

> In his dreams the man always walked out of the court-
> house in a suit while he laughed and shook hands with
> people, but when he awoke the man was always lying in
> a jail cell, wearing an orange jumpsuit—

A commotion outside interrupted him. A door had opened. Nell's back door. Darrel was yelling. It sounded like he was on the phone. He said Belinda's name. Then he yelled Belinda's name. The door closed and the yelling became muted. Somewhat. He could still make out some of the words. Most of them were words he was forbidden to say. He peered out an opening and saw that Norah was sitting on Nell's back step.

His movement startled her, and she looked up at him. In the dusky moonlight and the yellow glow of Nell's back-porch light, Luke could see she was crying. He thought perhaps she would look away or walk away when she saw him looking at her. But she just stared at him with those ancient eyes of hers. He didn't know why—he certainly never would have been able to explain it to his parents, or anyone else for that matter—but he held up his hand to her, fingers curled down except for his pointer finger, which he pointed with to the plywood ceiling above him. It was an invitation to join him in the tree house. His place of escape.

For a second, Norah did nothing. Then she nodded once and got to her feet. She walked barefoot across the little adjoining lawn and began to climb up the wooden planks nailed to the trunk.

She emerged from the opening in the floor and hoisted herself inside, looking around, taking in the view. Two camping stools were in one corner along with a box of comic books and Ethan's Hush Puppies shoebox of Creepy Crawlers. Luke was in another corner, sitting on the floor with an old sofa cushion behind his back. An old cigar box was on the floor by his feet, and the lantern sat between them. Norah took a seat on one of the stools and dried her cheeks with her hand.

Neither one said anything.

"I like to come in here to write," Luke finally said.

"To write? What do you write?" she asked softly.

"Stories."

"What kind of stories?"

Luke paused for a moment. "Stories about places I'd like to go, or things I'd like to do. Or things I hope I never have to do."

"Is that what you're doing right now?" she said, looking at his notebook open on his lap. "Writing a story?"

"Yeah."

Silence.

"You want to write something? I can give you some paper," he said.

"What would I write about?"

Luke shrugged his shoulders. "Anything you want."

"I like to write poems," Norah said.

"Then write a poem," he answered, tearing out a piece of paper and handing it her. He pulled a pencil out of the old cigar box and handed that to her, too. "You can use Ethan's shoebox to write on."

Norah picked up the Hush Puppies shoebox and put it on her lap, laying the piece of paper on the lid. She cocked her head and squinted: the look of someone searching for an idea.

Luke went back to his own paragraph about the man in the jail cell. A few seconds later he heard the sound of Norah's pencil on paper.

"What rhymes with 'water'?" she said a few seconds later.

Luke tapped his cheek with his pencil. "Daughter?" he said.

She considered it. "Yeah. That works."

The next day, Norah and Kieran sat with the Foxbournes during the parade that marched past the Janvik and Foxbourne houses an hour before sunset. Nell and Darrel had left—without saying much of anything to the Foxbournes—to head to the bar in Carrow, the next town over, where nothing special at all was happening that night. If Luke and his parents had been able to read Nell Janvik's mind they would have understood she could no longer watch the Wooden Shoes Festival Parade because army veterans bearing the American flag always led the way and she could no longer bear to look at a man in an army uniform. Not after what had happened to Kenny. But the Foxbournes were not mind readers, of course, so Nell and Darrel's casual way of leaving Norah and Kieran with them, without really asking, was looked upon with astonishment.

Two days later, while the carnival workers packed away the Tilt-a-Whirl and the carousel five blocks away, Darrel loaded up his car. Luke heard the sound of car doors opening and closing as he ate his breakfast, and he went and looked out the screen door, watching as Darrel prepared to go back to California. Norah came out of Nell's house then with a grocery bag and a pillow, and she put these in the car. She looked over at his house right then and saw him standing there. She held up her hand and kept it still. She was saying goodbye. He held up his hand, too.

9

The summer Luke turned fourteen, his father declared he was old enough to earn money at the *Halcyon Herald*. Real money—not a dollar here and there for running this ad copy over to the co-op, or that missing issue to the nursing home. Luke finally got to write his name on a yellow time card, and Lucie, the office manager, showed him how to punch it so the time landed on the line it was supposed to.

That summer, Luke learned how to use the Nikon 35mm camera and how to develop film in the darkroom. He also began to write the simplest of news stories, like announcements of concerts in the park and diabetes support-group meetings and benefit auctions for good causes. He proved to be dependable and thorough, as many firstborns typically are, but there was an unspoken agreement between father and son, and though it was never mentioned audibly, both understood it. The agreement was this: Working at the paper did not mean Luke wanted a career in journalism. Luke was sure he did not, and Jack hoped in time his son would change his mind.

When school began that fall, Luke had to cut back on his hours, but he spent two or three afternoons a week at the paper, doing what he could in between basketball practice and spending time with Matt. His friendship with Matt was changing as the years progressed: Matt was becoming more and more the superstar athlete, and Luke was becoming more and more the studious academic. Matt was a starter for the junior-varsity basketball squad, and sometimes suited up for varsity games. Luke sat on the bench most games and played only when a twenty-point spread at the two-minute mark assured a win. Their ideas of good entertainment were changing, too. Matt was a frequent guest at upperclassmen's parties and had already admitted to experimenting with alcohol. Luke was not extended those same invitations, nor did he want them. He felt torn between his loyalty to Matt as a friend and his own desire not to mess things up for himself.

When the basketball season was over, he saw less and less of Matt; they no longer had sleepovers, of course, and playing tricks on Nell had also lost its appeal. And Matt had a bigger circle of friends than Luke did. They were still good friends, but they were growing apart, and each knew it.

Knowing this made Luke long to find respite in the tree house. It was almost exclusively his now, as Ethan had long since lost interest. But when basketball ended in March, snow still covered the ground, and the limbs of the tree outside his window were often still glazed with ice. He had made a cubby of sorts for himself in the attic, but he found he could not write there. The chill of the unheated room was the smaller of two distractions; the inability to look out a window was the larger one.

In late April, the last of the snow melted away, and the earth renewed itself as it always does. And Luke began to climb into the tree house again, to escape and to dream.

The day after his fifteenth birthday, on the last day of school, Luke came home to find an old Chevy pickup truck with a beige camper shell parked in Nell Janvik's driveway. Somehow he knew as he neared his house that the pickup would have California plates. He was right.

Darrel was back.

There was no one in the Janvik yard, no sounds coming from the open windows. Darrel had probably arrived several hours ago, and the hoopla or the hullabaloo over his return, whichever it had been, was long over. Luke walked into his house wondering if Darrel had brought his kids with him. He grabbed a Pepsi from the fridge and a bag of Fritos and headed upstairs to his room. He didn't have to work at the paper that day, and Ethan was helping their mother clean out her classroom for the year, so he had the house to himself.

His room was stuffy inside from the early June heat, and he opened the window before he plopped down on his bed. He drank the soda and munched on the Fritos, all the while contemplating the long, lazy summer that awaited him. Then he heard the sound of a child crying. Kieran. It was a mad cry. The cry of someone who had not gotten his way. It was coming from one of Nell's upstairs windows. Luke turned his head toward the sound.

"Will you just go out to the camper and get it!" a man's voice yelled. He cursed the camper as he bellowed. Darrel.

Cautiously, Luke got off his bed and walked over to the window. He could hear Nell's front door opening but couldn't see who was coming out. Then from under the cover of the porch roof, a teenage girl with honey-blonde hair emerged. She stepped barefoot onto the grass between Nell's house and her driveway. Even from the back he could see it was Norah.

She opened the back door of the camper, went inside and then came back out with a stuffed toy dinosaur. When she turned Luke could see her face. She had matured in the last three years. She looked up then at his tree house—looking for him, it seemed—and then her eyes naturally traveled to his bedroom window. There would be no point in moving away. She had already seen him. The corners of her mouth raised a fraction of an inch, and she cocked her head slightly. She raised one hand and kept it still, just like she had three years ago when she was ten and he was twelve and she had said goodbye. This time, however, it was hello.

Luke raised his hand in return.

She paused for a moment, like she was considering coming to him, climbing his tree, ambling across the branch that led to his room, and filling him in on the last three years. But then she turned back toward the house, went inside, and all grew quiet again.

∽

That night after supper, Jack stated to his wife the obvious.

"I see Darrel is back."

"Yep," she said in return.

"Are the kids and Belinda with him?"

"I don't know."

Luke knew.

"The kids are with him. I don't think Belinda is," he said, and his parents turned to him. They seemed surprised. He wished they would hurry up and get over their aversion to his becoming an adult and participating in their conversations.

"Did you see them?' his mother asked.

"Saw one. Heard the other one," Luke said, taking his plate to the sink, where his mother was standing.

"Can I go to Ryan's tonight?" Ethan said, oblivious to the human drama next door and taking his plate to the sink also.

"I guess so," MaryAnn said. "We can take you over there on our way to the Nelsons' if you want. Luke, you have somewhere you want to go tonight? Do you mind being home alone?"

Matt had asked him to come to a last-day-of-school party at one of his new friend's houses that night, but Luke knew there was going to be a keg there. He had declined, feigning family obligations.

"Mom, I'm fifteen. I can handle being alone."

"Okay. Just making sure."

Forty-five minutes later the house was quiet. Luke went down-stairs into the basement, where it was perpetually cool, but there was nothing good on TV. He came back up to his room, climbed out his window, and scooted along the branch to his tree house. He would listen for sounds from Nell's house so that the next time his parents speculated about the goings-on there, he would be able to clue them in. If nothing happened, he would write.

He stretched out along the floor and peeked through open spaces in the roof. Stray starlight, filtering through the branches, greeted him. It was a beautiful evening.

He had been there for maybe ten minutes when he heard noise at the front door of Nell's house. He turned his head, and through a gap, he saw Nell and Darrel walk over to the camper. They did not go in. They started to talk. Then Luke heard Nell's back door open slowly, and by moving his body slightly he could see that Norah had quietly slipped out onto the back step just below him. She sat down and hugged her knees, leaning forward. It was ob-vious she wanted to hear what her father and grandmother were talking about.

"I think I have a right to know what is going on!" Nell said.

Luke could see that Norah had raised her head. He shifted his weight so he could see Nell and Darrel better. The floorboards creaked. He knew then that she knew he was there. Norah knew he was there.

"Is she in jail again?" Nell.

"Ma, it's worse than that."

There was a pause.

"Well?"

"Well, first she split on me, Ma," Darrel said. His voice sounded angry. "She left me and the kids and moved down to Mexico with some guy. I told her I wouldn't let her take the kids, and at first she didn't care. She didn't care! A couple months later when she decided she did want them, I hid them from her. She was high on something and pulled a knife on me, but I wouldn't tell her where they were. Well, she went back to Mexico anyway, and she and this guy got messed up in some drug deal and a Mexican cop got shot. I think she's in jail down there. Some friends told me she's being charged as an accessory to murder."

Luke sensed his heart beating faster. He knew Norah was hearing all of this, probably for the first time. He crept to his knees and looked at her, staying back as far as he could. Even shadowed in twilight, her eyes were huge, vacant, wet. She held a slender hand over her mouth.

"So what's going to happen?" Nell said after a long pause.

"She's going to rot in a Mexican prison, that's what!" Darrel was seething. "She and that loser she left me for."

Norah's eyes were closed now, and she was slowly rocking back and forth, but making no sound. Her grandmother and father hadn't a clue they were being overheard. Luke had an insane desire to slide down the rope and beat the heck out of Darrel Janvik.

"So what have you told these kids?" Nell said softly. There was the slightest hint of compassion in her voice.

"I told them she ran away. I told them, when she gets tired of running she'll come back."

"That's a bunch of bull."

"No, it ain't! She did run away. She ran away from me, and she ran away from them."

Nell was silent for a moment.

"She loves those kids, Darrel. She loves them, and you know it."

More silence.

"Yeah…well, she loves her heroin more, and *you* know it."

"She doesn't love it more, she *needs* it more. She was a prisoner long before she got put in a Mexican jail."

"And whose fault is that? Huh? Whose fault is that!" Darrel yelled. "I been clean for ten years, Ma! Ten years! She wouldn't stay off it. She wouldn't."

"Hush! You want the kids to hear you?"

"I've just had it with her, Ma. I've had it. I'm not going back to

California. And I don't care if she's in prison for two months or two years or the rest of her life, she's never going to get these kids."

"So you want to punish her."

"She's not getting these kids."

Luke could hear Nell sigh.

"So how long are you stayin'?"

"For good, Ma. I'm gonna get me a job at the paint factory and get a little house on a few acres, and I'm gonna make a good life for Norah and Kieran here. And you'll get to watch 'em grow up, Ma. You can see 'em on their birthdays and at their school functions and on Christmas morning. I just need a place to stay until I can afford a place of my own. Just till then."

"You get a job here and you better find a way to keep it, Darrel. They won't give you more than one chance at the factory. You better not blow it."

"I won't!"

Luke kept his eyes on Norah as Nell and Darrel moved on to less explosive matters. He watched her try to gather her composure, watched her dry her cheeks. She stood and then turned toward him, seeking his gaze. He moved so she could see him fully. He wanted to communicate to her somehow that he felt awful for her, that he knew how badly she must be hurting. But to say anything aloud would reveal them both. So he just looked at her, hoping she could tell he felt sorry for her.

She looked at him for only a second before she turned and quietly slipped back into the house.

The following morning—his first full day of summer vacation—Luke woke up late. He came downstairs at ten-thirty to find his parents already deeply immersed in the Saturday rituals of yard work and laundry. Ethan had stayed the night at his friend Ryan's house. Luke ate a quick breakfast and then headed back to his room to dress and make his bed. He was supposed to wash both cars today, and he wanted to get them done before he called Matt to see if he wanted to go to Goose Pond this afternoon. It was one of the few things they still enjoyed doing together.

He stepped outside into the shimmering June heat, grabbing his father's car keys. He got into his dad's classic Dodge Dart, eased it out of the garage, and then grabbed the nearby bucket, sponge, and detergent kept inside. He squirted the detergent into the bucket, filled it with water from the hose, and then brought it and the running hose over to the car. He sprayed the vehicle, humming a Three Dog Night song while he squirted. When he turned the hose off, he noticed a boy with dark curly hair watching him. Kieran Janvik.

"You washin' this car?" Kieran said.

"Yeah," Luke said apprehensively. Wasn't it obvious?

"Can I help?"

"Well, um, I only have one sponge, so…"

"I can get one from my grandma's garage!" He scampered off, returning a moment later with a faded rag frozen by time and neglect into a stiff terry-cloth fossil.

"See, I can help!"

The sight of the younger boy with his ocean-blue eyes and mop of curly dark hair, coupled with his eagerness to help and all that Luke knew that Kieran didn't, weakened him. He would let him help.

"Sure, you can help. You can wash the tires and the hubcaps, okay?"

"Okay!" Kieran said. He plunged his rag into the bucket of soapy water and brought it back out again, limp with water and suds. "Like this?" he asked, rubbing the tires and hubcaps.

"Yep, just like that."

"My name's Kieran," he said as he scrubbed the front tire.

"Yeah, I know. I'm Luke."

"My sister told me you took us swimming once. To a pond with rocks you can jump off of."

For some reason Luke found this strange, that Norah would want to remind Kieran of something that happened when he was four. Something he probably did not now remember doing.

"Uh, yeah. My brother, Ethan, and I took you there last time you visited your grandma. You were only four then."

"How old is your brother?"

"He's ten."

"Is he home?"

"No, he's at a friend's house."

"Oh."

"Can you take us there again?"

Suddenly there was a voice behind them.

"Kieran, you should wait to be invited." It was Norah. Luke whipped his head around. He almost smiled at the thought of her telling her brother to wait for an invitation. She had never waited for one. But then, that was when she was younger. She looked different now. Taller. More slender, with the obvious beginning curves of a woman's body. Luke looked away.

"Hey, Norah," he said, rather sheepishly.

"Hello."

"So can you take us there again?" Kieran repeated.

"Yeah, sure," Luke said, not looking up. His voice felt awkward. He wondered if he should tell them he was thinking of going there today. He felt Norah's eyes on him. He looked back at her. Her eyes still had the color of a rain cloud ready to burst. "I'm probably going to go this afternoon. You guys can come if you want."

"I want to come!" Kieran said, stopping and turning to Norah. "Can we? Can we go with them?"

"I'll have to ask," she said softly. She had not taken her eyes off Luke. She was communicating something to him. He didn't understand what it was.

"I'll go ask!" Kieran dropped his rag and sprinted into the house, yelling, "Daddy!" as he opened the screen door.

Luke felt a heavy drape of awkwardness fall between himself and Norah.

She cleared her throat, looked back at her grandmother's house and then at him.

"Can I talk to you later?" she said, almost in a whisper. She sounded like an adult.

Luke pretended to be interested only in the car he was wiping. "Ah, sure," he said casually.

"Not when Kieran can hear, though. Maybe after he's in bed tonight?"

Luke scrubbed harder. "Um, yeah. Okay."

Kieran came dashing out of the house. "We can go! Daddy says we can go!"

"So, when are you going?" Norah said plainly.

"I, uh, have to finish these cars first, then I need to call my friend Matt. So I'll probably go after Ethan gets back from his friend's house. And after lunch."

"You riding bikes there?"

"Yeah."

Norah nodded. "I don't think I can ride a bike with Kieran in my lap anymore," she said. Was she smiling?

Luke blinked. "Oh, well, I am sure you can ride my mom's bike," he said. "Kieran can ride Ethan's old bike. It just needs some air in the tires."

"Thanks. Kieran, come in when you're done there and I'll make you lunch." She turned and walked back into Nell's house. Luke watched her.

"I'm ready for the hose," Kieran announced. Luke threw his sponge back in the bucket and picked up the hose, wondering why he was wishing Matt wasn't coming to the swimming hole that day, too.

∽∾

The swimming hole was usually a popular place on warm Saturdays in the summer. When Luke, Ethan, Norah, and Kieran arrived a little after one in the afternoon, a sizeable crowd had gathered on the beach. Matt and a mutual friend of his and Luke's named Derek had already arrived. They had a huge black inner tube with them and were leaning against the *Warning! No Lifeguard on Duty!* sign. When they saw Norah get off Luke's mother's bike they gave each other a funny look. Luke didn't like it.

Luke made the introductions.

"Guys, this is Norah and Kieran. They're Nell Janvik's grandkids. Norah and Kieran, this is Matt and Derek."

Matt and Derek were grinning.

"Nice to meet you, Norah!" Matt said.

"Same here," Derek echoed. They seemed to be sharing a private joke. Luke was beginning to think it had been a mistake to invite Norah and Kieran to the pond.

"Let's swim out to the rocks and get away from all these people!" Matt said, and he turned toward the water, hefting the inner tube onto his shoulder.

"I want to jump off the rocks!" Kieran said, dropping the towel he'd brought onto the sand and dashing after them.

Ethan was pulling off his T-shirt. "I'm coming, too!"

Luke put his towel down and peeked out of the corner of his eye. Norah had slipped out of her shorts and tank top. She was wearing a two-piece swimsuit the color of tangerines. Little gold rings held the fabric together. He heard Matt and Derek laughing several yards over. They looked back at him and gave him a thumbs-up.

He walked to the water's edge. Kieran and Ethan were already swimming toward the rocks.

"You want to sit in the inner tube, Norah?" Matt said.

"And do what?" she said, looking at the black rubber behemoth.

"I'll push you!" Matt continued.

"No, thanks," she said, walking past into the water. She plunged in headfirst and swam, gliding through the water like a mermaid. She surfaced several yards out and swam away toward her brother and Ethan. Luke joined his friends.

"Man, are you one lucky dog!" Matt said, slapping him on the back.

"She is one foxy chick!" Derek said, grabbing the inner tube away from Matt and plunging into the water with it.

"Hey!" Matt yelled, splashing after him.

Luke fell in behind them, unsure of just about everything.

Norah didn't climb to the top of the rock face like she had when she was ten, nor did she mention having jumped off of it. She took turns with the rest of them jumping off the jumping rock, and seemed to be oblivious to or unmoved by Matt and Derek's attempts to flirt with her. When the beach area had cleared out a bit, the six of them swam back, and Matt and Derek decided to see which of them could stand astride the floating inner tube and jump off before falling off. Luke wondered if he was the only one who could see that they were putting on quite a show.

When they had exhausted that idea, Matt suddenly turned to Norah, who was floating on her back in the water, and challenged her to a race to the other side of the pond.

"A race?" she said, in a rather blasé tone.

"Yeah. A race," Matt said, smiling.

She looked across the expanse of water and wrinkled her nose, then turned to Matt. "Are you a sore loser?"

Matt's grin doubled. "Are you?"

She shrugged her shoulders. "I don't know. I haven't lost a swimming race yet."

Matt laughed. "This will be great! Luke, you tell us when to go!"

Luke furrowed his brow. Beside him Derek was laughing.

"I don't know if this is a good idea," he said.

"Norah can beat him with her eyes closed!" Kieran piped up.

"We'll start right here," Matt said, stepping over to ankle-deep water. "Tell us when to go, Luke!"

Norah followed Matt casually and stood by him. She leaned forward, ready to spring when Luke gave the word.

"See you on the other side," Matt said, winking at her.

"Eventually," she said, not looking at him.

Derek laughed, threw the inner tube into the water, and paddled out to watch the event.

Luke sighed. "On your mark. Get set. Go!"

The two plunged into the water.

Kieran began to jump up and down and cheer for his sister. Ethan joined him. Luke stood at the shoreline with his arms folded across his chest, watching. Norah was as graceful as a dancer in the water. And fast. She was already several strokes ahead of Matt. It would take them several minutes to reach the other side. Derek continued to paddle after them in the inner tube, and Ethan swam out to meet them coming back.

Kieran continued to yell and cheer, even when it was obvious Norah was going to win. She reached the opposite side. They were too far away to hear distinctly, but Luke thought he could hear Matt laughing. He didn't seem to mind losing to Norah. Kieran whooped and hollered, jumping up and down in the water.

"I told you she would win!" he was saying, but it didn't appear that he was talking to Luke. "Guess you lost that bet, now, didn't you!"

Luke looked more closely at Kieran splashing in the water.

"Guess you'll listen to me next time!" he continued.

The younger boy appeared to be talking to himself. Luke's eyes widened as he watched and listened.

Kieran plunged into the water to join Ethan, who was treading water near Derek at the halfway mark. But as Kieran swam away

Luke heard him say just under his breath, "Don't go so fast. Wait for me."

Again, Kieran was talking to no one. It sent a chill down Luke's spine despite the summer heat.

⁓⊗⁓

They left the swimming hole at five, coming back into town just as fathers all up and down the streets of Halcyon started pulling out bags of charcoal for their grills and mothers started flattening ground beef into hamburger patties. Matt and Derek waved goodbye when they reached the corner of Tulip Street and Seventh Avenue, particularly interested in making sure Norah waved back. When Luke, Ethan, and the Janviks arrived back at the Foxbourne house, Kieran parked the bike he'd used next to Ethan's new one.

"Thanks for taking us," Norah said as she lowered the kickstand on Luke's mother's bike.

"Sure," Luke said.

"Can we go again sometime?" Kieran asked.

"Um, yeah," Luke answered.

They walked out of the garage, and Norah seemed to linger for a moment. The tree that separated the two houses towered above them. Norah glanced over at Ethan and Kieran, who were talking together about something they had seen on TV. She looked quickly back at Luke and raised her eyes to the tree house. Luke followed with his own eyes.

She curled her fingers downward except for her pointer finger, which she raised almost imperceptibly toward the sky. It was the invitation to join him in the tree house—only this time *she* was extending it instead of him.

"Tonight. After ten o'clock," she whispered.

He nodded, and she walked away.

10

Luke was restless that evening knowing that he had an up-coming meeting with a "foxy chick" in his tree house. His parents were thankfully distracted with their Sunday school preparations, but Ethan kept coming in and out of his room for one thing or another. First he wanted to borrow a Creedence Clearwater Revival record. Then he wanted to play cards. But Luke kept shooing him away. He passed the evening trying to read *The Two Towers*, eating malt balls, and watching the clock.

Finally, a few minutes before 10, his mother knocked on his door to tell him good night.

"Good night, Mom," Luke said through the closed door and then listened for the sound of her bedroom door closing.

At five minutes after ten, Luke opened his window wide, slid the screen up, and climbed out. He scooted quickly across the branch but almost fell off when he reached the tree house.

Norah was sitting there, waiting for him. Seeing her had startled him. He had an excellent view of the tree's trunk and the steps that were nailed to it. He couldn't believe he'd missed seeing her climb them.

"How long have you been here?" he said softly, pulling himself inside and trying to mask his surprise at finding her there.

"A few minutes," she said. She was sitting with her knees up to her chest, her arms around them in a tight embrace. Her eyes were like gray wool—very out of place for a summer evening.

"How…how did you get in?" he stammered.

"Same as you. I climbed out a window. Then I walked across the garage roof."

Luke could not hide his shock. The tree limb outside his window was wide, sturdy, and strategically placed. The limb near the bedroom window where Norah was staying was narrower and was several inches away from the edge of Nell's garage roof.

"If my mom knew how you got in here, she'd have a fit."

"Why?"

"Because it's…it's not very safe."

Norah looked over her shoulder to the route she'd taken—the narrow branch, the sloping roof, her open window. "I didn't have any trouble."

She turned back around.

"Did you tell your parents what you heard last night?" she said.

Luke's mouth opened a little. He shut it. Then he opened it again.

"No."

"Good," she said. " 'Cause it's not true."

"None of it?"

She looked away and then looked back. "Some of it is, and some of it isn't."

Luke waited.

"My mom didn't kill anybody," she said defensively, as if she were in a courtroom and not a tree house.

"Well, your dad said she was charged with being an accessory. That's different."

"It's not different to me. She didn't kill anybody."

Again, Luke waited.

"And it's not true she left Kieran and me. She didn't leave us. She was getting things ready for us. We were going to move to

Mexico with her and Marco. We were going to have our own place. I was going to have my own room. In a house. On the beach. We weren't going to have to live in that camper anymore."

"You...you were living in the camper?"

"Kieran and I have been living in that camper for two years."

Luke was silent.

"I didn't know she'd come back for us," Norah continued. "My dad took us to some friends in Riverside one weekend because he said he had to go away for a few days. I think that's when Mom came back for us. But he never told Kieran and me. Then she went back to Mexico. And something bad happened. Some cop got killed. But she didn't do it."

"What about...the drugs?" Luke said softly. He couldn't bring himself to say the word "heroin" in front of her. He wasn't entirely sure why.

Norah looked down at her feet.

"That part is mostly true." She wouldn't look at him. "But she can't help it. She can't help it. She loves Kieran and me. Please don't tell anyone," she whispered, still looking at her feet.

"I won't," he whispered back.

"Don't tell Matt or Derek. And please don't tell your parents."

"I won't tell Matt or Derek," Luke said, but he couldn't make the other promise. He wanted to, but something kept him from it.

"Or your parents," she said, looking up at him.

He paused.

"Or my parents," he finally said. He decided he would break the promise only if he had no other choice.

"Thanks," she said softly, but she made no move to leave.

"I...I might need to ask you to help me," she continued, looking away again.

Luke blinked. "Help you what?"

"I need to find out where my mother is. Which jail she's in, if she even *is* in jail."

"I don't see how I can help you. I don't know anything about that kind of stuff."

"But your dad works at a newspaper. He must know how to find out if someone is in jail."

"But you said you didn't want me to tell my parents," Luke said, wrinkling his brow.

"I don't."

He paused. She wanted him to get information from his dad without making him wonder why he was asking. It would be like being a spy. It intimidated him and thrilled him at the same time.

"I guess I can try," he said.

"She was in Baja California when this happened. It happened last month or maybe the month before—I'm not sure."

"Okay."

"My mom's last name is Hickler. She and my dad…well, they never got married."

"Okay," he said again.

"So you won't tell anyone?"

"Well, I'm going to *try* not to."

"What? What does that mean?" she said, unhooking her arms from her knees.

"It means if my dad gets suspicious and starts asking *me* questions, I'm not going to lie to him."

"Why not?"

Luke paused. *Yes—why not?*

Because he simply knew he would not.

"Because my dad can always tell when I am lying," he answered. "My mom can, too. I'm not good at it. And I don't like doing it."

She looked irritated but said nothing.

"Besides, what difference will it make if my parents find out, Norah?" he continued. "They're not the kind of people to think badly of someone just because of something their parents did."

"My mother didn't *do* anything!"

"Or *didn't* do!" he said quickly. "Look, I'm not saying I'll tell them, I'm just saying, if they ask I'm not going to lie for you!"

She let her knees drop so she now sat Indian-style. Her arms and hands lay limp in her lap.

"You should never have eavesdropped," she said coolly.

"I wasn't eavesdropping!" Luke countered. "I was already in the tree house when your dad and grandma came outside. I couldn't help hearing what they said. Besides, *I* wasn't the one eavesdropping. *You* were."

She stared at him for a few minutes. "You would have done it, too, if you were me."

He had to admit to himself she was right. It was true he didn't like lying to his parents, but he wasn't above listening to their conversations when he wasn't supposed to. Especially when the conversation was about him. He wondered if there was a difference.

They were silent for a few moments. Then he remembered something that had been bothering him, something that had been tugging at him since they'd come back from the swimming hole.

"Norah...is Kieran okay?"

Her gray eyes widened a little. "What do you mean?"

He licked his lips. "I mean, is he, you know, mentally okay?"

"Why are you asking?"

Luke noted that she seemed angry but not surprised. "Well, he was, like, talking to himself at the swimming hole today," he said. "It was a little, I don't know, weird."

She seemed to be breathing a little fast as she looked at him and formulated an answer.

"Kieran is fine, okay?" she said evenly. "You leave him alone."

Leave him alone?

"What?" he said.

"I said, leave him alone."

"What are you talking about?" Luke was thoroughly perplexed.

Norah's angry features softened a little, and her steel-gray eyes seemed to mist over the tiniest bit. "Please just leave him alone," she said—she pleaded.

"Is he okay?" he said again. He wanted an answer. He wanted the truth.

"He'll be fine. He...he just needs some time."

"Time for what?"

Norah looked away in disgust, then whipped her head back around. "Time to get used to things the way they are right now! So leave him alone about it, okay?"

He considered her request. "So who was he talking to?" he said, not quite ready to acquiesce.

"I don't have to tell you anything," Norah said simply, after a momentary pause. "It's none of your business."

"You want me to ask questions for you and keep secrets for you and lie for you and leave your brother alone for you—and now you tell me it's none of my business?" Luke was starting to get a little peeved.

"I never should have trusted you," she said, shaking her head.

He was about to say, "You got that right," but before he could, she looked up at him. Her expression had changed from irritation to fear. Her eyes were brimming with tears.

"Please, I'm begging you. Don't say anything to anyone about Kieran. If the adults find out, they might...they might send him away," she whispered, her voice breaking.

"Why?" Luke was whispering also. "Why would they want to do that?"

Norah wiped her cheeks, swallowing hard. "Because...well, Kieran has this imaginary friend. He's had him the last year or so. He calls him Tommy. It used to not be so bad, but ever since Mom left, he's been talking to Tommy more and more. He really thinks he's real."

Luke felt the hairs on his neck come to attention.

"I've tried to get him to stop, but he gets all frantic when I talk like there is no Tommy," she continued. "His teacher at his school in San Diego was starting to get worried about him. She called my dad to talk to him about it just after Easter. She wanted Kieran to see a child psychologist because he was acting strange in class. I don't think she knew about Tommy, but I think she was getting close to finding out. I heard my dad talking to one of his friends about the call. He said the teacher told him sometimes kids like Kieran need to go to special places to get well. That sometimes kids like Kieran get sent away."

Luke wanted to say, perhaps that was exactly what Kieran needed, but he didn't. "So you're just going to let him keep doing this?" he asked.

Norah shook her head. "He just needs some time! If he gets sent away...he won't make it!...He won't..." But she didn't continue. Fresh tears started to slide down her cheeks.

As Luke sat there, watching Norah trying to staunch the flow of tears, he felt oddly and suddenly drawn to her pain. He didn't know why. But he slowly began to be aware that a sense of loyalty for Norah and for Kieran was swelling inside him. He wondered, as he felt it growing, if it was God himself talking to him, arousing in him the desire to protect them from further harm. Or perhaps it was just the growing awareness of his own physical and mental attraction to Norah. He did not know. He only knew he felt like he had been handed a responsibility—a responsibility to protect and defend.

"I won't tell anyone about Kieran," he said softly.

Norah raised her head to look at him.

"And you weren't wrong to trust me," he added. "I'm going to try to help you."

The following day, Luke and his family came home after church and eating lunch at the Golden Griddle in Carrow to find a note taped to their front door:

I hope you don't mind that we borrowed two bikes to ride down to the swimming hole. Kieran just had to go swimming today. I'm sorry if you really do mind. We will bring the bikes back this afternoon.

Thanks,
Norah Janvik

Luke's mother thought it was quite nice that Norah had left such a nicely worded, grammatically correct note. Luke thought it was strange that those two were going swimming. Again. Didn't they enjoy doing anything else?

"Maybe we should invite them all over for supper tonight," MaryAnn said as she stepped into the house with the note in her hand.

"Nell, too?" Ethan said, grimacing.

"I seriously doubt Nell would accept the invitation since she never has before," Jack Foxbourne said, following his family inside.

"Well, I can ask, can't I?" MaryAnn said.

"Do you want to go down to the swimming hole and meet them there?" Ethan said to Luke.

Luke was irked that deep down he really did.

"No," he replied. "Matt and I are playing baseball with friends this afternoon."

"Well, I'm going to go."

Luke had been looking forward to playing baseball, but he was aware now of being slightly resentful of Ethan's preparations to head to the swimming hole. He felt a crazy need to protect Norah and Kieran from even his own brother.

He ended up having a lackluster game, striking out more than once and dropping a fly ball that any other time he would have been able to catch. But he was distracted by thoughts of who might be at the supper table that night and perhaps sharing a meal with Darrel Janvik, a man he sort of wanted to punch in the face.

When he arrived home just before five, he was surprised to see that Norah and Kieran were at his house, standing in the kitchen with Ethan and his mother. He tried not to look too stunned.

"Luke, there you are," his mother said when he came into the kitchen. "Can you go get another leaf for the dining-room table? Norah and Kieran are joining us for supper tonight."

"Sure," he said, making eye contact with Norah but saying nothing.

As he went down the hall, he heard Kieran ask his mother what she was making. He heard Ethan say she was making a lemon-meringue pie, which was his favorite. Luke opened the hall closet, grabbed the table leaf, and carried it into the dining room, leaning it against a wall. Norah eyed him as he walked past. He stepped back into the kitchen to ask Ethan to help him put the leaf in.

"Hey! You have her!" Kieran was saying in a cheerful, excited voice.

"What's that?" MaryAnn said, turning to him with a yellow box of Argo cornstarch in her hand.

Luke looked at Norah, but she was looking at the box in his mother's hand.

"You have her, too! My grandma has that same box in her cupboard! That's my mom!" Kieran exclaimed.

"What?" MaryAnn said, smiling but obviously confused.

Luke kept his eye on Norah, but she wouldn't look at him. What in the world was Kieran talking about?

"That's my mom! That lady!" Kieran said. "See?" He pointed to the dark-haired woman with a body made of an ear of corn on the front of the box of cornstarch.

She did look like Belinda.

MaryAnn turned the box to look at the lady. "Well, how about that?" she said. "That's an amazing resemblance."

"Looks just like her, doesn't she?" Kieran said softly to the air on his left.

Luke raised his eyebrows, as did Norah. He quickly stepped into the vacant spot where an imaginary friend was surely standing.

"She sure does," he said to Kieran.

His mother looked up at him. "I had never noticed that before," she said. "She does look like their mother."

Then the moment thankfully passed.

"Ethan, I need help putting the leaf in," Luke said.

"I can help you," Norah said, and before he could say anything else, she walked past him into the dining room. He followed.

He silently removed the vase of fake tulips in the center of the table and placed it on the china hutch.

"You pull that side," he said to Norah.

She pulled one end of the table, and Luke pulled the other. When enough space had been created, Luke stopped, picked up the leaf and gently laid it across the frame.

They pushed the table back together until it clicked into place.

Luke looked up at Norah at the other end of the table. He was about to thank her for helping when she beat him to it.

"Thank you," she said softly. It was obvious her gratitude had nothing to with the dining-room table.

"You're welcome," he said.

Her gray eyes held his gaze, and Luke thought that in them he could see she had decided to trust him after all.

11

The first week of Luke's summer vacation solidified a routine that had begun to fall into place from the first day. He was usually up by nine and at the paper by ten. When he came home for lunch at noon, his mother's bike and Ethan's old bike would usually be gone, and sometimes Ethan's new bike would be gone, too. Norah and Kieran went to Goose Pond every day to swim. Sometimes Ethan went with them. MaryAnn had told the two neighbor children that first Sunday they'd joined them for supper that they could borrow her bike and Ethan's old bike anytime they pleased. They didn't have to ask, and they didn't have to leave a note.

Luke got off at two o'clock on most days, and sometimes he would join them at the pond. On more than one occasion Matt and Derek and some of his other friends were already there when he arrived. He didn't like the thought of Norah being ogled by Matt and Derek, and he was surprised he also didn't like the thought of Norah being befriended by some of the girls in their circle of friends. The only exception was Patti Carmichael, a classmate who lived at the far end of his street and whose father pastored the little Bible church on the north end of town. Patti was safe enough. Besides, he knew that the two girls were probably so different—at least they seemed different enough to him—that they would not get terribly close. And he liked that. It also annoyed him that he liked that.

He knew it was normal for a guy his age to be attracted to a girl, but it was a strange, new feeling for him. And it wasn't happening the way he thought it would. He'd always envisioned being suddenly and unexplainably attracted to one of the girls in his class at school. He'd always thought it would have to happen suddenly and without warning because he had known most of the girls in his class since grade school.

But then along came Norah. Someone he didn't really know, but sort of did. Technically, he had known her since she was six. Sort of. She lived next door to him. Sort of. She had been inside his tree house, which no other friend but Matt had done before. She needed him. Sort of. He felt drawn to her. Sort of.

It was all very weird.

The thing that was the strangest was the assignment she had proposed and he'd accepted. It was like he was suddenly a private detective with a job to do. It gave him a heady feeling of responsibility, and it surprised him how much he wanted to come through for her, especially since when she had first mentioned it, he'd thought it was the craziest idea in the world.

The second week of summer vacation Luke attempted to ferret out the information Norah needed, beginning his secret investigation with Lucie, the office manager. He was typing up the traffic-court report for the week when he turned to her and said,

"Say, Lucie, what happens if you go to a foreign county and get a speeding ticket?"

She was filling her stapler. She slipped a row of staples into the runner and closed the lid.

"Well, why would you have a car in another country?"

"If you were living there you might. Or if you lived in Texas or California, you could drive to Mexico, you know."

She shrugged her shoulders. "I guess it's the same as here. You pay the fine and promise to be a better driver."

Luke hesitated a moment. "What if you did something worse than speeding?" he eventually continued. "Like robbed a bank or tried to kill someone?"

Lucie turned to him. "What brings all this up?"

He continued to type. "Just wondering."

"Well, I'm sure no matter what country you're in, robbing banks and killing people are both against the law."

"So you'd get arrested."

"Well, I'm sure you would."

"And get put in one of their jails."

"Certainly."

"And there'd be a trial?"

"Well, I would hope so."

"Would you get a lawyer?"

"I guess if you could afford one, you would."

"What if you didn't have any money?"

"I would guess you'd be looking at a nice long stay in a foreign country." Lucie placed the stapler back on her desk.

Luke pretended to be musing on another question.

"What if the police only *thought* you robbed the bank or tried to kill someone, but you really didn't do it, it was really someone else?"

"That's precisely why I go to Florida for my vacations!" she said, putting the box of staples away.

"But what could you do?"

She thought for a moment. "Well, I guess that's what the embassy is for. I suppose you could contact the American embassy to see if they could help you."

"But what if no one will let you use the phone?"

"Then you better hope you have someone on the outside looking out for you," she said gravely.

The phone rang then, and the conversation was over.

Luke was pretty sure of at least one thing. He would need to tell his dad. There was no way he could call the American embassy in Mexico without his dad finding out. He wasn't even sure he would know what to say.

He finished the report, put it in the proofreading basket, and got ready to leave.

It was hard trying to find a way to talk to Norah secretly. Kieran was always with her. And they hadn't been alone at the pond for a while, now that school was out and the temperature was steadily rising every day. When he got home that day after talking with Lucie, he waited until Norah and Kieran were outside in Nell's driveway shooting hoops. He stepped outside and stood at the edge of his own driveway, watching and waiting for an invitation to play with them. He knew Kieran would offer. Within seconds, he did.

"It's me and Norah against you!" Kieran said joyfully, then he turned aside and whispered something to no one.

Luke cast a glance at Norah but her face was expressionless.

"Okay, let's see what you got," Luke said.

Kieran dribbled up the driveway past Luke's outstretched arms and lobbed a shot over his head. The ball hit the warped and peeling backboard at an odd angle and went sailing across the driveway onto Nell's lawn.

"I'll get it." He dashed off after the ball.

Luke turned quickly to Norah and gave her the "meet you in the tree house" sign. She nodded and held up both hands. Ten fingers. Ten o'clock.

He nodded back as Kieran came racing back with the ball.

That night when he met Norah in the tree house she did not warm up at all to Luke's idea that they involve his dad.

"Not yet," she said. "I'll try to call the American embassy. I'll find a way."

"But you don't even know where in Mexico it is. Or the telephone number."

"I'll call Information. They have the number for everything."

"But where will you call from?"

She hesitated. "I'll just use Grandma's phone when she's sleeping."

"But what happens when she gets the bill? Norah, she'll have a cow!"

She looked away and shrugged. "So, she'll have a cow."

Luke was afraid for her. Nell's anger wasn't a pretty sight. "Let me tell my dad. I think he'll be able to help you."

"But why would he?" she said, turning to look at him.

Luke blinked back his surprise. Norah was apparently not used to the kindness of adults.

"Because you need it."

Several seconds of silence passed between them.

"Let me try calling the embassy first. I'll let you know what happens."

∾

On the following Monday afternoon, the beginning of his third week of summer vacation, Luke and Ethan arrived at the swimming hole at two-thirty. Ethan had arranged to meet his friend Ryan there, and the moment they arrived, he dashed off to the jumping rock with his friend.

Norah was sitting on a towel reading. Kieran was far out in the pond, paddling to the other end with a Styrofoam cooler top as a flotation device. His legs, kicking, produced mini-volcanoes of water. Only one other family was at the pond, and it looked like they were getting ready to leave. Luke decided to play lifeguard and put his towel down not too far away from Norah's where he could see Kieran, Ethan, and Ryan with no trouble.

Norah looked up when he sat down.

"Hey," he said.

"Hi."

She looked past her book to her brother out at the other end of the pond. He was now swimming toward Ethan and Ryan, apparently happy to have other boys to jump off the rock with.

"So, you guys are still coming here every day?" Luke said. He knew they were.

"Yeah, I can't keep Kieran away. He loves to swim. He wants to swim in the Olympics someday."

"Really?"

"Yeah. Kind of a big wish, isn't it?"

"Yeah, I guess so."

"Well, at least he doesn't want to grow up to be a whale anymore."

"Yeah."

"My dad finally got a job at the paint factory," she said after a pause.

"That's great." Luke supposed it was good news. It was hard to tell what Norah thought of it. He imagined it meant they were staying.

"Yeah."

He had not been able to ask her about calling the embassy, but now that they were alone, he wanted to know if she had found out anything.

"So did you call?" he asked.

She nodded. "They took information from me. And they asked how old I was. I told them I was seventeen."

"Why?"

"I don't know. I didn't think they'd take me seriously if they knew I was thirteen."

"What did they say?"

"Some lady said she would look into it and call me back," Norah said, looking out over the water.

"You gave her Nell's number?"

"Of course." She turned to look at him.

"But what if Nell answers the phone when that lady calls back?"

"Well, the lady will ask for Norah Janvik. That's me. Grandma will tell me I have a call."

"And then?"

"And then I'll find out what the lady has to tell me."

"What if she tells you it's true, that your mom *is* in jail because they think she helped kill a cop?"

Norah raised her chin, her face resolute. "My mother didn't kill anybody. I'll have to find a way to help her. And I will, too. If I have to go to Mexico myself."

She paused for a moment.

"I'm hot," she said simply. She put her book down and stood up, then walked gracefully into the water. She strode forward until she was in waist-deep and then plunged into its depths and swam away from him.

Three days later, at a little before ten in the morning, Luke went out to the garage to get his bike and go to the newspaper office. He had just grabbed the handlebars when Norah ran in, stopping short when she saw him.

"Hey," Luke said.

Norah looked scared and breathless.

"Can I use your mom's bike?" she said, all six words seeming to run together.

"Sure, no need to ask," he said, a little curious about her expression.

She looked past his mother's bike to the place where Ethan's old bike usually sat. He followed her gaze. There was no bike.

She rushed over to the other bike and grabbed its handlebars.

"Something wrong?" he asked.

"No—no." Barefoot, she was struggling to get the kickstand up.

Luke stepped over and kicked it up for her.

"Did Kieran go somewhere without asking?"

"Yes. No. I don't know!" she said quickly, climbing onto the bike. Then she stopped and turned to him. "I think he might have gone to the swimming hole alone."

His eyes widened. The town's worst fear was that one day a child would find his or her way down to the swimming hole when no one else was there and drown. "By himself?" he said.

"Well, that's what 'alone' means, doesn't it?" she said sharply, but her eyes were growing clouded with fear.

"I'm coming with you," he said and got onto his own bike. He thought Norah might protest but she didn't.

They took off.

Luke had never ridden to the swimming hole as fast as he did then. To an onlooker it would have appeared the two of them were racing. And in a way, they were. They were just not racing each other.

They arrived at Goose Pond, breathless and sweaty. There were no cars there, and the beach was empty, as it usually was at ten in the morning. The only thing visible in the pea-gravel parking lot was Ethan's old bike.

"Kieran!" Norah began to yell, even before she was fully stopped. "Kieran!"

The two dashed off the bikes, letting them fall to the gravel, and sprinted across the grass to the sandy beach, looking across the sapphire-blue water. Its surface was serene and peaceful—and that fact alone sent a cold arrow of fear into Luke's gut.

"Kieran! Kieran!" Norah wailed, stepping out into the calm water.

Luke kicked off his sandals and joined her, his heart pounding in his chest. Then out of the corner of his eye he saw movement. On his far right a tiny head broke the surface of the water by the rocks. It bobbed up and down. Then it arose from the water, and he could see it was attached to a living torso. Arms came up out of the water and touched the rock.

Kieran.

"Norah!" he said and pointed to the rocks.

She turned toward his voice and then followed his pointed finger. She saw her little brother hoist himself onto the first rock ledge and then slide off into the water again. He was playing some sort of game.

Norah strode right into the water, fully clothed, taking the biggest steps she could. Then she dove in, swimming hard toward her brother. Luke headed in to follow her.

She reached Kieran first and had already begun to scold him, when Luke arrived slightly out of breath.

"I told you we weren't going today!" she yelled. "Get up on this rock!"

Kieran climbed out of the water and sat on the first ledge. Norah climbed up next to him. Luke climbed out onto the next one, a couple feet away.

"But I wanted to go swimming!" Kieran said.

"And I said *not today!*" Norah yelled.

"But I don't need you to take me! I can swim fine," he replied angrily. "I can swim better than you!"

"But you're not allowed to go swimming by yourself!"

"But I wasn't by myself. Tommy came with me."

Norah's next reprimand froze in her mouth. Luke was aware that his own mouth had dropped open a little.

"Oh, God," Norah whispered.

Oh, God, indeed, Luke thought.

Kieran waited for his sister to respond but she did not. The look on his face said, *I win!*

Finally she found her voice. She quietly but authoritatively told her brother to please swim back to the beach and she would meet him there in a minute. Feeling thoroughly vindicated, he slipped into the water and began heading back.

Luke waited for Norah to say something. When she didn't, he did.

"Norah, you gotta tell somebody."

She shook her head. "No."

"But he could have drowned."

"But he didn't!"

"But he could have! He could've slipped on the rocks, hit his head, and drowned! He could have—"

"Stop it."

"Well, if you aren't going to, then I will." He started to ease his way back into the water. Norah sprang across the ledge to him and grabbed his arm.

"Don't! Please don't tell anybody!" Her deep-gray eyes were wild.

Luke was certain something had to be horribly out of place for a seven-year-old to believe in imaginary people. It was far too peculiar. This was not like pretending. This was not like playing a game where you're a cop and your friend is a robber. When he had played pretending games as a kid he'd always known it was just *pretend*. He'd known what was real and what wasn't.

"He can't keep this up, Norah. It's not right. And you're not helping him by keeping it a secret."

"I know, I know, it's just…it's just I think I may need help with him. Maybe *you* can help me, Luke. He likes you. He talks about you all the time. You're like his hero."

This was news.

"What?" he said.

"He will listen to you. You can figure out a way to let him know he can't come here with just Tommy. And I think maybe *you'd* be the best one to convince him Tommy isn't real. He would believe you, Luke. He would listen to *you!*"

"No way," he said, shaking his head.

"Please, Luke!" she begged. "Please! They will send him away. I promised my mother I'd look after him! I promised her I wouldn't let anything happen to him! Please! When she comes back for us, he *has* to be here!"

Norah's tears were falling freely down her face, making her gray eyes shimmer like rain in a gutter. Her pull on him was difficult to ignore.

"Please?" she said again.

He looked across the water. Kieran was near the beach now; soon he would be where his feet would be able to touch the bottom. The water would no longer be above his head.

He decided in that moment he would give it a shot. For Norah's sake. He would attempt to make Kieran understand Tommy didn't exist. But he wasn't going to be at it forever, no matter how much he was attracted to her. He'd give it three or four months, maybe a little longer. Norah said it had been going on for over a year; he figured there was no way Kieran would just suddenly stop. It might take a while. It might have to happen a little bit at a time. He'd give him six months at the most. But that was it. If by December that kid still believed Tommy was real, he was going to tell his parents.

"Okay, I'll try. But if it doesn't work, we have to tell someone," he said. "I'm giving him until Christmas. If nothing has changed, I'm telling my parents."

Norah blinked several times as she considered his offer. "All right," she finally said. "Just be gentle with him, Luke. Please? Don't try to kill him off in one day."

"Kill him off?"

"Tommy. Don't kill him off in one day. Kieran needs time to let go of him."

Luke said nothing, just slid into the water. He took even strokes back to the beach. Norah stayed behind him several strokes, though he knew she could outswim him any day of the week.

When they got to the shore, Kieran was sitting on the edge of the beach, making a mountain out of wet sand.

Norah looked to Luke, nodded to him. *You make the first move,* she wordlessly indicated.

He took a deep breath, prayed a silent prayer for wisdom, and sat down next to Kieran. Norah sat down on his other side.

"Kieran, you and I need to talk, man-to-man."

"Dontcha mean boy-to-boy?"

"Okay, boy-to-boy. Kieran, I know about your friend, Tommy. Norah told me about him."

Kieran whipped his head around to his sister. "You told me we had to keep Tommy a secret!"

"We do, but it's okay for Luke to know because he's your best friend," Norah said.

Kieran swung his head back around.

"Uh, the thing is, there are rules about the swimming hole and since you and, uh, Tommy, are new here, we're going to give you a break this time," Luke said, trying to sound very grown-up. "But you need to know that kids who are younger than twelve can't swim alone, even if there are two of them together."

Kieran thought for a moment. "But Tommy's older than twelve. He's your age," he said, like he had just suddenly discovered this.

Luke gave Norah an exasperated look, and she shot one back at him.

"Yeah, but Tommy is one of those special friends that only you can see, right?" he continued.

Kieran gave him a knowing look. "Yeah," he said, obviously amazed that Luke knew this.

"Well, um, special friends that only you can see are always *your* age, never anyone else's. Everyone knows that."

"Really?"

"Yep."

"So, Tommy is seven like me."

"I'm afraid so."

"So we can't come to the swimming hole unless you or Norah comes, too."

Luke saw Norah visibly relax.

"Yeah, that's how it is."

Kieran tossed a handful of wet sand on the little mountain he had made. "Well, okay, I guess."

Luke paused for a moment, a question poised on his lips. He was almost afraid to ask it.

"So, Kieran—where is Tommy right now?" He let the question escape.

Kieran threw another handful of sand on his mountain of dirt and didn't look up. "He went back to Grandma's."

"He did? When did he go?" Luke said, looking at Norah—but her eyes were on her brother.

"He left when you guys got here and Norah started yelling at me," the younger boy replied. "Tommy doesn't like yelling."

At this, Luke stood up, grabbing his sandals. He was ready in many ways to get away from the pond. "I need to go home and change. I'm late for work."

Norah stood up, too. "Sorry," she said.

"It's okay. I don't think my boss will fire me."

Norah gave a smile, but it was nervous and forced.

He turned and walked up the grassy area to the parking lot. She followed him.

"That was really great what you did," she said softly as he reached down for his bike.

Luke wasn't so sure it was that great. He felt like he'd just told all the kids who'd finally realized there is no Santa Claus that, hey, there really is one after all.

"I don't know about that," he said, swinging his leg over his bike seat. "It doesn't seem right to go along with him, Norah. This had better work."

"It will," she said softly but confidently.

"It better. I meant what I said about Christmas. If by then he still thinks Tommy is real, we have to tell somebody. We have to."

She said nothing. He turned, put his feet on the pedals, and began to ride away.

There was, of course, no way for him to know that by Christmas Norah and Kieran would be gone again.

12

The Foxbournes' annual mid-July vacation to South Dakota took place right on schedule that year, the week before the Wooden Shoes Festival. As Luke packed his duffel bag the morning they were to leave, he was aware this was the first year he wasn't really excited about going. Perhaps it was because he was fifteen and just beginning to realize that family vacations take a person seriously out of their current social world. There would be no Matt or Derek or even Norah or Kieran to pass the time with. He'd be stuck with Ethan for company—not just in the backseat during the long drive, but during every day of their vacation and on every excursion. He packed a fresh spiral-bound notebook to jot down story ideas and character sketches. He would escape into a tree house in his mind if he had to.

Norah seemed both relieved and annoyed he would be gone for a week. He imagined the relief came from knowing that the only person capable of squealing on her brother would be gone for seven days. But she also seemed irritated that his absence would prolong Tommy's hoped-for departure. It might even set Kieran back. Her little brother was becoming very attached to Luke. Most of the time Luke didn't mind. It was kind of cool to be someone's idol. But then Kieran would laugh out loud at absolutely nothing or whisper long, animated sentences to no one—and each time Luke would involuntarily shudder. He even noticed his mother giving Kieran a sideways glance several days after the swimming-hole incident, when the two Janviks were again invited to Sunday dinner and Kieran had whispered, "Use your napkin!" to the bowl of peas on his right. Luke had quickly asked his mother for the salt. Nor had there been much progress with regard to Tommy after that.

Norah had climbed up to his tree house on two different occasions since that scary day at the pond—once to tell him the lady from the embassy had not called her back and, at last, another time to tell him she had.

"What did she say?" Luke had quickly asked.

And Norah had sighed. "She just wanted to let me know she was still looking into it, that she hadn't forgotten. And she wanted to know my mother's birth date and where she was born. But when I told her, she just said, 'Thanks. I'll be in touch.' And then she hung up."

"So has Nell gotten her phone bill yet?" he'd asked next.

And she'd only shook her head. That ordeal was still to come.

Luke wondered if it would happen while he was gone visiting his grandparents. He wondered if he wanted it to.

The vacation turned out to be more enjoyable than Luke had imagined. His family and his grandparents spent part of the week camping in the Badlands, a place Luke loved because there was nothing earthly about it. It was like being on another planet. Lots of ideas for stories came to him while hiking with his grandpa and listening to the coyotes howl at night and watching the sun rise over the Mars-like landscape. And Ethan proved to be more of a comrade on the trip and less of an annoyance. He was no longer asking nearly as many questions as he used to, though he did begin a conversation one morning at the breakfast table with, "So why do we call grapefruit 'grapefruit'? They don't look like grapes. They're huge and grapes are small. Grapefruit grow on trees. Grapes grow

,ly:

on vines. They're nothing like grapes at all. They're more like oranges. Except they're not orange."

Luke had excused himself to find a tree to climb.

And though he enjoyed seeing his grandparents and getting out of Halcyon for a little while, the day they packed their car to head back to Iowa he was anxious to get home. He was looking forward to sitting with his friends during the parade at the Wooden Shoes Festival, eating corn dogs, watching his teachers get dunked in the dunking booth, riding the Octopus, playing in the Festival softball tournament, and standing around at the street dance trying to look cool. He had to admit he was hoping to show Norah the Festival. The last time she and Kieran had been in Halcyon they had only seen the parade, nothing else, and they had sat with him and his parents. Luke no longer sat with his parents during the parade. The parade for him was now a hugely social event where Halcyon teenagers sat in pre-determined cliques along the parade route. Luke sat with his friends in front of the Texaco station. It was their spot. And he knew it always would be.

So he was understandably disappointed when he got home from South Dakota and found the Janvik house empty. And it surprised him, because Nell never went anywhere. When he went to bed that first night home from his family vacation, it was the first time he could ever remember falling asleep without a light burning in a Janvik window next door.

The next day, a Friday—and the day the town crowned the new Miss Halcyon—he waited for the Janviks to arrive back home from wherever they had gone. Luke thought maybe Norah would like to come to the pageant, and maybe she'd be impressed with watching him take pictures for the paper. Maybe she'd come down to the newspaper office afterward and watch him develop the film. Maybe she would think it was exciting to watch the images appear magically on white paper in the eerie red glow of the darkroom.

But the Janviks didn't come home. And he developed the pictures alone.

The next day, the first full day of the Festival, Luke kept an eye out for the family, watching the crowds to see if Norah and Kieran were walking around the city square in a daze, wondering where he and Ethan were. He'd invite them to come sit with him and his friends at the parade. He'd even let Kieran come, though he'd have to pray that God would keep the younger boy from having a Tommy moment during any lulls between marching bands.

But there were no Janviks. Luke stood around at the street dance that night with Matt and Derek, hands in his pockets, striking cool poses, but he didn't see Norah. He walked home at eleven, and while many townspeople were still engaged in revelry, including Matt and Derek, his street was quiet. When he was within sight of his house he noticed with disgust that the snot-green house was dark.

He scowled as he threw open the front door.

Who in their right mind leaves Halcyon during the Wooden Shoes Festival? No one! Leave it to the Janviks to do the stupidest thing in the world. Bunch of morons. He trudged up the stairs to his room.

" 'Night, Luke," he heard his mother call out from his parents' half-closed bedroom door.

"Night, Mom," he mumbled back.

Bunch of morons.

The following morning, the faithful of Halcyon gathered in the park for the community worship service. Folding chairs with stencil-stamps on the backs like *TACRC* (Tenth Avenue Christian Reformed Church) and *ORLC* (Our Redeemer Lutheran Church) and *HCBC* (Halcyon Community Bible Church) were strewn about the shaded grass, making a lopsided half-circle that faced the band shell. Luke and Ethan sat at a picnic table with Patti Carmichael and her sixteen-year-old cousin, who was visiting from Waterloo. Patti's father was on stage with the other pastors, and Luke and Ethan's parents were on the stage, too, along with the other members of the community choir.

Patti kept looking at him. He pretended not to notice. He was in a bad mood.

After a community potluck to beat all potlucks, Luke did the barest amount of volunteer work to help clean up. He walked home as soon as his father told him he could. He was out of spending money and out of ride tickets, and he didn't know where Matt and Derek were. He was scheduled to take pictures at the evening talent show in the band shell, but that wouldn't start for another four hours.

As he neared his house he saw that Darrel's camper was back in Nell Janvik's driveway. So the Festival was nearly over and the Janviks had finally decided to come home. *What a bunch of morons!*

Luke stopped walking toward his house. He did not want to see any of them. Not even Norah.

He turned around and walked quickly back to the park, all the while formulating a plan. The high-school food booth always needed more volunteers to work the last shift of the Festival. He'd work it. Then he'd take pictures at the talent show. He'd get home late. He'd be tired and would smell like grease from the food booth. He'd take a shower and go to bed. He'd be too tired to consider writing or thinking in the tree house tonight. He'd be in bed at ten. Lights out. No tree house. He quickened his step.

On Monday morning, an overcast sky greeted Halcyon. Carnival workers, still sleepy from tearing down the rides at midnight the night before, smelled rain in the air and doubled their efforts to hoist the collapsed rides onto their trailers before the storm hit. By noon, the sky was dark and angry, and the trailers of portable amusements and concession stands were making their way out of town. The Wooden Shoes Festival was officially over.

Luke climbed into the tree house after lunch to wait for the storm to arrive. He loved being there during a storm. His mother flat-out refused to let him sit there when there was lightning, but sometimes he could manage to convince her to change her mind if the lightning was off in the distance, like today. She had relented with the condition that if thunder followed the lightning by less than four seconds, he had to come in.

He had made some improvements to the roof, tacking on a few new boards here and there, which had made the tree house nearly waterproof. He sat under the improved roof now in a lime-green beanbag chair he had bought at a garage sale for two dollars. The leaves in the tree were clattering against each other as an energized breeze hurled itself against them. A low booming sounded far off to the west.

He leaned back in the beanbag, looking out through an opening and anticipating the debut of the first drops of rain. But then he heard a different kind of booming—high-pitched and near. It was coming, not from somewhere off to the west, but from right below him.

It was Nell. She was yelling and cursing. From her open kitchen window her voice carried on the agitated breeze and reached him in the tree house where he waited for the storm.

"Who do you think you are, that you can do whatever you please like you own the place!" she yelled.

Then another booming. Lower in pitch, again from within the snot-green house. It was a man's voice. Darrel. Curses flowed from his mouth, too. And they were far worse than Nell's damning of this and that. Luke had never heard such profanity spoken so loudly and so completely. It made him blush.

"She won't do it again—I swear she won't, Ma!" Darrel yelled. "You touch that phone again, Norah, and I swear I'll break your arm! You understand me? Do you? This is none of your business!"

He cursed again, choosing a particularly profane word to describe the business that was not Norah's.

Luke sat up. Nell had gotten her phone bill. He was sure of it. "And close that window!" Nell yelled. "It's starting to rain."

He heard a window being heaved down, cutting him off from the horrors taking place in Nell's kitchen. He could feel his heart beating faster. He wondered if Norah was going to be hit. Slapped. Beaten. Should he tell his parents? Should he climb down and look in a window? Should he call the police?

"God," he breathed, "don't let them hit her."

He wondered where Kieran was. And he suddenly pictured him hiding with his invisible friend—who didn't like yelling—in an upstairs closet and having a hushed conversation about whales. He breathed a six-word prayer for Kieran, too. He didn't know how to make the prayers longer, so he just kept repeating them, over and over, as he climbed down the wooden slats.

Raindrops, hard and heavy, pelted his body as he stole across the lawn that separated the two houses. He crouched low in the scraggly juniper bushes that sat under Nell's side and front windows, wanting to look over them and yet being terribly afraid he'd be seen. If Nell and Darrel saw him, would they haul him in and beat him, too? He suddenly decided he didn't care if they did. What could fat, lazy Nell do? And Darrel? He had wanted to punch him in the face for a long time. This would be his perfect opportunity. And if he came home from the Janviks with a black eye from Darrel, his parents would call the police. The cops would come and take him away. No more Darrel. He stood cautiously, looking into the large front-room window. Rain fell all around him, obscuring his view somewhat. He saw a figure on the couch. He moved in closer.

It was Norah. She was crying, but not bleeding. And she didn't appear to be hurt. To his surprise he saw she was folding laundry. He could see Darrel behind Norah in the kitchen, pacing back and forth with a beer in his hand. He and Nell, whom Luke could not see, appeared to be arguing about something. Luke took another step toward Norah, and his movement caught her attention.

She raised her head to look through the window. Shock at seeing him standing there in the rain was evident on her tear-stained face. She turned briefly toward the kitchen, then swung her head back around.

"Go!" she mouthed to him, waving him away with a hand that held a holey sock.

"Are you okay?" he mouthed back.

She hesitated for a moment, and he wondered why.

She nodded her head, turned her head toward the kitchen and then back to him.

"Go!" she mouthed again.

But he was reluctant to leave her sitting there—and Kieran, too, in that madhouse. That house made of snot. The familiar feeling that he was supposed to protect her and her brother swept over him. He wanted to talk to her.

He made the sign that she was to meet him in the tree house; a closed fist and a pointer finger raised to the sky.

She nodded.

He raised his other hand and spread his fingers.

Ten o'clock.

She nodded.

By ten that night the storm had moved east to water Illinois, and the July sky seemed especially proud of its clean, freshly washed face. The stars shimmered in the darkness like harnessed, wiggling fireflies. A few minutes before ten, Luke crawled out to the tree house with an armful of old towels. Rainwater had seeped in through cracks and one of the openings. Part of the beanbag chair was sitting in a puddle. He'd have to bring it down to the driveway tomorrow and let the sun dry it out.

He was draping the last wet towel across a tree branch to dry when he heard movement behind him. Norah was working her way across the narrow branch that reached to within a foot of Nell's garage roof. Luke took a seat on the dry part of the beanbag and waited.

She didn't say anything at first. She just made her way in and sat down on the floor, using the old sofa cushion as a backrest. Luke thought he saw a red mark on her cheek, but it was dark so he wasn't sure, and he was afraid to ask.

"I take it Nell got her phone bill," he said quietly.

Norah sort of grinned. It was not a true grin, though. It was a sad one. He didn't think there was a word for it.

"You heard, huh?"

He nodded.

"I am now not allowed to even *touch* the phone," she continued in a hushed, mocking voice. "But all evening long, I've been walking past that phone and touching it. I've been touching it for hours. And neither one of them knows it."

Luke didn't know how to respond to this. "So what are you going to do?" he finally said.

"I don't know," she said, shrugging her shoulders and looking out the window opening where Luke had seen the storm's approach. "My dad told me this thing between him and Mom is nobody's business but his. He said if I go messing around in his business again, he'll leave me here and he'll take Kieran and he'll go somewhere I won't be able to find them."

Two tears worked their way out of Norah's eyes and slipped silently down her cheeks.

"He can't do that," Luke said.

"Oh, yes, he can. Adults can do whatever they want."

"He can't keep you from finding your mother. He can't keep you from your brother."

She turned to him. "Yes, he can, Luke. You don't know anything."

He felt anger welling up inside him. "I know I'd like to punch his lights out."

"Be my guest," she said, but then quickly added, "But it wouldn't do any good. He'd still get his way. He always does."

A few seconds of silence passed between them.

"So what's going to happen when that lady from the embassy calls back?" he said.

Norah just shook her head. She looked hopeless. Like she was dying a little inside.

"I know what you should do," Luke said, leaning forward. "How many phones does Nell have?"

"Two," she said lifelessly.

"Where are they?"

"One's in the kitchen, one's in her bedroom."

"Okay. She sleeps most of the day, right? And your dad works days, so he's gone from morning until five, right?"

She nodded her head but added, "Four-thirty."

"Okay, when you wake up in the morning, tiptoe in her room and unplug her phone. Then if you get a call while she's asleep, it'll only ring in the kitchen, and you just answer it right away. Or have Kieran answer it right away."

"I won't have any trouble answering it right away," she said and Luke could picture her walking by Nell's forbidden kitchen phone earlier in the evening and stealthily caressing it.

"Then when Nell wakes up to go to work, sneak back in her room when she goes into the bathroom and plug her phone back in."

Norah nodded. "I guess that might work. That lady may call me later in the day, though. What if tries to call me after three o'clock? That's only one PM in Baja."

"Yeah, but the embassy's in Mexico City, right? That's where this lady is. And Mexico City is on Central Time, just like us."

"It is?"

"I'm pretty sure."

She pursed her lips together. "But she still might call me after three."

"Well, we'll just...we'll just have to pray that she doesn't," he replied.

"Pray?" Norah said, as if the thought were wholly foreign.

"Well, yeah."

"Will that work?"

Luke didn't answer right away. He knew enough about God to know you never could tell what He might do. Or might not do. And yet Luke usually prayed anyway, about all kinds of things, and had for as long as he could remember. His parents had always told him God answers every prayer. Every one. Sometimes, though, the answer is "no."

"It might. If God wants it to, it will," he finally replied.

Norah seemed to ponder this for a moment. He thought he saw in her eyes a sad understanding that, just like all the other adult figures in her life, God, too, was someone who always got His way, regardless of what she wanted. He felt an itching urge to explain that with God it was different, but he hadn't a clue where to begin. He didn't even know why he knew that. Nor why it was okay. He said nothing.

"She'll probably call when we're at the swimming hole," Norah said, "and I'll miss it anyway." The dying look came back.

Luke licked his lips. He had another idea.

"Or I could ask my parents if they would let the lady call back here. At my house."

She turned her head toward him. "What if they say no?"

"What if they say yes?"

She turned away and sighed. "I'll try unplugging her phone, first," she said. "We'll see…"

A few seconds of silence followed.

"Where were you guys?" Luke finally said. "You missed the Festival."

Norah picked at a cuticle. "My grandma wanted to see her sister—my dad's Aunt Eleanor. She lives in Albert Lea. In Minnesota. So my dad took us there in the camper. They didn't ask Kieran and me if we wanted to come, they just said, "Get in the camper, we're leaving.""

He waited.

"It wasn't so bad. My dad's aunt is kind of nice. She's a widow, but she has a little dog Kieran likes. Her kids, my dad's cousins, have all moved away. She never sees her grandkids, so she was kind of happy to see Kieran and me. She bought us each a long rope made of red licorice. Kieran ate his in ten minutes. I still have part of mine."

Luke ate red-licorice ropes all the time. He said nothing.

"Kieran and I got to sleep in the camper by ourselves," she continued. "That was nice. Grandma slept in the house, and Dad took Aunt Eleanor's little car to Minneapolis for a couple days. I don't know why."

"So, I guess it was like a vacation?"

She looked up at him. "Yeah," she said, as if considering this for the first time. "It was kind of like that."

She did not ask him about his vacation or the Festival.

"Is Kieran doing all right?" Luke said.

Norah looked away again. "I guess. Nothing has changed, if that's what you mean."

"Yeah, I guess that's what I mean."

"I still have until Christmas," she said, rising to sit on her knees. "I better get back. They may want to come in where Kieran and I sleep and yell at me some more before they go to bed."

She scooted past him before he could say anything and eased herself out into the canopy of branches. Luke watched her pick her way across the limbs, sometimes crawling, sometimes climbing, until she reached the pitched roof of Nell's garage. She made her way across it to an open window with a beige curtain fluttering out of it and she disappeared inside.

July eased into August, and still there was no call from the embassy in Mexico. After two fruitless weeks of sneaking into Nell's room and unplugging and re-plugging the phone, Norah announced she was ready for Luke to ask his parents if they would let her receive a phone call at his house. They decided he would ask his mother first. A mother would better understand Norah's plight, Luke thought—especially a mother who is a drama teacher and deeply drawn to the theater of real, human pain. At least it seemed likely she would be quick to understand. Then, hopefully, the three of them could convince his dad that it wasn't meddling to let Norah receive a phone call from Mexico about her mother. Jack Foxbourne hated meddling.

MaryAnn was a little shocked at first to hear that Belinda was mixed up in the murder of a Mexican policeman. Luke left out the part about Belinda's apparent addiction to heroin. One problem at a time seemed like the smart way to go. But his mother readily agreed that Norah needed to know where her mother was and if she needed help. That evening, Luke invited Norah and Kieran over to watch reruns of *Hawaii Five-O* and eat caramel corn. While Ethan and Kieran munched on the caramel corn and watched Steve McGarrett cleanse Honolulu of crime and lawlessness, Luke, Norah and MaryAnn quietly convinced Jack to allow the call to come to the Foxbourne house.

Luke could tell his dad was a little uneasy about the whole thing. He did not want to cause trouble or be accused of sticking his nose in other people's business. But in the end, he reluctantly agreed. Compassion for Norah and Kieran won him over. It was decided that the following day, Norah would make another call to the embassy, this time from the Foxbourne house. She would let the lady there know she wanted any information about Belinda to be given to Jack, MaryAnn, or Luke Foxbourne and would give her the new number.

The following morning, a few minutes before eleven, Norah made the call. The woman at the embassy had not been able to devote much time to the case and had nothing new to tell her. She promised to make a concerted effort within the next few weeks.

But the long days of summer wound down and there was no

call. Darrel Janvik registered his children to attend school in Halcyon. He continued to tell his mother he was saving for that down payment on a little farm site, though he was a frequent and generous patron of bars all over the county. Norah and Kieran continued to sleep in the little bedroom above Nell's garage and swim every day at Goose Pond. Kieran continued to have whispered conversations with his invisible playmate, and Nell continued to smoke, complain, sleep all day, and bowl on Saturdays. Summer ended and school began.

And there was no call.

13

*L*uke began his sophomore year at Halcyon High School doing something he had not done before: He spent the first month looking over his shoulder at the younger students. As often as he could, and without drawing too much attention to himself, he stole glances at chattering groups of squirrelly junior-high students, looking for signs that Norah was finding her way all right. Most of the time she was where she needed to be, but Luke noticed she always seemed to be a few paces behind her classmates. Luke rarely saw her giggling with the other thirteen-year-old girls. She did not seem to be bothered by her own aloofness or apparent inability to attract new friends. Or maybe it was that she had quickly taken inventory of the eighth-grade girls at Halcyon and determined none of them were particularly interesting or worthy of friendship. Either way it seemed to be of no consequence: Norah appeared to be quite comfortable by herself.

Luke and Norah's paths did not cross much at school, though they shared many of the same hallways and ate in the same cafeteria. On occasion he would pass her on the way to the library or the gymnasium and would offer a nod of his head or a soft-toned "hey." He thought she seemed quietly at ease. And while he cleverly hid his sideways glances in her direction, she never seemed to likewise seek him out, never seemed to be looking past her junior-high world to catch a glimpse of him. He didn't know if she was purposely keeping herself from becoming dependent on him or if fending for herself socially was something with which she was already very familiar.

Sometimes Norah would come to the tree house in the evenings and share a few highlights of her day or week with Luke, but she usually kept the focus off herself and on other people. Luke's parents didn't seem to mind that Norah often joined Luke in the tree house, at least they never said anything to indicate they minded. Luke was pretty sure Nell and Darrel had no idea how often Norah snuck out her bedroom window to crawl into the tree house. He was also pretty sure that if either of them were to find out, they would put a stop to it, if for no other reason than to rob Norah of a little joy. When she did come she always asked if the lady from the embassy had called—she hadn't. She always asked if he would be spending any time with Kieran—he did sometimes. And occasionally she would ask if she could read one of the stories he was writing. He usually and sheepishly declined.

One crisp evening in mid-October, however, Luke agreed to read her the first chapter of the science-fiction story he was working on. It was about a family whose car had gotten stuck in a snow-drift during a blizzard when they were just a few hundred yards from their farmhouse. They left their stranded vehicle, and as they groped through the blinding, icy whiteness, they had come upon a barn. Thinking it was their own, they had opened the door, relieved to be able to wait out the storm in its safe confines. But once they were inside they realized it was not their barn. And then they were somehow transported to another time, another place—a place where they were not safe. A place where they were being hunted. The strange barn was still their hiding place, but not from a snow-storm. From something else. Something far more dangerous.

"That's a really good story," Norah said when he was finished.

Inside he was beaming, but he pretended to shrug off the compliment. "I've got a ways to go," he said.

"Yeah, but I can almost feel the snow, I can almost feel their fear. It's almost like you know what it's like to be afraid."

He didn't know what to say to this observation. Of course he knew what it was like to be afraid. Every kid grows up being afraid of something—big dogs, the bogeyman, shots. But he also sensed that Norah was somehow seeing past all that; past all the little childish things to what everyone eventually learns to fear no matter how old they are: the bad things that happen over which they have no control.

"Um, thanks," he mumbled.

"Did I ever tell you I like to write poems?" she said after a long pause.

As she spoke, a chilly early fall breeze swept though. Luke wrapped his arms around his knees. He remembered sitting in the tree house on a long-ago, disquieting day when she was ten, and giving her a piece of paper from his notebook because she wanted to write a poem.

"Maybe," he answered.

"Not all of them rhyme, but some of them do. My seventh-grade English teacher told me not all poems have to rhyme. Do you like poetry?"

He shrugged his shoulders. He did not. "It's okay, I guess."

"Do you want to see one? I mean, I could go get one and you can read it."

Luke was envisioning a trite roses-are-red-violets-are-blue nursery rhyme and was already dreading trying to pretend he liked it. But he nodded anyway. "Um, sure."

"I'll be right back."

Norah scrambled out of the tree house, picking her way back across the limb to Nell's garage roof. He watched her crawl back inside her bedroom window.

It seemed like she was gone a long time. When she finally

emerged from the window she held a plastic bag in her hand. A corner of a blue paper stuck out of her pants pocket. She made her way back and set the bag down. Inside were two chocolate cupcakes. Then she pulled out the piece of blue paper and handed it to him.

"I wrote it for my mom. It's about whales."

He took the paper and held it up to the light of his battery-powered camping lantern. The evenly spaced writing flowed across the page.

> *Underneath the rocking sea*
> *In the shadows of the deep*
> *The mighty kings in silent rule*
> *Swim the lengths of the salty pool*
> *Blast of steam, plume of spray*
> *Tails and fins like pennants wave*
> *But barely touch the world of man*
> *Content to stay where time began*
> *No show of force to change or scorn*
> *Nature's way, Earth's slow turn*
> *Unconcerned or unaware*
> *That a world of light and air*
> *Is not far; just there it lies*
> *Just above their hooded eyes.*

He read it again, seeing the giant fins, tasting the salt water, and feeling the deep vastness of the ocean. It scared him how good it was. It suddenly seemed—to his surprise—that Norah had an innate talent for writing that outmatched his own. And she was younger than he was. He felt a tiny coil of jealousy wrap itself around his awe.

"Wow," he said softly. "This is good, Norah."

"Really? You think so?"

"Yeah. Sure. Don't you think it is?"

"I don't know. I like the way I felt when I wrote it," she said. "I had to use a dictionary for some of the words. I needed another word for feathers. When whales breach and blow water out their blowholes, the water looks just like those feathery things knights wear on their helmets. I found the word 'plume' in the dictionary. I love the way it sounds. And I love the word 'pennants,' too. When whales wave their tails, it looks like fans waving those triangle-shaped flags at a football game. They're called pennants. Did you know that?"

"Um, yeah," he said, swallowing his envy and handing the blue paper back to her. "I mean it. It's really good, Norah."

But she made no move to take the piece of paper.

"You know, the whales don't know what they're missing, but they don't seem to care. They don't know there's this whole other world above them. No one knows how to tell them."

She still made no move to take it.

"Yeah, I can see it all, just like you said you could feel the snow and sense the fear in my story," he said, his arm still extended. "Don't...don't you want it back?"

She looked at the piece of paper in his hand. "Maybe you can keep it for me in your notebook there. Sometimes things get lost in my room."

She didn't say it, but he wondered if maybe Nell had a habit of throwing stuff out she could see no purpose for.

"Sure," he said, withdrawing his hand. He folded the piece of paper and stuck it in the pages of his notebook.

Norah seemed to relax when her poem was suddenly safe from people who wouldn't understand why she wrote it. She reached down and picked the little bag up. "Want a cupcake?" she said, opening the bag. "I made them, but they're pretty good."

"Okay." He reached to take a cupcake from her. "Special occasion or something?"

"It's my birthday, " she said casually. "I'm fourteen today."

Something in the way she said it, so nonchalantly, made Luke pause. "It's your birthday?" he finally said.

"Yeah. My mom usually makes the cupcakes..." She stopped

mid-sentence and turned her head toward the window opening, looking past the houses on the other side of the street, past the treetops, past the silvery, moonlit Halcyon water tower.

"Well…happy birthday, Norah," he said clumsily.

She turned her head back to him. Her gray eyes were moist. "Thanks."

"Did…you get anything?" He couldn't help asking. He hoped to God she did.

"Grandma's still mad at me about the Mexico phone call. She gave me some socks today, but she told me it was 'cause I needed them anyway. My dad gave me a ten-dollar bill. I think I might give it to Grandma to pay for the phone call. Maybe she'll forget about it then."

Several long moments of silence passed between them. Luke suddenly had an idea.

"Sometimes I like to imagine things in here, in the tree house." He was instantly aware he was blushing. No one else knew this about him. Certainly not Matt or Derek. But he continued. "Sometimes I close my eyes and pretend I'm somewhere else. That I *am* someone else. It gives me ideas for my stories."

Norah said nothing. Her gray eyes blinked.

"It's a good place for imagining things different than how they are," he continued.

Still she said nothing.

"Want to try it?"

"Okay," she said, tentatively.

"Okay. Close your eyes."

She obeyed.

"Now, picture something you would have liked to have gotten for a birthday present today. Can you picture it?"

"Yes."

"Can you picture it wrapped up in paper you like?"

"Yes."

"What does the package look like?"

"Well, it's…it's square. The paper is dark blue with silver stars on it. And the bow is made of shining white ribbon that my mom curled with her scissors. She used the whole roll."

"You want to open it?" Luke was unable to keep from smiling. Norah knew how to play his game.

"Yes!"

"Okay! Open it."

Her hands made movements like she was untying a ribbon and tearing away paper.

"What is it?" he asked.

"It's Navajo jewelry," she answered, eyes still closed. "The turquoise stones are creamy blue, and the silver shines like sunlight. There's a bracelet. And a necklace. And earrings. And they're just like the ones my mom saw in a store in Arizona, the ones she said she would buy me if she won a million dollars."

"So put them on."

And Norah smiled with her eyes closed and placed the imaginary jewelry on herself. She opened her eyes and laughed.

Luke snapped off a twig from outside, removed the leaves, and broke it in half. He placed the tiny stick in the middle of her cupcake. "I'll just light the candle here," he said.

He pretended to strike a match and then held the imaginary flame to the pretend candle. "Now make a wish."

"Aren't you going to sing 'Happy Birthday' to me?" she said, grinning.

"If you can picture the flame, you can picture me singing. Now, make a wish and blow out your candle."

Norah smiled and took a breath, deciding on her wish. "Okay," she said. "I've got it."

She leaned over and blew air over the tiny stick. Luke clapped. "Well done."

She laughed. "That was fun!" She picked up her cupcake, and then she shook her head as she took the stick out of it. "That was really fun."

She paused for a moment, then said, "No wonder."

"No wonder, what?" Luke said, picking up his own cupcake and starting to peel the paper away.

"No wonder Kieran loves Tommy so much. Pretending makes you happy even if it's not real."

They ate their cupcakes in silence.

⤫

Later that evening as he was getting ready for bed, Luke told his mother that it had been Norah's birthday that day. He told her about the cupcakes, the socks, and the ten-dollar bill.

Four days later, on a rainy Sunday afternoon, MaryAnn invited Norah and Kieran over for supper. She made Mexican food. And served cupcakes for dessert.

⤫

By the end of October, the weather had turned frosty. It was a time of year that Luke both loved and hated. He liked sledding, playing ice hockey on the outdoor rink with his friends, and waking up to find out school had been cancelled because of snow. But it also meant the end of his evenings in the tree house. By the first part of November, a dusting of snow already covered the ground, and the tree house was officially closed for the winter. At least it was according to his mother. He had never thought a little snow and ice was that big of a problem, but his mother did not allow him to climb out his window once the first snow fell.

He saw less of Norah and Kieran once the weather changed. With the onset of winter weather—which, in the Midwest, always arrived before the calendar said it should—and the freezing of Goose Pond, Norah began taking her brother to the indoor pool at the high school to satisfy Kieran's addiction to swimming. They went almost every day after classes were let out. Luke worked at the

Herald after school, so he couldn't join them, though sometimes Ethan did. His mother began inviting them for Sunday dinner every week, and most Sundays they came. Sometimes Norah and Kieran came with them to church, too. The invitation was always extended to Nell and Darrel as well, but they never came.

Norah and Kieran were speechless with wonder when the first real snowstorm blanketed Halcyon in bridal white. Neither of them had ever seen that much snow before, and their amazement amused Luke. The day of that first big November snowfall instead of going swimming, they joined Luke and Ethan after school on the snow-covered hills at the Halcyon Golf Course for their first experience with sledding. Half an hour into their fun, when Ethan and Norah were taking their turns on the sledding run, Kieran turned to Luke and said under his breath, "Tommy really likes the snow!"

Luke turned to him, noticing he was making a circle of perfectly formed footprints in the mini-drift under his booted feet. It had been a couple weeks since Luke had been alone with Kieran, and not much headway had been made—since then or before then—with regard to Tommy. Norah had told Luke that her brother was becoming more secretive about Tommy, which was both good and bad. It was good in that his new teacher hadn't seemed to notice anything strange about Kieran other than that he was a bit behind academically. It was bad in that Norah's brother was still firmly attached to his imaginary friend—attached to the point he felt he had to protect Tommy from being discovered by the grown-ups. Kieran apparently feared for Tommy's safety.

Luke watched him for a few seconds, swallowed, and then *casually* called his name.

"Yeah?" Kieran answered, still plodding around in the snow.

"I don't see any of Tommy's footprints."

He stopped but didn't look up. There was a long pause.

"He has magic snow boots so they don't show," he finally said, but he sounded unsure of himself, like he, too, was troubled that his friend made no prints in the snow.

"Too bad," Luke said, looking away nonchalantly. "Making footprints is fun."

Kieran said nothing more, and neither did Luke. Ethan and Norah returned then with the sleds so they could have a turn.

Luke didn't say anything to Norah that day, but he was pretty sure there was no way he was going to pry Tommy out of her brother's hands before Christmas. No way at all.

A few days later, basketball season began. Luke's schedule got a little more complicated. In addition to schoolwork, basketball practice, and working at the paper, he operated the sound board for his mother's fall-play rehearsals and then the performances in mid-November. Despite his full days, though, he found himself especially looking forward to playing basketball, more so than in years past. First, he was now on the varsity squad, and second, Norah and Kieran had said they would come to all his home games. He'd been working on his three-point shot, and his coach was very pleased with his averages. He was making eighty percent of his attempts during practices. He was looking forward to impressing Norah with a tie-breaking, game-saving three-pointer. He was certain it would happen sometime during the season.

Life was busy but he felt content. Sure of things. In control.

As it turned out, Norah and Kieran only made it to one home game. Four days before Thanksgiving, on a Monday night that showered most of Iowa with an unpleasant mixture of ice and freezing rain, Darrel Janvik got into a fight with another man at a bar in Carrow. Both were drunk. Both were angry. Both should have listened to the advice of friends and other patrons who told them to "just let it go."

But Darrel had followed the other man, who had insulted him, out to the parking lot. He'd staggered over to his truck—the camper shell had long since been sold—and taken out his hunting rifle and waved it around, telling the man if he didn't learn to shut up, he, Darrel, was going to give him "shutting-up lessons." The man had reeled over toward Darrel, shouting curses and challenging him to go ahead and try it. Darrel had raised the barrel of the rifle, and the other had reached down into his boot and pulled out a knife. When Darrel had laughed and cocked the rifle his opponent had lunged at him—and as he yelled, "bang!" the other man threw himself at him and knocked him to the ground. As he fell, his attacker had plunged the blade into his chest, slicing through skin and muscle and arteries. Darrel had landed with a thud on the icy parking lot, and the skin above his right eye had torn away in a ragged gash. The man fell next to him, the rifle in Darrel's hand cracking him over the head.

"I can't see," Darrel had mumbled as he raised a shaking hand to the wound on his forehead. Someone ran into the bar to call for an ambulance.

By the time it arrived to whisk Darrel Janvik away to the hospital, he had bled to death.

14

*L*uke, his brother, and his mother were asleep when a pair of sheriff's deputies drove quietly down Seventh Avenue shortly after midnight on the night of the ice storm. Only Jack, who was up getting a drink of water, saw the squad car stop at Nell's house. He watched from the kitchen window as the deputies got out of the car, walked up to the house, and knocked. Nell was still up; Jack could see the blue glow of her television screen. She had only been home for half an hour from her shift at the paint factory.

He'd shaken his head in parental sympathy. Nell's trouble-making son was probably in jail, and the deputies were telling her what it was he'd done this time. Jack sipped his water and wondered why she hadn't just gotten a phone call, why the deputies had driven over on a night like this one. He set his cup in the sink and turned off the light, preparing to go back up to bed. But then he saw the lights in one of Nell's upstairs windows come on. He waited and watched for what seemed like a long time. Maybe five minutes later, the deputies came out of the house, and so did Nell, bundled in a coat and hat. Behind her trailed Norah and Kieran, their pajama pants visible underneath their heavy jackets. They all quickly got into the squad car, and the car drove off.

"What in the world...?" Jack whispered to the kitchen curtains.

He left the kitchen and started back up the stairs, wondering what Darrel had done that required his children to be roused from their beds at midnight on a school night.

In the morning, while he ate his Wheaties, he found out.

Royce Harkin, Halcyon's chief of police and a personal friend, came by the Foxbourne house a few minutes before seven. The storm had passed, and a glistening infant sunrise was making the ice-covered tree limbs and electrical lines twinkle and shine like strands of white Christmas lights.

MaryAnn welcomed Royce into the kitchen, took his hat and coat, and poured him a cup of coffee.

"What's up, Royce?" Jack asked, moving the pages of the *Des Moines Register* so the other could sit down.

"Bad news, I'm afraid. There's an arraignment at the county courthouse at two o'clock this afternoon, and I wanted you to hear from me what it's about rather than from your fax machine or the coffee gang, seein' as you're Nell's neighbor and all."

Jack said nothing, and MaryAnn took a chair next to her husband as she waited to hear what horrible crime had been committed. Darrel must have really done it this time.

Royce took a breath. "Look, Darrel Janvik was killed last night."

MaryAnn sucked in her breath, and her eyes grew wide. Jack was motionless beside her.

"What?" Jack managed to say.

"There was a fight in the parking lot at The Eight Ball last night sometime before midnight. Darrel was drunk, and so was this other guy. Darrel got his hunting rifle out of his truck and was waving it around in the parking lot, making threats. He and this other guy got into a tussle. The guy had a knife. Several witnesses say Darrel was just waving it around. But the fact is, he had the gun and was making threats with it. The guy came at Darrel with the knife and stabbed him. He bled to death before help could get to him."

"Oh, dear Jesus," MaryAnn whispered.

"The other guy's not from around here, and he's got a record. And he was already in violation of his parole just by being in Carrow last night. But I wouldn't be surprised if he gets off with a self-defense plea. The lousiest public defender in the world could probably get him off."

"Nell…" MaryAnn whispered. "And the kids…"

"No one else was hurt?" Jack said, rising from his chair and wiping his mouth with a napkin. He had to get going. A murder was a rare occurrence in the county. The last one had been years earlier. As sad as the news was, it was front-page material. And today was press day.

"No, no one else was hurt. And there were half-a-dozen witnesses. They're all listed on the police report." The police chief took another gulp of his coffee and rose from his chair, too.

"Where's Nell? And the kids?" MaryAnn exclaimed, the third one to rise from the table.

"The kids are in foster care at the moment. Nell's in bad shape. She stayed the night at the hospital."

Tears began to form in MaryAnn's eyes and slip down her cheeks. "Royce," she said, "can't those kids stay with us until Nell…" but she did not finish.

The lines around Royce's face softened when he saw her tears. "MaryAnn, you know that isn't up to me," he said gently. "The county will take good care of them."

"But why can't they stay with people they already know? Do they know what has happened to their dad?"

"Well, I guess…"

"I don't see why they can't stay with us! Couldn't they stay with us, Jack?" she pleaded.

Jack wrapped a scarf around his neck, preparing to leave. "Hon, of course I wouldn't mind if they did, but it's not our decision to make. The folks at Social Services don't know us."

"Well, where are they? Do you know where they are, Royce?"

"I'm afraid I don't, MaryAnn. I know they're with a licensed foster family in Carrow, but I don't know which one. I am sure whoever the family is, they will take good care of those kids."

MaryAnn shook her head and rubbed her tears away.

"Has anyone called Nell's sister in Minnesota?" she said angrily. "Has anyone tried to reach the kids' mother in Mexico?"

Jack handed Royce his hat and coat. "MaryAnn…" he began.

"Well, has anyone?"

The chief shrugged. "I don't know. Maybe."

Jack walked over to his wife and touched her shoulder. "MaryAnn, let the county take care of this. They'll do the right thing. And when Nell comes home, you can be the neighbor and friend she's going to need, okay?"

Her cheeks were wet again, but she nodded her head.

"I'll call you later," he said, kissing her on the cheek.

"What am I supposed to tell our boys?" she said softly, not looking up.

Jack paused for a moment in the doorway. "Tell them the truth." And he left.

When Luke came downstairs for breakfast at twenty past seven he found his mother standing by the kitchen window, looking across the driveway to Nell's house. She held a cup of coffee in her hand. He couldn't really read the look on her face, but she was clearly deep in thought. And it didn't appear she was contemplating the preparations she still needed to make for Thursday's Thanksgiving meal. He walked past her, and she seemed not to notice him.

He grabbed a bowl from the open dishwasher and looked back at his mother as he reached for the box of Sugar Smacks. She was now looking down at her coffee cup.

"Luke," she said softly, but it startled him anyway.

"Yeah?"

"Ethan is up?"

"Yeah, he's in the bathroom."

She paused for a moment.

"When he comes down I need to tell you boys something."

Luke felt a strange flutter go through him. Something was wrong. He noted his dad's half-eaten bowl of Wheaties on the kitchen table and the pages of the paper in disarray at his own place. His dad usually took the *Register* with him to work, yet there it sat. And he didn't usually leave for the office until after Luke and Ethan left for school, so where was he?

"Where's Dad?" he asked.

His mother fiddled absently with her wedding ring. "He's left already."

He set the bowl and cereal box on the table but didn't sit down. His mom looked over at him, saw the ingredients for his breakfast, and then smiled an obviously forced smile. It was like she threw a mask over her face. She set her coffee cup down.

"Why don't you eat something first?" she said lightly.

"What's wrong? What's happened?" he said, making no move to take her up on her suggestion.

She moved away from the window and walked briskly over to the open dishwasher, taking out a bowl and spoon for Ethan. She set them on the table at his place. "You boys need to eat something first," she said. She turned and pulled two juice glasses out of the dishwasher's top shelf.

"Did something bad happen? Is Dad okay?" he said, following her with his eyes.

"Dad is fine, he's just fine. Please, Luke—just eat, okay?"

"Is Dad sick?" Ethan said, coming into the kitchen and hearing only his mother's last two sentences.

"No, Dad's not sick. He's fine. Eat."

Luke dutifully filled his bowl, and Ethan did the same. He ate, but the cereal felt strange and tasteless in his mouth. Something wasn't right. Something bad had happened. Maybe it had to do with his grandparents in South Dakota. Or maybe it had to do with his other grandparents in Florida. No, not them. Dad wouldn't leave early if something had happened to his mother's parents. He'd still be here, comforting his mom. It had to be his South Dakota grandparents. One of them had had a heart attack. He was sure of it. His grandpa, probably. He was older. A sick feeling rose up inside him, and he pushed his bowl away. He couldn't eat anymore.

Ethan was still crunching away. Luke looked up at his mother, wanting her to just say it but also not wanting her to. He felt afraid. Just like the people in the barn in his story. MaryAnn returned his look. She looked afraid, too. She was afraid to tell him whatever it was that had so horribly altered their normal morning routine.

Ethan gulped down his juice. "So, where's Dad anyway?" he said, putting the glass down and wiping his mouth with the back of his hand.

MaryAnn took her chair at the kitchen table. She took a breath, and Luke thought he heard her whisper something to herself.

"Boys, last night…Darrel was…Darrel got hurt," she said anxiously. "It was sort of an accident, and sort of not. I mean, I don't think it was planned or anything. He didn't even know the man who hurt him. They…he and this other man had been drinking and they got into a fight. And Darrel had his hunting rifle with him. And.. "

She stopped. She was rambling.

Luke was torn between concern for Norah and Kieran and his own relief that the bad news had nothing to do with his grandparents. He waited for her to continue.

"And…he was stabbed by the other man," she finally said. "He…didn't make it. He died."

Strained silence encircled the trio of mother and sons.

Luke felt very weird inside, like it had all just happened right there in the kitchen while they were sitting there. Like Darrel was lying in a pool of blood at his feet and a strange man with a knife was standing over him. He saw Darrel's lifeless eyes looking up at him. He tried to blink away the image. And he imagined he saw Norah, too, standing there in his kitchen, looking at the body.

"Darrel's dead?" Ethan said, drawing him away from the images in his head, but only for a second.

"Yes, I'm afraid he is," his mother answered, and she sounded different, like she was relieved to be free of at least one burden—that of having to tell her sons their next-door neighbor had been murdered.

"He got stabbed?" Ethan sounded dazed.

"Yes," MaryAnn replied gently to him, but she turned her head to look at her older son. "Luke, honey, are you all right?"

He nodded but said nothing. His mother looked alarmed as she watched him.

"So where did he get stabbed?" Ethan asked, trying to piece it all together.

"Well," MaryAnn said nervously. "He was in Carrow last night at a bar, and he and this man both had too much to drink. They were in a parking lot."

"Where did he get stabbed?" Ethan repeated.

"Well, they were in the parking lot in Carrow, Ethan. It didn't happen here."

"He means where in his body," Luke said stiffly. His voice sounded funny. He didn't know why he knew Ethan wasn't asking about the location of the killing. He just did.

MaryAnn turned back to Luke, clearly unnerved by the lifeless tone of his voice.

"Well, I guess I don't know."

Ethan was quiet, imagining, as they all suddenly were, where steel had met flesh.

"Where are Norah and Kieran?" Luke suddenly asked.

"They're with a foster family in Carrow today," she answered. "I think this was really hard on Nell. She couldn't take care of them last night."

Ethan looked up as a fresh realization washed over his face.

"Nell's kids are both dead," he said. "First Kenny and now Darrel. Her kids are both dead."

MaryAnn looked up, too, but said nothing, apparently too afraid to look for words that would address Ethan's discovery.

"How long will they be gone?" Luke said, and again his mother seemed to welcome his question.

"I don't know, Luke."

"Do they know? About Darrel?"

She swallowed. Luke imagined she was wishing his father had stayed behind to help her tell them.

"I don't know."

Several quiet seconds fell about them.

"Do you guys want to stay home from school today?" MaryAnn finally said.

"No," Luke said quickly, getting to his feet. He didn't want to stay at home. He didn't want to be here where there were no answers. He didn't want to be stuck in his room looking out his window at that hellish house next door.

"I guess I don't either," Ethan said, getting to his feet.

MaryAnn sighed. "Okay. Well, we'd better get going then. But…if you guys change your mind, just ask to come down to my room, okay? We can leave if we change our minds, okay?"

Luke was aware of his mother's eyes on him as he left the kitchen and headed upstairs to brush his teeth. He wanted her to look away from him. He did not want to be watched.

Jack Foxbourne had scrambled to change his front page for the Tuesday-morning print run. He'd called the printer and gotten a later print time, sending up a hastily assembled front-page galley just before noon that included coverage of the stabbing death of Darrel Janvik. When Luke arrived at the newspaper office after school later that afternoon, his father had just returned from Carrow and the arraignment of Darrel's killer.

His father seemed surprised to see him.

"I thought maybe you might want the afternoon off," he said as Luke slipped into his dad's office and sank into one of the chairs that faced his desk.

"No," Luke said, but nothing else.

"So, you'll be going to basketball practice at five, too?"

"If I don't practice with the team I can't play in Saturday's game," he said tonelessly.

"Luke," his father began, leaning forward on his desk, "I know how close you are to Norah and Kieran. I know this must be affecting you. It's okay to take some time off to deal with it."

Luke looked away. He really didn't want to think about Norah and Kieran at that moment. Aside from them there simply was nothing to deal with. Nothing.

"I don't need any time to deal with it," he said. "Darrel was a lousy father. He was a scumbag. I hated him."

His father said nothing at first.

"He probably was a lousy father, Luke," he said gently a moment later. "But he was the only father Norah and Kieran had. And the only parent, at the moment. I don't know everything, son, but I do know that even lousy fathers are loved by their kids."

Luke fidgeted in his chair.

"I'm okay, Dad," he finally said. "I've got film to develop from the girls' game."

He stepped out of his dad's office, again sensing parental eyes following him, probing for assurance he was not in some kind of danger.

The following day, Wednesday, basketball practice was cancelled so team members who needed to travel with their families to

Thanksgiving destinations could get an early start if they wanted. Luke didn't usually work at the paper on Wednesday, so he rode his bike home from school to begin his four-day break from algebra, biology, and studies on Western civilization.

Ethan had gone to a friend's house, and his mother had stayed behind at the school to get caught up on grades, so Luke was alone in the house at three-thirty when the phone rang. He answered it.

"Is this the Foxbourne residence?" a man's voice said.

"Yes," he said, preparing to tell the telemarketer he wasn't interested in anything he had to sell.

"My name is Edward Lobos, and I am calling from the American Consulate in Tijuana, Mexico. Whom am I speaking with, please?"

Luke felt a rush of adrenaline sweep through him.

"Uh, this is Luke Foxbourne. You have a message for Norah Janvik?"

"Yes, I do. Is she there?"

"No—no, she isn't. But I can take the message for her."

"Well, I am calling in reference to an inquiry from one of our embassy employees regarding Miss Janvik's mother, Belinda Hickler."

"Yes?"

"It looks like Ms. Hickler is currently serving a five-year sentence for driving a getaway vehicle in a drug arrest where a Mexican policeman was shot and killed. The incident happened outside Rosarito in Baja California on April third of last year. The documents we received from Mexican law-enforcement officials show that she is presently incarcerated at a state prison in Ensenada."

"Ensenada? Where's that?" Luke said, rifling through a pile of mail by the phone and grabbing an empty envelope and a pencil.

"That's in Baja, not too far from Tijuana and the U.S. border."

"And is it true? I mean, did she do it? Is, um, is there an appeal?"

"No. No appeal. She pled guilty."

"She did?"

"Yes. The court documents say she did not know a policeman had been killed, but she admitted to driving the vehicle."

"So, is there an address? Do you have an address where she's at? Can she get mail?"

"I am sure she is allowed mail. I can give you an address. You have something to write with?"

"Yes." Luke was trying not to imagine how things could get any worse for Norah and Kieran. The man gave him the address, and he wrote it down.

He rubbed his head, trying to think like a reporter. Trying to remember what his dad asked when he worked a news story about a crime.

"Did she have a lawyer? Do you have his name?"

"Yes, she had a public defender. His name is Ernesto Trujillo. He has an office in Tijuana. You want that address, too?"

"Yes," he said, and he scribbled down the second address.

"Okay, then. Does this take care of all of Miss Janvik's concerns?"

Luke thought for a moment. Of course it didn't. But he knew what the man meant. "Well, is there anything you guys can do to…to get her out?"

"Get her out?"

"Norah and her brother just lost their father. They really need their mother right now."

"Oh. I see. I'm very sorry to hear that, I truly am. But you understand Ms. Hickler pled guilty to the charge?"

"Yes," he said, sighing.

"She may be released early for good behavior. It happens sometimes."

"Sure. Okay."

"I'm really sorry about the loss of Miss Janvik's father. She is seventeen?"

Luke cleared his throat. "Actually, she's fourteen. Her brother is eight."

"Ah, that's too bad. Really it is. But I would think they'd be well cared-for in the States. I am sure Iowa has a program to take care of kids whose only living parent is in prison."

"Yeah, I guess."

"Well, you can give Miss Janvik my number if she has any additional questions."

He wrote down the number as the man recited it.

"Thanks," he said.

"You're welcome. Goodbye, then."

The man clicked off.

Luke stood at the kitchen counter with the phone in his hands. The air around him felt heavy. The scribbled-on envelope in his hand felt even heavier. He had no idea how to get this information to Norah. He wasn't even sure he wanted to be the one to give it to her. But someone needed to know what he now knew. Someone with the power to make decisions for Norah and Kieran needed to know where Belinda was and why she was there. He didn't know who that someone was.

But he did know in whose hands he wanted the envelope to begin its journey to Norah, if those hands weren't his.

He dialed the number for his dad's office.

15

Luke awoke on Thanksgiving morning with his head turned toward his window. When he opened his eyes, the wooden walls of his tree house were the first thing he saw. Denied its leafy clothing, the elm that bore his refuge looked naked in the grayness of a Midwest November morning. And the tree house itself looked exposed and vulnerable. He hadn't been inside it for weeks. He could see Norah and Kieran's bedroom window beyond the awkwardly pitched roof of the tree house as he lay in his bed. There was no light behind the glass, and the curtains were drawn. He turned his head, threw back the covers, and got up.

Nell Janvik had returned to her home the previous evening—none of the Foxbournes were entirely sure when. At five, when dusk was approaching, the house had still been dark. But at seven-thirty, his mother had noticed a light was on in the living room. Luke had seen it, too. MaryAnn had grabbed a parka and headed for the front door.

"Do you want me to come with you?" his father had asked.

"No," she'd said as she pulled on her winter boots. "Not yet."

She hadn't been gone very long, maybe twenty minutes. When she'd returned, her eyes betrayed that tears had been shed.

"Everything okay?" his dad had said. It was not a well-worded question, but the three of them knew what he meant.

"She's so angry," MaryAnn had pulled off her parka and stepped out of her boots and had made her way to the kitchen with Jack and Luke following.

"But she let you in. She let you talk with her," Jack had said.

"Yes," his mother had replied, and then she'd sat down at the kitchen table. "It was the longest stretch of conversation I've ever had with her in the thirteen years we've been here. And actually I said very little. She just kept going on and on. I think she mistook me for God. It was like she was reading off a list of every horrible thing He's allowed to happen to her. And it was such a long list."

MaryAnn had looked up then and noticed Luke was in the kitchen listening as well. She'd quickly gotten up, walked over to the stove, and grabbed the teakettle. "I think I'd like some tea."

"Were Norah and Kieran there?" Luke had asked.

"No," his mother had answered, filling the kettle with water at the sink. She'd said nothing else about it last night. Not to him, anyway.

He now pulled on a pair of jeans and a sweatshirt, leaving his pajamas on the floor. When he opened his bedroom door, the savory smell of sautéed sage, onion, and celery greeted him—his mother was preparing the stuffing for the turkey. He descended the stairs, hands in his pockets, and walked past Ethan, who was lying on the couch watching a parade on TV. He went into the kitchen.

"Hey, sleepyhead," his mom said when she saw him.

"Hey," he said in return. He thought his mom looked tired.

"I made cinnamon rolls for breakfast," she said. "They're on the table."

"Okay." He reached into the cupboard for a juice glass, poured a glass of orange juice, and looked at the cinnamon rolls, their tops glossy with white icing. He didn't feel in the mood for something so dreadfully sweet.

"After you eat, can you get a leaf out for the dining-room table?" his mother continued. "We'll just need one."

His grandparents were coming from South Dakota and would be staying through the weekend. MaryAnn had invited the Janviks, too, and it had been looking favorable that they were all going to come. Even Nell and Darrel. But that was before. The Janviks weren't coming now. None of them.

"I'll just do it now," Luke said, setting his juice glass down and leaving the room.

∽∽∾

The morning passed slowly. Ethan and Jack began to watch the first of a string of college football games while waiting for the grandparents. But Luke found he had no interest in watching football. Nothing seemed to interest him.

After lunch, he went back upstairs to his room and closed the door. Through the window, his tree house beckoned him. He walked over and stood there for several long minutes, then raised the sash and screen and storm window. A sharply cold November wind blew across his face, and he shut his eyes. It was invigorating. He opened his eyes and looked out at the limb that would take him to his tree house if he dared to climb out onto it.

His parents would most likely ground him.

So what?

He grabbed a hooded jacket off his desk chair and pulled it on over the sweatshirt he was already wearing, pulling the hood over his head. Then he grabbed the blanket off his bed, wadded it up as best he could, and climbed gingerly out onto the limb. The branch felt icy and petrified, and it swayed a bit in the wind. He crept across it slowly, throwing the blanket into the tree house as soon as he was close enough. His hands were numb when he finally climbed inside, and he grabbed the blanket and wrapped himself in it, covering his hands and hunkering down. After a few moments, the icy chill left his fingers and his own heat began to warm him. The walls kept out most of the wind, and there was only a trace of snow where he sat. It was not as bad as he thought it was going to be.

Once he was warmer he leaned back against the wall that faced Norah's window and gazed out at the unforgiving November sky. He wondered what the weather would be like at Darrel's funeral tomorrow. He wondered if everyone would sit in their cars at the cemetery if the ceremony was accompanied by an icy wind.

He decided he wouldn't be a bit surprised if a freak, unpredicted blizzard swooped down on Halcyon tomorrow morning, burying mourners in their cars as they tried to pay their last respects. Bad luck followed the Janvik family. It just did. Or seemed to.

Was it really bad luck?

His youth pastor had told the youth group a few months ago there was no such thing as bad luck. Or good luck. There was no luck to anything or for anyone. Nothing happened by chance, because there is a God who is in control of everything.

If that was true, Luke thought to himself, if God was in control of everything and nothing happened by chance, and there was no such thing as luck, then it was God himself who had brought such unrelenting misfortune to the Janviks. There was no other way of looking at it. God was either in control or He was not. If He was not, then no wonder life was sometimes a picture of chaos. *If He is in control, though, then what on earth is He doing? This planet is a crazy mess!*

"I don't understand You," Luke whispered aloud, but he was afraid to whisper anything else. He was afraid a cosmic hand would reach down out of heaven, pluck him from the tree house, and fling him to the frozen ground.

He sat there with his troubling thoughts for a long time. He didn't hear his father come to his window or see him look out of it. He was not even aware his father was climbing out of the window and inching his way along the branch until he was nearly in the tree house.

"Dad!" Luke said when he saw him.

"It's okay, Luke," Jack said gently. "Can I come in?"

Luke was completely shocked. His father had never come into the tree house before. Never. And here it was the end of November, twenty degrees with a measurable wind chill, and his father was perched on a tree limb, asking to be let in.

"Yeah. Sure," he said, dumbfounded.

His father gingerly approached the entrance and crawled inside.

"Here," Luke said, unwrapping himself from his blanket and handing it to his dad. "I've got on another sweatshirt."

"Thanks." His father wrapped the blanket around himself.

The two sat in silence for a few seconds.

"Your grandparents are here," Jack finally said.

Luke nodded.

"You've been out here doing some thinking?" his dad continued a moment later.

He nodded again. "Yeah."

"What about?"

He was hesitant to confess to his father that he had been accusing God of being ridiculously unfair. But on the other hand, he desperately wanted reassurance God was still good.

"It just seems like God has been unfair to the Janviks," he said after a long pause. "Every time I turn around something bad is happening to them. It's just like Mom said last night. Nell has that huge list of horrible things that have happened to her. It seems like God is against her."

His father nodded. "It does seem that way," he said, letting out a sigh that let Luke know his dad knew exactly how he felt and it wasn't a damnable crime.

"So is He? Is He against her?"

Jack looked up at the roof of the tree house, studying it. He waited a few minutes before he began to speak.

"Do you remember when I built this tree house and your mom and I told you there were two rules? Do you remember what they were?"

"Sure," Luke said. "I had to share it with Ethan, and we weren't allowed to roughhouse in it."

"And why weren't you allowed to roughhouse in it?"

He shrugged. Was his dad playing a trick on him? "Because Mom was afraid we might fall."

"And what would happen if you fell?"

"Dad—"

"Just tell me."

"Well, if I fell, I'd probably get hurt. Might even break something important."

A grin broke across Jack's face. "And why would you get hurt? Why is it possible you might break something?"

Luke smiled now. "Because when people fall from trees they usually get hurt. You know, there's that thing called gravity."

"And the frailty of the human body," Jack added.

"Yeah, that too."

He knew his dad was trying to communicate something to him. He just couldn't see what it was.

"We live in a world with limitations, Luke," his father said. "The body is frail, and the laws of our planet confine us. You know you cannot jump out of this tree house and expect to fly. You know your limitations. You also know, Luke, that God made the world perfect, even perfect in its limitations, but we kind of made a mess of it. So now we live with limitations that can hurt us. Do you see where I am headed, Luke?"

"I...don't know," he said. Some of it was making sense. Some of it wasn't.

"Part of the reason Nell has known such sadness is she has made bad choices, and so have some of the people she has loved. And of course some of her sadness is because of things that were beyond her control, things that came up against those limitations."

"You mean like Kenny getting killed in Vietnam?"

"Yes, like that."

"So why doesn't God ease up on her, then?" Luke said. "He hasn't let even half as much bad stuff happen to us as He has to Nell. Or Norah. I don't see what Norah has ever done to deserve what is happening to her, Dad. She's not like Nell. And only bad stuff happens to her."

"Well, I don't know all that God knows about individual people, Luke. I believe He works in each life in whatever way that will draw that person to Him."

"Yeah, but Dad—this will just drive them all away from Him!"

Jack nodded. "Tough times will bring that out in people, Luke. It's in the worst of times that a person will either run to God or turn his back on Him. I think it's always been that way."

Luke was silent for a moment.

"Don't you ever wonder why, Dad? Don't you ever wonder *why* it's that way? Why He made us like that? I mean, why are we even *here* if life is going to be so hard that it turns some people away from God?"

"I've wondered those things, too, Luke," Jack said. "Sometimes I still do. I'm not sure why God made us the way He did. I know we were made in His image, so there's something about us that is uniquely like Him, but there's probably much more to it than that. As to why we're here, well, I think maybe we're here to learn to love Him. To learn to love God and to want to be with Him. I think we're here to cultivate our longing for heaven."

Luke sighed. "Heaven," he said, "seems like a long, long way off, Dad."

Jack nodded. "It does. But I think God gives us glimpses of heaven from time to time to help us nurture the desire to want to be there at the end of our lives."

place humans on a planet with limitations, that He would give those same humans the ability to make choices, but that He would also instill in every person a tiny longing for heaven, a longing designed to blossom. He even began to feel that tiny longing stir within his own heart and soul. It all made sense except for one thing. It did not explain why God had allowed such an abundance of tragedy into Norah's life. She never saw glimpses of heaven. Ever. How could she? He wouldn't be surprised if all she saw were glimpses of hell.

"But Dad," he said. "What about Norah? What about Kieran? When do they ever get to smell the turkey? When do they ever get to smell the pumpkin pie? Dad, their world is like a nightmare."

Jack leaned forward and placed his hands on Luke's shoulders. "Luke, listen to me. Every time you've showed kindness to Norah and Kieran—and I've seen you do that for years now—I've seen the love of God in you. I know their lives are harder than yours, but Luke, God hasn't forgotten about them. They have smelled the turkey and the pies. They've smelled it all. Every time they came over to our house. They smelled it every time you cared for them."

Luke could think of nothing to say in response. Nothing at all. He had never heard his dad compliment him in such a way. It made him feel hot inside, despite the ice-cold air.

His dad smiled at him, squeezed his shoulders, and let go. "Ready to go in?" And Luke nodded.

They carefully made their way back to the window and eased their chilled bodies back inside the house. From the open doorway of the bedroom, the heady fragrances of a Thanksgiving meal floated into the room, welcoming them inside.

Carl Janvik was laid to rest on an upper slope of the Halcyon under a cottonwood tree the day after Thanksgiving. The

"What do you mean?" Luke asked, feeling at that momen[t] he greatly needed a glimpse of heaven.

"Well, I see glimpses every spring when the earth ren[ews it]self. And sometimes I see glimpses in a worship service w[hile] singing about Jesus and all of a sudden I feel like I'm right [in] His arms. And sometimes I see glimpses at dawn after a [snow,] before the plows come through, before the sunlight to[uches the] new snow and only the dying moonlight is falling on it. [All] the time."

Luke looked away toward the window opening an[d the] sky. "But those things all seem like, like, *earthly* thing[s," he] said quietly.

"Yes, I suppose they are. I guess it's like the bea[uty] here on earth is a taste of what's to come. It's not the [thing,] it makes me think of the real thing. It makes me *lo[ng]* [for the real] thing. And I think that's what we're meant to do. W[e're meant] to long for heaven."

"Not the real thing…" Luke was trying to [follow] what his father was saying.

"But like it. It reminds you of it," Jack said[.] "Like—like right now, if you went into the hous[e what would you] smell?"

"What would I smell?"

"Yes. What would you smell?"

"Well, I guess I would smell the turke[y and the] pumpkin pies. All the food Mom's making fo[r us."]

"And will you eat the smell?"

"Well, no—I'm not going to eat the *sm[ell.]*"

"No, you'll eat the real thing when Mo[m calls us,"] Jack said. "Until she does, the smell will be [there,] almost. It'll make us *want* her to call us to[... The smell] is not the real thing, it just makes us long [for it."]

Luke leaned back against the wall of t[he barn, pondering] his father's words. He could understand [...]

casket that bore his body was placed in the plot next to that of his brother, Kenny. City workers had managed to coax out the semi-frozen earth so Darrel could be buried the same day as his funeral. And there was no freak blizzard. The sun peeked through the clouds off and on, and the temperature hovered around thirty degrees.

Luke attended the funeral with his parents with the sole purpose of making sure Norah and Kieran were all right.

There hadn't been much of a crowd at the funeral. It hadn't been at all like Kenny's, whose patriot's death fourteen years before had brought out the whole town, as Mrs. Liekfisch described it. There was instead a scattering of people—distant relatives, a few neighbors and friends, the owner of the paint factory, and several of Darrel's co-workers and former high-school classmates.

After the interment, the four dozen or so people gathered back at the church for little ham sandwiches, Jell-O salad, chips, and Rice Krispies bars.

Luke waited impatiently for the moment when he could talk to Norah alone. A large, sixtyish woman hovered over her and Kieran constantly. He didn't know who she was—the foster mother, maybe. Finally she left the two alone at a table and went to sit with Nell, who was also sitting at a table and looking rather dazed. Luke made his way over to them.

"Hello, Norah, Kieran," he said when he reached them.

"Hi," Norah said softly. Kieran said nothing.

Luke sat down by the younger boy. "You doing okay, Kieran?"

Kieran toyed with his fork. "We're going to live in Minnesota."

Luke turned to look at Norah. "You are?"

Norah's flannel-gray eyes blinked. "We're going to live with Aunt Eleanor for a while." She nodded her head toward the woman who had been hovering over them.

"How long a while?"

"I don't know."

"Grandma doesn't want us," Kieran said, squishing a Jell-O'ed marshmallow on his plate with his fork.

"Grandma is too sad right now to take care of us," Norah said to her brother, without expression.

"So where will you be?" Luke said. He wondered if she could sense his disappointment.

"In Albert Lea. It's a few hours away."

She seemed flat. He could think of no other word to describe her. He wished he could talk to her alone.

She must have sensed this because she suddenly asked Kieran if he would go get her another cup of lemonade. He slipped off his chair and started walking toward the beverage table.

"Thanks for getting that information from Mexico for me," she said when her brother was out of earshot, but again her voice was without emotion.

"So, you know about your mom?"

"We have a social worker with the county. She told me you took the call. She gave me my mom's address."

"So...are you going to write her?"

Norah looked away. "Maybe."

"Does she know what happened?"

"The social worker wrote to the prison officials. I'm sure she knows by now."

"Norah, I—" he began, but she cut him off.

"He's coming back," she said. A second later Kieran was at the table with a cup of lemonade.

"I'm tired of being here," he said.

Norah held out her arms and her brother came into them, falling against her chest. She bent her head, and her honey-blonde hair fell against his brownish-black curls. Luke suddenly felt like an intruder. He rose from his chair, and she raised her head.

"Do you want me to write to you?" he said softly, impulsively.

Again, the gray eyes blinked as she considered his request.

"I guess that would be okay."

"What's your new address?"

She looked back down at her brother's head nestled against her. "I don't know what my new address is."

Luke wasn't sure what to do. He didn't want to go ask that big hovering woman for her address.

"I'll write to you first," she said. "Then you'll have my return address."

"All right."

Luke kneeled down to look at Kieran. "I'll miss going sledding with you," he said. "If you come back to visit your grandma, make sure you come over to say hi, okay? Maybe we can go sledding."

"Okay," Kieran said, but he didn't look at Luke.

Luke stood up and waited for Norah to look at him.

"I'm sorry about all this, Norah," he said when she finally did.

She looked at him for a second without saying anything. "Why are you sorry? You didn't do anything," she finally said.

He didn't know how to say he was aching for her and Kieran.

"I know I didn't do anything," he said instead. "But I wish I could."

She held his gaze for a moment and then rested her cheek on Kieran's head.

" 'Bye, Luke," she said softly.

And for a moment, her voice did not sound flat.

16

November eased into December in typical fashion, in a flurry of pre-Christmas activities that kept Luke busy and distracted. Basketball practice and games dominated his schedule, followed closely by capturing all the local holiday happenings on film for the *Halcyon Herald*. When he wasn't on the court or behind the lens of a camera, he was doing homework or learning how to drive on glare ice or writing stories. He found he didn't miss the tree house as much as he had in previous winters. He wondered if that was simply because he was growing up. He wasn't the scrawny twelve-year-old who first climbed into the tree house imagining there were elves nearby. He was now nearly as tall as his father, with a deeper voice, and he'd given up the fantasy genre to write science-fiction stories. He supposed that his decreased interest in the tree house could possibly also be because his most recent memories of being in it included Norah, and she was no longer around.

In the days after she and Kieran had left, Luke was unclear in his mind how he felt about their absence. His home life was certainly less complicated without them right next door, but there was a new kind of emptiness at home. He wasn't sure if it was just another sign he was maturing, that home was becoming less and less his favorite place to be because he would soon be leaving it. He was surprised he felt more comfortable writing at the library than in his bedroom, since he couldn't write in the tree house. And he wasn't sure he even wanted to.

Coupled with this odd sense of restlessness was the mounting knowledge he and Matt were continuing to grow farther apart. Matt enjoyed living life on the edge of trouble, sometimes falling smack into it and barely registering any remorse. The only thing that kept him away from trouble on the weekends was his desire to keep his place on the basketball team. Luke had a horrible feeling that when basketball ended in March and there was no longer a team eligibility issue to keep him from partying, Matt would throw caution to the wind and lose himself to bad choices. Luke had no desire to go down that road. And Matt had no desire to stay away from it.

Luke had never thought of Norah as his second-closest friend until she disappeared at the same time that his decade-long friendship with Matt was finally disintegrating. As Christmas approached, he found himself feeling alone and out of place, like he was living someone else's empty life. He pretended it didn't bother him that day after day there was no letter from Norah. But it did bother him.

His parents were concerned for him—his mother especially. MaryAnn knew her son had feelings for Norah. And though she'd never said anything to Luke, she worried about where those feelings were headed. In the beginning, she'd been proud of her son's compassion for Nell's troubled grandkids. But then Norah began to grow up. And so did Luke. It wasn't difficult to see Norah was becoming a young woman young men would be drawn to. It wasn't that she was beautiful—there were prettier teenage girls in Halcyon—but she was definitely striking. Those eyes of hers were strangely stunning. How could Luke not notice her?

And while MaryAnn still felt compassion for the Janvik kids, she was starting to realize she was glad they no longer lived next door—and infinitely glad her spontaneous offer to take Norah and

Kieran the night their father died had not worked out. She had pity for those kids, genuine pity. They came from a family of problems, which was precisely why she didn't want Luke falling for Norah. She didn't want her firstborn to fall in love with the daughter of trouble. She had said as much to Jack, and he had reminded her that most of the time one cannot stop and catch what has already started to fall.

MaryAnn began to pray there was nothing to try to catch.

Together she and Jack decided a change of pace was probably the tonic Luke needed—and Ethan, too. The death of Darrel Janvik had been hard on all of them. So for Christmas, they took their sons to Florida to spend the holidays with MaryAnn's parents at their new winter home. It was only the second time in fourteen years that Jack had left the paper in the care of employees over Christmas and New Year's.

The Florida sun melted much of the lingering gloom Luke felt, but as the eight-day reprieve drew to a close, he became aware he was already itching to graduate from high school and leave Iowa for good. The brilliant sun on his face, the wild call of sea birds, and the breeze off the Atlantic convinced him he was not meant for small-town life and small-town woes. He wanted the anonymity of big-city life, where he would only socialize with the people he wanted to and *they* would be the only ones who knew his business, not every living soul within a four-mile radius. He wanted to write books in a New York City apartment where he didn't have to know his neighbors on a first-name basis, where no one scrutinized the contents of his garbage can as they walked their dogs on early Tuesday mornings, where swimming holes were unheard of, where mosquitoes did not exist, and where people like Nell Janvik would not be interested in residing.

The thought of spending two-and-a-half more years stuck in

Halcyon darkened his mood somewhat as he and his family boarded their plane on the last day of the old year. But on the flight back to the Midwest he mentally sketched out his three-point plan to make the next thirty months pass as quickly as possible. It was blessedly simple: school, work, write.

It was late afternoon when the Foxbournes drove up Seventh Avenue the day they returned. Fresh snow had fallen since they'd left, and a misty twilight was not far off. As they climbed out of the car after the long drive from the Des Moines airport, every one of them noticed that fresh footprints led across Nell's snow-covered lawn, her messily-shoveled driveway, and the adjoining lawn to the base of the elm tree, where the wooden slats began. Someone had been in the tree house. Perhaps was even still there.

"Luke," his mother said, but he didn't answer her and instead walked over to the elm and began to climb. He heard his father say, "Leave him be, MaryAnn."

When he reached the tree house he could see it was empty, and he was surprised at the disappointment he felt. Snowy footprints showed inside, though. If Norah was the one who had been there, it couldn't have been that long ago. He was about to climb down to see if she and Kieran were back, when he saw an envelope thumb-tacked to one of the walls. On the outside, in Norah's handwriting, was his name. He reached for it, pried it loose, and opened it.

Luke,

We came to visit Grandma over Christmas vacation. We only stayed for a few days. I think seeing Kieran and me still reminds her of everything that happened. Aunt Eleanor thought it would be best if we didn't stay long. I keep looking at your house, but I never see a light come on so I figure you guys must have gone somewhere for Christmas. Kieran is kind of sad you aren't here. He really wanted to go sledding with you. I hope you don't mind that we borrowed your sleds. I also hope you don't mind that I came into the tree house while you were gone. I just needed a place to think. It is always very quiet and peaceful in here.

Aunt Eleanor is pretty nice, but she worries a lot. There is an indoor community pool a few blocks from the house, so I take Kieran swimming almost every day. I think he'd die if he couldn't swim. He still talks about Tommy sometimes, though not as much. We are both seeing a counselor. She's okay, I guess. Her name is Margaret. Kieran won't see her without me in the room. I think he thinks Margaret will try to take Tommy away from him. I just tell him not to tell Margaret about Tommy. How can she take away what she doesn't know he has? But he thinks she'll see Tommy. He thinks she'll see him and won't like him. But she's not insisting Kieran see her alone. At least for now.

The school here is big, more like California. The girls are kind of mean, though, and the boys just stare at me all the time. Kieran has met a kid named Bertie, who lives a couple houses away. He's been to his house a couple times. Kieran would like to have him come over, but Aunt Eleanor gets a little uptight when there are too many kids in the house.

I decided to write my mom and send her a Christmas present. Aunt Eleanor thought it was a crummy idea, but she helped me wrap it and send it. I bought her a red scarf. I thought it would brighten her room. She hasn't written back yet.

Today is New Year's Eve and we are driving back to Albert Lea. Aunt Eleanor is paranoid about driving with all the drunk people on the road so we have to leave before noon.

I wish you had been here.

Norah

Luke read the letter three times and then sat in the tree house for many long minutes before climbing down.

Norah had written to him after all. But she had not left her return address, and he did not know what to make of that.

His mother waited until bedtime to ask him about the note. She knew there had been one because he'd had it in his hand when he'd climbed down and come into the house.

"Is it from Norah?" she'd said as she grabbed a suitcase and started to head upstairs with it.

"Yeah," he'd replied.

"Are Norah and Kieran here?" his father asked as he, too, grabbed a suitcase.

"They were. They're gone now. We missed them."

Luke grabbed his own suitcase and said nothing else.

When his mother knocked on his door later to say good night, she asked if she could talk to him.

"Yeah," he said.

She opened the door. He was sitting at his desk, an open spiral-bound notebook under his hand. He was holding a pen.

"So, are Norah and Kieran doing okay?" she asked.

"I guess."

"Did they come for Christmas?"

Luke shrugged his shoulders. "I don't know how long they were here. Just a few days. But they left today. At noon."

"Mmm," MaryAnn said.

She lingered at the door, and he sensed she was waiting for him to ask if she wanted to read the note.

He didn't ask her.

He couldn't. Tommy was in the note. The deadline was up—it was past Christmas—but he didn't want to explain to his mother about Tommy. And she would wonder who he was if she read Norah's note. She would ask. And he would not be able to lie to her.

"Well, good night, then," she finally said.

"Good night, Mom."

She closed his door, and he turned back to the letter he was writing to Norah. He knew he wouldn't be able to send it, because he had no idea what her address was and there was no way he was going to ask Nell for it. He wasn't even sure he wanted Norah to see it. It was filled with all the things he wanted to do when he was free of Halcyon. And since she was part of his life in Halcyon, it meant he would be free of her, too.

No—even if he had the address he knew he wouldn't send it.

Spring arrived early that year. Halcyon's tulips burst through the chocolate-brown ground the third week in March, blooming the first part of April in showy wonder. Basketball season had given way to baseball, and though Luke had not played in his freshman year, the coach was anxious to fill his bench, and he let Luke join the varsity team based on his impressive work on the basketball court. There had to be something that crossed over onto the diamond, even if it was just determination and a good eye. Luke joined for rather selfish reasons, though he shared them with no one. First, Matt was pretty much out of his life now. Two, Patti Carmichael was starting to make him nervous with her constant watching. If he left school the same time she did, he usually ended up walking with her or riding his bike next to hers. Baseball practice took care of that. Three, staying busy made the time pass more quickly.

In all that time there were no more letters from Norah. Some days Luke found he could forget about her and Kieran. But as the weather got warmer and people spent more time outdoors, Luke saw Nell more often, and whenever he did, he could not help but think of Norah.

It wasn't that Luke ever spoke to Nell or was closer to her than several yards, but seeing her hardened face reminded him of what her life was like. And that Norah was wrapped up in the middle of it whether she liked it or not. It seemed to him Nell had changed a great deal with the murder of her second and only remaining child. She became someone who didn't need garden shoes and who would never have thought to hang a wind chime from her porch, because things like homegrown vegetables and music of angels held no interest for someone like her. She stopped bowling. It seemed the only time she went out was to work her shift at the paint factory. He rarely saw her in town. He wondered if maybe Nell drove to Carrow to get her groceries to avoid having to see people she knew. Or maybe she just didn't buy groceries anymore. Maybe she fed on her grief and anger and had no need of food.

One Saturday in early April, his father came to him at the breakfast table and told him that when he was finished with his scrambled eggs, he wanted him to come outside. They were going to take down Nell's storm windows. He cringed.

Ten minutes later he stood outside Nell's ghastly green house while his dad climbed an extension ladder and handed him the storm windows one by one.

"Does she even know we're doing this?" he asked his dad as they stacked the panes in Nell's garage.

"Mom called her," Jack replied. "She knows. And though she won't say it, I know she's grateful, Luke. If she hadn't wanted us to do it, she would have said so. You know she always makes clear what she *doesn't* want."

"You got that right," he mumbled.

"Luke," his father said, softly, gently, but with authority.

He turned to look at his dad.

"Even Nell needs to be reminded, from time to time, how wonderful a roasting turkey smells." Then he turned to go back outside.

❧

On the last day of school, a Friday and the thirtieth day of May, Luke turned sixteen. That afternoon his father took him to Carrow, where he passed his driving test with a near-perfect score. Two weeks later he flew to South Dakota to spend a month with his grandparents. Then his parents and Ethan drove to South Dakota to pick him up and spend the traditional seven days' vacation.

He was lying in his grandfather's hammock when his family arrived on a hot, early July day. His grandmother had just brought him a glass of lemonade, and he was making notes for a story he was concocting about an undercover agent for the government who could see into the future. He saw the family Buick pull into the driveway, and he sat up as Ethan and his parents got out. He stretched and lazily got to his feet, pretending like he wasn't anxious to see his family, though in truth he was.

"Luke!" his mother said, coming toward him and wrapping him in her arms. "We've missed you! Phone calls just aren't the same!"

"Hey, Mom," he said, returning her hug.

"Luke, how's it going?" his dad said, slapping him on the back and giving him a manly, one-armed embrace.

"Good."

"Hey!" Ethan said. "Whose hammock?"

"Grandpa's. I helped him put it up."

"Grandma and Grandpa inside?" his dad said as they began walking toward the house.

"Yep. Things the same at home?"

"Pretty much," his mother said as they walked.

"I got a new skateboard," Ethan interjected. "And Patti Carmichael's dog had puppies. Mrs. Liekfisch's cat died. And Norah and Kieran are back."

He whipped his head around. "They are?"

"Yep," Ethan said, running ahead.

Luke searched his parents' faces for confirmation. His mother's face was expressionless. He turned to his dad. "Is that true?"

"Yes," Jack said.

"For good?"

His father kept walking toward the house. "I don't know. I didn't actually talk to them or Nell. Ethan saw Kieran for a few minutes when we were loading up the car to leave."

"Oh."

He looked at his mother but her eyes were trained on the steps of the porch as she climbed them. "Can we talk about this later?" she said. Her hand reached for the doorknob, and she went into the house without waiting for an answer.

∽

He spent the next seven days relishing his final week in South Dakota one moment and anxious to get home the next. Even the camping trip to Custer State Park, one of his favorite places, failed to completely hold his interest. He didn't know why it was so important to see Norah and Kieran, but it made him restless to picture them, especially Norah, in Halcyon, probably swimming in Goose Pond, perhaps with Matt and Derek. That thought alone annoyed him.

When the vacation was finally over, the drive home had never seemed so boring and monotonous. The Foxbournes finally pulled into Halcyon around nine-thirty at night. Luke could see lights on in the Janvik house, but he had no intention of going over there and ringing the doorbell. He helped his dad and brother unload the car, stealing multiple glances at Nell's front windows, wondering if a face might appear through the curtains. But it did not happen.

He took his suitcase up to his room, opened it, and began to unpack, needing something to do. Usually he let it lie open in his bedroom for several days after the family vacation until his mother would nearly explode in frustration and demand that he unpack it and put it away. He had nearly emptied it when it occurred to him that maybe Norah would come to the tree house that night. If she had noticed that the Foxbourne car had pulled up into the driveway, maybe she would try to sneak over and say hello. He looked at his wristwatch. It was a few minutes before ten o'clock, the usual meeting time. He walked over to the window, raised the glass and the screen, and climbed out. He inched along the massive branch and ducked inside the tree house.

There seemed to be a dark shape in the corner.

"Norah?" he whispered.

But there was no answer.

He bent down and switched on the camping lantern. The dark shape was just his old beanbag chair. She wasn't there. Luke crawled over to the beanbag and eased himself into it, inwardly chiding himself for imagining Norah would suddenly decide to climb into the tree house after having been away for seven months.

He leaned his head back and gazed up at the stars through the window opening. They were shimmering in the heavy velvet sky. Wisps of cloud fell about the moonlight like illuminated gauze. The songs of crickets and bullfrogs began to lull him, and he started to relax. Then the sound of a motorcycle broke the music of the evening. The sound got closer until it was right below him. He sat up and looked out the opening. In a pool of amber light cast by the streetlight, he saw Norah climb off the back of the motorcycle. Her arms had been around the driver's waist. The driver turned as she got off, and he saw his face. It was Matt.

A thin bolt of anger, or something like it, coursed through his body.

What was she doing with Matt?

" 'Bye!" Norah was saying.

"See ya," Matt called out, and then his cycle bolted down the street like, as Mrs. Liekfisch was fond of saying, a bat out of hell.

Norah began to walk up the path to Nell's front door. Luke made no move to silently retreat from the opening. He continued to stare at her. Perhaps she caught a glimpse of his head as she got closer to the tree house, or perhaps she was just suddenly aware she was being watched. She stopped and looked up.

"Luke!" she said, and her voice sounded bright. "You're home! Did you get home today?"

"Yeah. A little while ago," he answered, purposely keeping his voice as flat as possible.

She took two steps toward him. "Kieran and I are here for a while."

"So I heard."

She took another step toward him.

The closer she got, the more he could see she had changed in the seven months she'd been gone. She was taller, and she had filled out in the places where a girl's body becomes a woman's.

"Can I come up?"

He swallowed. "If you want."

She walked to the tree and disappeared from view. He could hear her climbing up. Then her head poked through the opening in the floor, and she clambered inside.

"So you were in South Dakota at your grandparents'?" she asked as she swung her legs in.

"Yep."

He watched her settle into a cross-legged position. Her now womanlike face stared back at him. She seemed to be waiting for him to say more.

"Aunt Eleanor went on a cruise," she said when he did not speak up.

"Oh."

An awkward pause followed.

"Grandma came up to get us."

"So you're staying?" The question fell from his lips before he had time to consider if it mattered to him.

"I don't know. Grandma hasn't said. Sometimes she acts like she's glad to have us back, and other times it's like she can't stand us. She's different…I don't know. Sometimes I'll catch her looking at Kieran and it almost looks like she wants him. Like she loves him. And then the next minute she's yelling at him. It's weird."

Luke said nothing. That didn't seem weird to him. It seemed like good ol' Nell. Impossible to please.

"Living with Aunt Eleanor hasn't been all that bad," Norah said, moving on. "I mean, it's not the greatest, but she takes us places like the zoo and museums and stuff. I think she really misses her grandkids. They live in Nevada. She hardly ever sees them."

He knew it was his turn to say something, but all he could think of to say was, *What were you doing on the back of Matt's motorcycle?* He wasn't sure if he was angry, jealous, or concerned. Or maybe a crazy combination of all three.

"Luke, are you mad at me?" she said, giving him exactly what he needed—an opportunity to find out.

"What were you doing with Matt?"

"What?"

When he repeated the question, he felt the warm rush of embarrassment creep across his face. He knew how he sounded. He sounded like he was the wounded boyfriend. He told himself he was neither. Not wounded. Not the boyfriend.

"He gave me a ride home," she said plainly, studying his face.

"A ride home?"

"Yeah."

He wanted to ask, *From where?* But he felt silly even thinking it. That's what a parent would ask.

"He invited me to one of his friend's houses. Grandma said I could go if I was home by ten."

"You went to one of his friend's houses? And Nell let you go?" he said, feeling angry all over again.

"Well, yeah." Norah frowned in confusion. "Luke, are you and Matt, like, mad at each other or something?"

He turned his head to consider his answer without having to look at her. It wasn't that he was mad at Matt; he just didn't have that much in common with him anymore. The things that Matt liked to do with his free time reminded him too much of Darrel Janvik and all the things *he* had liked to do. He didn't want to end up like Darrel Janvik. He didn't want Norah to end up like Darrel Janvik. He found himself wondering for the first time if it truly was possible to break the curse. If Norah could grow up and be a Janvik without acting like one. If it were going to happen, she'd have to stay clear of people like Matt.

"He and I just don't like the same things anymore, Norah."

"Like what things?"

"Well, he likes to go to drinking parties, he likes to smoke pot, he likes to skip school, he likes to get into trouble," Luke answered. "I don't want to spend the rest of my life here in Halcyon. I don't want to have to work the line in the paint factory because I've got no other options. And I don't want the highlight of my week to be drowning my paycheck in beer at The Eight Ball in Carrow."

He had not meant for his explanation to sound like a sad commentary on the demise of Darrel Janvik, but there it was. "And that's where Matt is headed," he continued. "I don't want to hang out with people like that."

Her gray eyes held his gaze. They looked like metal in the mix of moonglow and lantern light. He wondered if she was seeing in her mind the lifeless body of her hopeless father, lying in a pool of blood and wasted opportunities.

"Do you think I'm like that?" she whispered.

Images of Norah caring patiently for Kieran, of her deflecting Nell's and Darrel's constant verbal abuse, of her tireless efforts to locate her mother floated across his mind. She was not like them. She was not like Nell and Darrel and Matt. But she could be. Anybody could be. All you had to do is want it. He did not think she wanted it.

"No," he said gently. "I don't."

She seemed to visibly relax. "You think I should stay away from Matt?"

"Matt and I have been friends since kindergarten, and I'll probably always think of him as my friend, but I don't think he's safe to be around, Norah."

"Then I won't hang out with him anymore," she said firmly. "I don't want to stay in Halcyon either. I want to go back to San Diego when I grow up. Maybe I can run a little hotel on the beach, and Kieran can work at Sea World like he's always wanted. And our mom can live with us. If she were happy, I don't think she'd do drugs. And if she lived with Kieran and me on the beach, she'd be happy. I got a letter from her. Did I tell you that?"

"No, you didn't."

"She's hoping to get out early, in two more years instead of four. She didn't know a cop had been killed. That guy she was with never told her he'd shot a cop. I told you she couldn't have had anything to do with killing anybody."

Luke didn't know what to say to this.

"She's doing everything they say and hasn't caused any trouble, except for one little fight, and that wasn't her fault either. When she gets out, she's going to come for us. Kieran is so excited. He keeps a box of Argo cornstarch by his bed. At first, Aunt Eleanor had a fit when she found her cornstarch in his room. I think she thought he was eating it or something. But then I told her Kieran just likes looking at the lady on the front 'cause she looks like our mom. She bought him his own box."

At the mention of Kieran's name and Argo cornstarch, Luke immediately thought of Tommy. He must have betrayed where his thoughts went because a look of uneasiness fell across Norah's face. It was like she could sense what he was about to ask next.

"So does Kieran still think Tommy is real?"

"Sometimes," she said, attempting to sound nonchalant.

"Sometimes?"

"He only talks to Tommy when he's having a really bad day. Most of his days are good."

"So he still thinks he's real?"

She stiffened. "It's not as bad as it was in the beginning. He's way better!"

"Yeah, but Norah—Kieran's, what, eight, nine?" Luke said. "Don't you think he's getting a little old for this?"

She leaned forward, and her voice took on a defensive edge. "So what if right now Kieran still needs Tommy from time to time. Look at everything he's lost! His home, his parents! There's nothing constant in his life except me and…"

"And Tommy," Luke finished her sentence when she would not.

"It's not as bad as it was in the beginning," she repeated. "Don't make a big deal about this, Luke. He'll be fine. When Mom comes back for us, he'll be fine. It's none of your business anyway!"

Her words stung as if she had slapped him. How could she say it was none of his business? She'd *begged* him for help with her brother last summer! She'd insisted he was the one best suited to ease Tommy out of Kieran's grasp.

"I'm sorry!" Norah suddenly whimpered. "I'm really sorry! I shouldn't have said that, Luke." She reached out and touched his knee. Her hand was warm and soft. Then she drew it away.

It was on the tip of his tongue to remind her they had had a deal and it was way past Christmas. But he looked into her troubled eyes and at the hand that had touched him. He didn't say it.

"I'm not going to say anything to anyone," he finally said. "Even though I probably should. *You* probably should."

"He's going to be all right. He will," she assured him. "I promise I won't let him live this way forever. Just for right now. And I still think maybe, in time, he'll listen to *you*, Luke. Maybe there's still a chance you could help him."

"I don't know, Norah. I'm not a psychologist."

"He doesn't need a psychologist! He just needs someone who understands him and who he can look up to."

Luke wasn't sure he did understand Kieran, so he said nothing.

"You know, sometimes I'm a little jealous that when things are really tough and he feels alone, Kieran has Tommy to talk to."

Luke felt a curious and scary compulsion, thanks to years of Sunday-school lessons, to remind her that no one is truly ever alone.

"He could talk to God. You could talk to God." He was embarrassed to be giving such lofty counsel. Who was he to be giving pastoral advice?

She was thoughtful for a moment. "Sometimes I do talk to God."

"Yeah?"

"It doesn't feel like He ever talks back."

Luke knew there had to be a good theological comeback for what Norah had just said, but he didn't know what it was. The moment to respond fluttered away.

"Kieran was so disappointed when we got here and you were already in South Dakota," she continued, as if there had been no holy moment just seconds before. "I mean, he was happy to see Ethan and all, but he really wanted to see you. He has really missed you."

At the mention of her brother's missing him, he nearly asked why she hadn't written to him. But he quickly decided it could only be because of one of two reasons. One, because she didn't want to write him—or two, because she really did but was afraid he didn't want her to.

He really didn't want to know which one it was.

"Well, maybe we can go to Goose Pond tomorrow," he said instead.

"Just like old times." Norah smiled.

When he went to bed that night and said his prayers, he added to his usual list of nighttime supplications the plea that God would indeed break the Janvik curse. That it would stop forever at Darrel. And that the next time Norah tried talking to the heavens, God would talk back.

17

The rest of the summer passed in a lazy, comfortable fashion. When Luke wasn't working at the newspaper, he was spending time with a new circle of people that didn't include Matt. Patti Carmichael's friends, mostly drama-club extroverts his mother already knew and liked, became his new social world. They were bold and daring without being foolish and delinquent. Best of all, they welcomed Norah into their group from the first day. It was this crowd that joined him and Norah in front of the Texaco station for the Wooden Shoes parade, since Matt and several other friends had moved to a curbside seat closer to the liquor store. And it was this crowd that hung out in his basement playing games, watching movies, and teasing his mother throughout the long summer days and nights.

He still made regular visits to the tree house on weekday eve-nings, though he felt like he was getting too old and too tall to be doing such things. Despite his age and height he still loved writing his stories cradled in the tree's embrace. And it was the only time he could be alone with Norah.

She continued to fascinate him in all kinds of ways. He still imagined he'd been commissioned in some crazy way to look out for her and Kieran. And he couldn't deny there was in him a deepening affection and attraction to her, though this unnerved him some-what. He didn't want to fall in love with her, and he didn't think he would. But she had a pull on him that intrigued him as a writer. And as a man. It felt a little dangerous to be on such close terms with her, but he liked it. The feeling of danger was key to his current collection of spy stories, and he found he fed on it. He could tell his mother was worried about his close friendship with Norah, too, that she worried he might fall for her and that nothing good could come from it. He was a tad ashamed to admit he found that intriguing, also. He almost felt challenged to prove his mother wrong. Almost.

Norah didn't come every night to the tree house. When she did come, she often didn't stay long. Sometimes Kieran whined at the window, urging her to come back. She didn't allow him to take the route across the garage roof, and usually by ten o'clock he was ready for bed, so climbing up from the ground wasn't an option. Sometimes she came with notebook paper to write her mother a letter. Sometimes she came with cookies she had made. Sometimes she came with nothing.

One evening Luke asked her if she still liked to write poetry. She sighed—lightly—but sighed nonetheless.

"No, not really. I feel like all my good ideas are gone. Or locked up somewhere and I don't know where they are."

The thought of not being able to write frightened him. Luke didn't want to know anything more about what that was like, and he didn't ask her about it again.

Norah and Kieran spent most of their Sunday afternoons with the Foxbournes, staying for supper nearly every week. Nell always got the invitation too and always declined. On these occa-sions Luke would stealthily look for signs of Tommy's imaginary presence. Kieran never mentioned him and hardly ever whispered things to the air beside him, but it did happen from time to time. No one else ever seemed to notice, and Luke was glad they didn't. Perhaps Norah was right. Perhaps in time Tommy would just fade away.

As summer neared its end, it appeared to Luke that Norah and Kieran would be staying. No one ever said anything, but the closer it got to the start of school, the more it seemed Nell was planning on having them stay. Luke asked Norah about it a couple times, but she just said she didn't know what her grandma was planning to do. And she was afraid to ask. Her grandma had grown quiet, she said, like she was brooding. Norah was afraid she was teetering on the edge of keeping them or sending them back to live with Eleanor. She didn't want to say something and push her over the edge. For the first time in her life, Norah had friends. She didn't want to go back to Albert Lea.

On a Sunday evening in late August after a meal of barbecued spare ribs, MaryAnn fixed a plate for Nell and handed it to Norah as she and Kieran got ready to go home.

"School starts next week," she said to Norah as she gave her a brownie to put on top of the foil-covered paper plate.

"Yeah," Norah said.

"You want me to talk to Nell about getting you and Kieran registered?"

Norah glanced at Luke and then turned back to MaryAnn. "No, I can take care of it. Thanks for supper. C'mon, Kieran."

"Okay. Glad you came. Say hi to Nell for us."

Luke saw his mother turn to his dad and give him a look. It was the Nell look. He'd seen it pass between them for years.

After he'd helped his dad put the grill away, Luke got out a basketball and started shooting hoops out front. He was looking forward to the start of the new year. He'd be a junior. He had new friends to replace the ones he'd grown apart from. He'd start getting college information in the mail. He'd be able to drive to away football games. Norah would probably come with him. Kieran, too. And that was okay.

As he shot the ball over and over, he began to hear voices in between dribbles. The voices got louder. Someone was yelling. He stopped shooting and held the ball to his chest. The voices were coming from Nell's open kitchen windows.

"You've got a lot of nerve telling me how you think things oughta be. How dare you tell me how to live my life? You don't know a thing about anything!"

Nell.

"I know a lot more than you think!" Norah's voice was raised, too, but it didn't match Nell's in terms of decibels.

"Oh, really! Well, Miss Smarty Pants, if you think things are so much better over at the Foxbournes, then you be my guest! You go live with *them,* you ungrateful nuisance!" Nell roared.

Luke felt his cheeks coloring. He'd never heard anyone say his last name with such venom. His breathing quickened. He heard the screen door to Nell's kitchen open. Someone was coming out. But Nell wasn't finished.

"No one ever asked me if I wanted to live next door to Paradise!" she screamed. "No one! No one asked me if I wanted to raise you kids. No one asked me anything!"

The back door slammed shut, and Norah emerged, chest heaving. She turned and saw Luke standing there with the basketball to his chest. Her face was flooded with a mix of anger, rejection, and fear.

He threw the ball onto the grass and motioned with his head for her to follow him. He began to walk toward the garage and his father's car. She hesitated a moment and then followed. He reached underneath the vehicle to the spot where an extra key was hidden.

"Come on," he said as he opened the driver's side door and got in. "Let's go for a drive."

Again, she hesitated for a moment. Then she opened the passenger door and slipped in.

"I don't want to talk about it," she said, barely above a whisper.

"I don't either," he replied.

He said nothing as he backed the car out of the driveway. He said nothing as he headed toward the water tower and the gravel road to Goose Pond, where the two of them would find peace and quiet. In his mind he heard Nell's menacing accusation about his house, his home—over and over.

No one ever asked me if I wanted to live next door to Paradise!

Next door to Paradise. His house.

As if it were really that close.

⁓

Luke didn't see Norah again until Tuesday. He came home from the paper for lunch at twelve-thirty and noticed a car he didn't recognize parked in Nell's driveway with its trunk open. He stepped into his house where his mother was making egg-salad sandwiches. Ethan was opening a can of Dr Pepper, and he looked up at him.

"I think Norah and Kieran are leaving."

Luke stood still for a moment, waiting to see if his mother would confirm or deny it, but she did neither. She just continued to mash bits of egg into a yellow Tupperware bowl. He turned and went back outside.

The woman from Darrel's funeral—Eleanor—was now outside putting two pillows into the trunk. Norah came out of the house then holding a tired-looking green suitcase. She looked up at him and then looked down, staring at her feet as she walked over to the car with it.

"Okay, now I'll just go get your brother's suitcase, and we'll be off!" Eleanor said brightly. "Trixie will be so glad to see you kids again! She just went to the groomer! You won't recognize her!" The woman walked back up the path to the front door and went inside.

Luke walked over to the car, where Norah stood like a statue, unmoving. "What's going on!" he said, but not like a question.

She shrugged her shoulders. "She's sending us back."

Familiar ripples of revulsion swept across him. He hated Nell Janvik at that moment. Truly hated her.

"Why!?"

Again she shrugged. She would not look at him. "I don't know."

The front door opened, and Eleanor came out with another green suitcase, Kieran behind her. Nell was behind Kieran. The three of them stepped out into the sunshine.

Kieran saw Luke standing there and turned to Nell. "Can't we stay, Grandma?" he said softly.

Nell said nothing.

"We'll be back to visit!" Eleanor said brightly. "And Bertie has missed you, Kieran. He always asks about you when I see him!"

Eleanor walked to the car and then noticed Luke for the first time.

"Oh! Hello! Why, you must be Luke. Kieran talks about you all the time. You're the one with the tree house, right?"

He just nodded. His eyes were trained on Nell. He wished his eyes were daggers, just like books said eyes could sometimes look.

"Well, we've got a long drive, we'd best be off," Eleanor said as she put the second suitcase in the trunk and shut it. "Say goodbye to your grandma, kids."

Kieran looked up at his grandmother, and there was no mistaking he was silently pleading for one more chance to stay in Halcyon.

" 'Bye, Grandma."

Nell reached out and tousled his hair. Luke thought that was quite possibly the only time he'd ever seen her show any kind of physical affection for either of her grandkids.

"You mind your Aunt Eleanor, now," she said, as if Kieran was prone to mischief. She said nothing at all to Norah.

"Goodbye," Norah said, but not to Nell. She'd finally raised her eyes to meet Luke's.

Before he could say anything in return, she opened the car door and slid inside.

There had been no time to talk of exchanging addresses this

time. As the car began to back up, he became aware that Ethan had joined him on the driveway and was standing next to him, waving goodbye. Kieran's eyes looked misty as he returned the wave through a half-opened backseat window. Norah was looking straight ahead. Eleanor punched the horn two times in a cheery, two-note farewell.

Ethan watched as the car drove down Seventh Avenue, but Luke turned his head to stare at Nell. He wanted her to feel the heat of his anger, the depth of his scorn for her. He wanted her to feel demoralized by his gaze. He wanted her to squirm under his scrutiny.

She met his eyes with her own, and for several long seconds she said and did nothing.

"What are *you* looking at?" she finally muttered at him.

He continued to look down on her, feeling none of the fear and aversion he'd felt when he was younger. Only loathing.

"Nothing," he said.

He hoped there was no mistaking he meant exactly what he said.

He spent the rest of the day in an irritable mood. His mother had obviously told his father, when he came home for lunch, what had happened because he told Luke he could have the afternoon off if he wanted. Luke didn't know what he wanted. No, that wasn't it. He knew what he wanted. He wanted to be free. He longed to be free.

But he took the afternoon off anyway, and so he was home at three when Nell left for her shift at the paint factory. He saw her get into her car and drive away like it was just an ordinary Tuesday in August.

He declined an offer by Patti and several others to see a movie that night in Carrow. He didn't want to watch TV in the basement. He didn't want to play a game of Risk with his dad.

When he went to bed a little after eleven, he couldn't relax. After fifteen minutes of lying awake and frustrated in his bed, he

climbed out and stood at his window, looking at his tree house—
the symbol of escape. After a moment he opened the window and
inched his way out to it. He kept the lantern off as he stretched
out on the floor with his arms crossed under his head and began to
imagine his future. He started to review his mental list of cities he'd
like to live in. Maybe he'd go to college on the East Coast. Maybe
he'd go to college in California. Maybe he'd start writing screen-
plays. Maybe he'd develop a TV series about spies and Interpol—
he'd have to travel all around the world to do the research.

As he mused on the possibilities he became aware of the odor
of cigarette smoke. And the sound of muted sobs. He came out of
his reverie, sat up, and turned his head. He saw Nell in a square of
moonlight, sitting on her back porch...sitting where Norah had
stood just two days ago. A lit cigarette dangled from one of her
fingers. But she wasn't smoking it. She was crying. As she tried to
stifle her anguish, what came out of her was utterly mournful, the
saddest thing Luke had ever heard. He wanted to scramble out of
the tree house, climb back into his room, and shut the window. But
he was afraid to move. She would hear him.

So he just sat there, hearing the agony of thousands of failed
days bleed out of Nell. He put his hands over his ears and closed his
eyes. He didn't want to hear her sobbing, didn't want to acknowledge she felt pain—nor that he knew she'd lived through more pain
than anyone else he'd ever known. That maybe she had sent Norah
and Kieran away because she knew Eleanor's home had to be hap-
pier than hers. Better than hers. He didn't want to acknowledge
that. He wouldn't be able to hate her then. He pressed his fingers
harder into his ears. But he heard her anyway.

His own eyes were starting to burn with unshed tears, and he
screwed them closed as tight as he could. But the more Nell continued to weep, the more he could not keep them back. He felt his
cheeks growing damp.

Then a thought occurred to him, so surprising that he snapped
his wet eyes open and pulled his hands away from his ears. For the

first time in his life he saw that he and Nell really weren't so different from each other in what they longed for.

His pastor had read something in church on Sunday. It was a strange verse from Ecclesiastes, one he'd never heard before. It had intrigued him then and it pricked him now as he remembered it:

> He has made everything beautiful in its time. He has also set eternity in the hearts of men; yet they cannot fathom what God has done from beginning to end.

The words of the ancient scripture tumbled around in his head as below him Nell wept.

He has also set eternity in the hearts of men.

Eternity in the hearts of men.

Nell longed for Paradise. So did he. They were meant to. The desire to be where God dwells had been imbedded in his being. And in hers, too, though he knew she didn't know it.

That's why it felt so close, just next door. Just above them.

That's why he longed for Paradise.

18

There were no letters, no phone calls, nothing tangible to remind Luke he had a friend named Norah, if that is indeed what she was. His parents did not speak of her or Kieran, possibly because they figured he was angry with Nell and didn't want to intensify the anger by reminding him of what she'd done. Luke *was* angry with her, but his parents did not know that the anger was daily giving way to a strange, compassionless pity.

That winter, his father asked Ethan instead of him to shovel Nell's driveway when snow covered it, and it was Ethan who helped his dad put up her storm windows. Luke didn't mind keeping his distance. It was sadly refreshing.

At Christmas, his parents again took the family to Florida, and this time when they returned there were no footprints in the snow to indicate Norah and Kieran had been to Halcyon for the holidays. Nell was gone, too, when they got back. Perhaps she'd gone to Albert Lea to spend Christmas and New Year's with Eleanor and her grandchildren but there was no way to know for sure. When she came home on the third of January, there was nothing about her mute, aloof presence to indicate where she had been. She was simply not there one minute and there the next.

Basketball, working at the paper, and helping his mother with the spring play did for Luke what he hoped—kept him crazily busy. The long winter months and muddy pre-spring weeks passed quickly.

His new circle of friends decided to go to the prom, which was on the third Saturday in May, as a group, but they agreed to pair off for the Grand March, which was always held in the high-school gym before the prom actually got started. At the urging of one of the other guys in the group, Luke asked Patti to accompany him, and she had promptly said she would love to.

The evening of the prom was balmy and slightly breezy, near perfect. MaryAnn began to get misty-eyed when he came down-stairs in a black tuxedo a few minutes before three.

"I can't believe how handsome you look!" she gushed. "Jack, look at our son!"

"Mom, please," he replied, rolling his eyes.

"You look downright respectable," his father said, smiling.

"Now, you're coming right back here so I can take pictures, right?" MaryAnn continued.

"Yes, we're coming right back."

"Don't forget Patti's corsage in the fridge!"

"I won't, Mom."

Ethan was sitting on the arm of the couch, watching.

"You look like you're going to somebody's funeral," he said.

Luke pushed him back onto the cushions as he walked past into the kitchen. "You better watch it, Ethan. It just might be yours."

"Luke!" his mother exclaimed, but laughed as she said it.

After getting the corsage, he headed out to the garage.

"Now, come right back so I can take pictures!" his mom re-minded him from the back-porch steps.

"Maybe, maybe not," he said, winking at his dad. He got into the Dart, which had been waxed and polished until the chrome shone like mirrors, and drove the six blocks to Patti's house. As he pulled up into the Carmichaels' driveway, Patti was standing in the front by a lilac bush, wearing a blush-pink gown that seemed to swirl like water when she moved. Her mother had a camera in her hand and was snapping away while Pastor Carmichael gave posing advice. Patti had her hair swept up into a bunchy pile except for a few stray ringlets about her face, and there were tiny rhinestones peeking out of the curls on the top of her head. He wondered how they stayed there. She looked very nice, and he knew he should tell her so. But he felt awkward saying anything with her parents standing right there.

"Luke!" Patti's mother said, turning to him. "Don't you look dashing? Oh, won't you two make a handsome couple! Now, come on over here, and let's get some pictures!"

He stepped over in his shiny rented shoes and handed Patti the box with a wrist corsage of pink tea roses.

"Pink. Like you wanted," he said softly.

"They're beautiful!" she whispered back, taking the corsage out.

"I can get that," her dad said, stepping forward and taking the box from her.

He backed away, and she slipped the corsage over her hand.

"You look really nice," Luke managed to say. He felt his face color.

"So do you," she whispered.

"Okay! Turn this way and smile!" her mother said.

After ten minutes of smiling, posing, and feeling rather silly, the pair was relieved when Patti's parents announced they were finished taking pictures and would see Luke and Patti at the Grand March in a little while.

He helped Patti get into the car—as Mrs. Carmichael took shot after shot—and they drove back down the street. Pulling up to his house, Luke could see Nell had just arrived home from somewhere. She was getting out of her car. And so was someone else. And then someone else. It was Norah and Kieran. Patti saw them, too.

"Oh my gosh, Luke! It's Norah!" she said as they pulled into the Foxbourne driveway.

An odd feeling of nausea, heat, and anticipation washed over him as he put the car in park. Norah was here. She was staring at the car as he shut off the engine. Nell had a suitcase in her hand and was stepping inside the house with it.

He got out of the car, almost dreading walking around to get Patti's door. Norah was watching them. It was impossible to read her face.

"Norah!" he said from across the roof of the car, attempting to sound cool and confident as he walked around it. But Patti was already opening her own door. He almost thanked her for doing it.

"Norah! You're here!" Patti said, running over to her as best she could in high heels. Patti wrapped her arms around her, and he saw she hesitated a moment before returning the hug. As he watched them, he noted that Norah hadn't changed much in the nine months she'd been gone. Her hair was longer, fuller. She *seemed* taller, too. But next to Patti, it was obvious she hadn't actually gained an inch. It was strange.

"Luke!" Kieran ran over to him. "Are you getting married?" Kieran was looking at his tuxedo, worry and awe etched on his face.

"No! I am not getting married! I'm just going to the prom."

"What's a 'prom'?" he asked, looking like he was imagining pain was somehow involved.

"It's just dinner and a dance," Luke said, watching as Patti and Norah broke away from each other.

"Why is Patti's hair like that?" Kieran whispered, leaning in close.

"Uh…well, it's supposed to make her look pretty and grown-up."

"Oh. Is Ethan home?"

"Yeah. Sure. Go on in."

Kieran walked away from him, and Luke went over toward the two girls.

"How've you been?" he said to Norah. He sort of wanted to

give her a hug, too. But not in a tux. Not with Patti standing there. Not while Norah was looking at him like she was right then.

"Okay," she said, studying his face like she was memorizing it.

"How long are you and Kieran here?"

She blinked. "For good."

"Really?" Patti said enthusiastically.

Dumbfounded, he waited for Norah to confirm it.

"Eleanor's daughter found out she's expecting triplets. She has two little kids already and is now supposed to be on bed rest until she delivers. Eleanor's moving to Nevada to live with them."

"Oh!" Patti said. "Well, I'm so glad you're coming back. We've missed you."

Norah turned to Luke when Patti said this. "I've missed you guys, too."

An awkward pause followed.

"So you guys must be going to the prom," Norah said, her face expressionless.

"Yeah," Luke said, feeling strangely like he should apologize.

"Oh, I wish you'd come home sooner! You could have gone with us!" Patti said.

"With you?"

"We're all going together! Luke, me, Tracy, Brendan, Max, Camille...everybody."

"Oh," Norah said, looking at Luke's glistening patent-leather shoes.

"You want to come to Grand March? You can see everybody!" Patti continued.

Norah seemed preoccupied. "No, thanks. I really need to help Grandma get our rooms ready. This happened kind of sudden."

"Oh. Okay."

"Well, I guess we'll see you later, then?" Luke said, not wanting to stand there another minute with Norah's odd gaze on him.

"Yeah."

He turned and walked back toward his house with Patti at his side. He could feel Norah's eyes on him through the smooth-fitting black back of his jacket.

He knew as sure as anything he'd be preoccupied with thoughts of his own at the prom that night.

༄

Over the next few days Luke slowly readjusted to the notion of Norah being back. It seemed to take longer this time, and he wasn't sure why. Perhaps it was because she'd said they were in Halcyon for good, and deep down he didn't believe it.

She and Kieran had moved back at a very strange time—two weeks before school got out. By the time they got registered for classes there were only ten days left. Luke didn't see Norah often during those ten days, and when he did, she seemed distant, like she was still in Minnesota. Or perhaps somewhere else altogether. On the last day of May, his parents threw a birthday party for him, and it wasn't until the final hours of the party that he finally saw a bit of the old Norah. As he and his friends sat around playing movie charades at one in the morning she laughed, and it was the sound of her laughter that reminded him of their previous years.

The next day, a Sunday, MaryAnn invited Norah and Kieran to supper, just like old times. As they were getting ready to leave afterward, Norah turned to Luke, and after making sure no one was watching her, she made the sign to meet him in the tree house—a closed fist, index finger raised to the sky. He nodded.

At ten, he went out there. As he eased himself inside, he could see she was already there.

"Hey," he said, crossing his legs and leaning against the wall across from her.

"Hey."

A few seconds of silence passed between them.

"So, did you need to talk to me about something?" he asked.

"No."

He waited.

"I just wanted to know if you still came here. If you still came to the tree house."

"Yeah, sometimes I do."

"Okay. I just wanted to know."

Silence.

"Kieran doing okay?"

"He'll be fine."

He asked no more questions, and neither did she.

June arrived with clouds, mosquitoes, and humidity. Afternoons at Goose Pond often ended in thunderstorms that sent kids and parents running for cover. There was talk among the farmers that something bad was brewing. Some bought extra hail insurance. Some put off buying a new implement. Some began to pray.

On a particularly cloudy Wednesday afternoon, while Jack and MaryAnn were in Cedar Rapids buying a new refrigerator, Luke agreed to help Ethan change the furniture around in his room. He had nothing better to do, and it looked like it was going to start pouring outside anyway.

About four-thirty, just after they'd moved Ethan's bed from the south wall of his room to the east one, the sky turned an odd shade of brown, and the room fell into shadow. A wind had begun to tug at the leaves outside. Luke switched on the bedroom light.

"Looks like a bad one," his brother said, stepping over to the window and looking out.

"Yeah," Luke said, joining him. Off in the distance a thickening wall of black clouds appeared to be moving toward them. "I think I'll go close the garage door."

He sprinted down the stairs, amazed at how dark the living room was for four-thirty in the afternoon. Ethan was right behind him. They stepped outside. The air was breezy and sticky at the same time. The black wall of thunderclouds was inching forward. He walked quickly over to the garage door and pulled it closed. He noticed Nell's garage door was open, too. Her car was gone, of course, as she was working her shift at the paint factory. He walked over and started to pull her garage door down. A strong gust of wind swept up around him and challenged him. He yanked harder. The wind answered back.

"Get inside," he yelled to Ethan as he managed to pull the door closed. He didn't like the look of what was coming. As the words left his mouth, the civil-defense siren five blocks away began to wail.

He knew this was no test. The high-pitched wail meant a severe thunderstorm was on its way—or worse, a tornado.

"Get inside!" he yelled again to Ethan.

Just then Norah appeared at Nell's front door.

"What's going on?" she hollered.

He ran over to her. "Where's Kieran?"

"I'm right here!" her brother called out from behind her.

"C'mon!" Luke yelled, holding the door open and motioning them out.

"What is it?" she exclaimed.

Kieran's eyes were wide with fear. Luke was sure they'd heard the siren go off before during tests—hadn't they?

"Bad storm! We need to get to the basement. Go inside our house with Ethan!"

"I need to close the windows!" Norah yelled. The wind was getting stronger. The sky turned a sick shade of green.

"No time!" he yelled. He yanked Nell's door shut and ran with the two others across the lawns and into the Foxbourne house.

Ethan was standing at the top of the basement stairs and his eyes were also wide with panic.

"Go!" Luke yelled to his brother.

He ran down the stairs while Luke fought with the front door.

"Go!" he yelled over his shoulder to Norah and Kieran.

He heard the door click, and then he ran for the stairs.

"Keep going!" he yelled to Ethan, who had stopped by the couch in the middle of the room. "Go into Mom's canning closet!"

Ethan pulled open the bi-fold doors and ran inside the unfinished part of the basement, the others behind him. The concrete floor felt cold on their bare feet. Then the single lightbulb winked out, and Ethan gasped.

"It's just the power," Luke said calmly, but his heart was pounding. "Sometimes the winds snap the lines."

"Is...is it a tornado?" Norah whispered.

"Maybe," he replied, and he heard Ethan whimper behind him.

"I hate tornadoes!" said his brother, and his thirteen-year-old man-boy voice was thick was dread. "I hate 'em! I hate 'em!"

As he watched Ethan, Kieran leaned into his sister.

Outside the siren continued to moan. The tiny window above their heads revealed nothing but flashes of branches and who knows what else, and the howling wind made the house creak. Something hit the window, and everyone jumped.

Suddenly Kieran shouted.

"Tommy! I forgot Tommy! I have to go back and get Tommy!"

He ran for the doors, and Norah screamed. Luke reached out and grabbed him. Ethan took a step back in astonishment.

"We have to stay here, Kieran! It's not safe to go up yet," Luke yelled.

"But I forgot Tommy! I have go back and get him!" He fought to free himself from Luke's grasp.

"No! Don't let him go!" Norah cried.

"Kieran! We can't leave the basement until the siren stops! Not until the siren stops!"

"Tommy! Tommmmmyyyyy!" Kieran yelled, tears coursing down his cheeks.

Help me, God! Luke breathed a prayer. Or maybe he yelled it.

He went for the first idea that came into his head. He prayed it was the right thing to do.

"Kieran!" he yelled, holding onto the squirming boy. "Listen to me! Listen to me! Tommy came with me! He ran down the stairs with me. He's right here."

Kieran stopped thrashing. Luke could see that his brother's face was pale in the dusky half-light. He surely must think the world was indeed crashing in all around them. Not just outside the house, but inside it, too. In that room.

"No, he's not! I left him," Kieran said, resuming his struggle.

"Kieran! Listen to me! I was the last one at your grandma's house! I closed the door, remember? And I closed the door at my house, too. I was the last one in! Tommy came with me. He's already here. He's…he's in the corner over there and…he's scared, too."

"He is?" Kieran relaxed in Luke's arms and looked over where Luke was pointing.

"Yes," he said, easing up on his grip.

Norah was staring at him, fixing him with a gaze that he couldn't interpret. He couldn't tell if she was mortified or relieved at what he'd just said to her brother.

Despite the shrieking outside of wind and siren, Kieran stepped away from them, walked over to the corner, and sat down.

"It'll be okay," he said to the wall next to him.

His sister walked over and sat down next to him. Luke joined her. A dazed Ethan followed.

Sitting down by Luke he whispered, "What is going *on?*"

"I'll tell you later," Luke breathed.

The four of them huddled together, and Luke began to whisper a three-word prayer he repeated over and over. *God, protect us! God, protect us!* As he prayed, he felt Norah's hand search for his. He let her find it.

Within five minutes the horrible howling stopped, quickly replaced by a pelting sound.

"What's that?" Kieran said, breathless.

"Hail," Luke answered, looking at the window and seeing the

blurry white shapes hit the glass. Then the pelting stopped. A few moments later the siren blew the all-clear sign, and he stood up.

"Is it over?" Norah asked.

"I think so," he said, listening for any sounds above that would indicate the house had fallen in on them. But it was quiet.

"You guys stay here," he instructed. "I'm going to see if it's safe to come out."

He pulled open the doors and saw that the rest of the basement was untouched. He ascended the stairs slowly, wondering if he would see open sky where a ceiling used to be. The front window was gone, and shards of glass, as well as dirt clods and roof shingles, were sprinkled about the couch and carpet. A child's wagon was sitting half on, half off the coffee table. He didn't recognize whose it was.

He headed up the stairs to make sure the house still had a roof. Ethan's bedroom window was broken, and a large tree branch was resting on the sill and on the bed they'd just moved. But the rest of the house seemed intact. He ran down the stairs to get the others and then see what the rest of the town looked like.

"It's okay to come up," he said as he went down into the basement. Ethan appeared at the bi-fold doors, and he brushed past Luke. When Luke stepped inside the canning closet, Norah and Kieran were still huddled on the floor in the corner.

"It's okay to come up," he repeated, a little less confident this time.

Norah looked up at him.

"What is it?" he said.

Kieran raised his head and blinked at Luke. "Tommy is shrinking."

"What?"

"Tommy is shrinking," he repeated, looking at the spot in the corner where Luke had pointed.

Luke looked at Norah, but she said nothing.

"He's...shrinking?" he asked, flabbergasted.

"He's getting smaller and smaller. I can hardly hear his voice," Kieran said gently. "I think he's leaving."

Norah implored Luke with her eyes. *This is it,* her eyes were saying. *This is the time. I knew all along it would be you.*

"Um, maybe that's because he did the job he was supposed to do for you, and now he's going to help some other little boy," he said, hoping she'd been right all along.

"No, that's not it."

Luke's mouth gaped open, and he fumbled nervously for more words, better words. "It's not?" Norah was staring at him. *Don't blow it,* he imagined her eyes saying.

"No. I was the scared one, and he was always the brave one. But then today I was the brave one. And he was scared. He doesn't like being scared. So he's going up to heaven where he won't be scared anymore."

"Oh…sure. Of course," Luke said.

"He was a good friend," Kieran continued.

"The best."

"So, is he gone, then?" Norah ventured.

"He's very small now," Kieran said. "All I can see are his clothes… He's gone."

Luke had no idea what to do next. "You…want to put…to put the clothes in a little box or something?" he asked and then cringed, realizing he didn't want little imaginary clothes in his mother's canning closet.

"Yeah. A box would be good."

Luke rummaged around on the shelves until he found a gift box that smelled like bayberry candles.

"How's this?" he said, handing it to Kieran.

"That's good."

Then he paused.

"Can I do it alone?" he said, looking up at Luke and his sister.

"Oh! Sure!" Luke said. Norah rose to her feet. "We'll just be right outside."

He led Norah outside the closet, and they waited by the foot of the stairs.

"Thank you for everything you did today," she said. Her eyes glistened with emotion.

"No big deal," he replied, but he knew how shallow that sounded. "I mean, you would have done the same for me."

She nodded. "Yes, I would have."

Kieran emerged from behind the doors with the gift box in his hands.

"Can we...give Tommy a funeral?" he asked, looking up at Luke.

Luke looked down at the little box. It was no bigger than the box he'd buried a hamster in a decade ago, and its contents weighed even less. But he knew it carried a troublesome weight Norah had borne for years.

"Sure," he said.

And they headed up the stairs.

19

The tornado that sent the residents of Halcyon fleeing to their basements took no lives, but it destroyed seven homes and one business on the south side of town and cut a swath across surrounding acres of juvenile corn plants, flattening them into tattered green ribbons. Many houses, like the Foxbournes', had superficial damage, and even this to varying degrees. It was almost like Godzilla had walked through the streets of northern Halcyon swishing his tail, smashing a few windows and knocking down trees, but when he got to the other end of town he'd raised his reptile leg and brought it crashing down.

On Luke's street, Seventh Avenue, the path of the monster was marked just by a broken window here, an uprooted tree there. Some houses had missing roof shingles, some had portions of siding peeled away like sections of an orange—and some were suddenly without clotheslines, American flags, and plastic lawn animals because these things had simply disappeared.

Luke's tree house received little damage, which surprised him. A portion of the roof was gone and was nowhere in sight, but that was easily fixed the next day with a fresh piece of plywood and a few nails. In fact, that first day after the tornado, it seemed the whole town was busy putting things back together. With nearly all of Halcyon distracted, it was easy for three teenagers and one ten-year-old to drive out to the cemetery unnoticed.

Earlier in the day, it had been on the tip of Luke's tongue to suggest Tommy be buried in Nell's backyard, but before he could even propose this plan, Kieran told him he wanted to bury his good friend Tommy in between Uncle Kenny—the hero uncle he never knew—and his father. Luke's initial response was to protest, since the cemetery was owned by the city and he figured they would get into trouble if they were caught digging in the Janvik plot. But then it occurred to him that the tiny gift box that held imaginary clothes would require no more than a small hole. In all likelihood no one would ever know what they were about to do.

Ethan had taken the news of Tommy's existence and then sudden nonexistence rather well, Luke thought, and he actually surprised Luke by wanting to come to the "funeral." Luke told Norah and Kieran after lunch that day that while the adults were busy with insurance adjustors and other clean-up efforts, he would take them to the cemetery at two o'clock. He was prepared to tell his mom, if she asked why he needed the car, that he was taking the Janvik kids to visit Darrel's grave, which wasn't exactly a lie.

At two o'clock, Luke, Ethan, Norah, and Kieran got into the Foxbournes' Buick, and the four of them headed to the cemetery. It took only minutes to get there and park the car. Luke was grateful that no one else was around. The way to the Janvik plot was familiar; it hadn't been all that long ago that Norah, Kieran, and Luke had been there on the cold November morning Darrel was laid to rest. Luke carried a small shovel as they walked up the knoll to the tree that kept the departed Janviks in shaded repose. Norah had plucked a few begonias from Mrs. Liekfisch's yard, and she held these in her hand. They got to the Janvik plot and stopped. Luke waited for Kieran to choose the place.

"This is a good spot," he said, pointing with his toe to the grass in between the Janvik brothers' headstones.

"Okay," Luke said, and he plunged the blade of the shovel into the earth, scooping out a scalp of sod first and then several more shovelfuls of dirt. Within seconds the small opening was ready. He stepped back.

Kieran knelt down and placed the box in the hole, touching the lid with his fingers before he stood back up again.

"Shouldn't we say something?" he said to Luke.

"Well, sure. You can say whatever you want."

Kieran looked back at the little white box. "Thanks for being a good friend, Tommy. I will never forget you."

He stopped and Norah reached down and placed the begonias on top of the box.

"Can we sing something, too?" Kieran said, turning his head to Luke again.

"Yeah. Sure."

"I want to sing 'Away in the Manger.'"

"The Christmas carol?" Norah said as she rose to her feet.

"Not the verse about no crib for a bed or about baby Jesus never crying. The other one about all the dear children."

"I don't know that verse," Norah said.

"I know it," Luke said, quietly.

"So do I," Ethan said, and Luke turned to him, oddly grateful.

"Can you sing it? I don't know all the words," Kieran said.

Luke took a breath. He hated singing in front of people. Ethan nodded. *Start and I'll join you,* his eyes said.

Luke began, his voice sounding rough and tuneless in his ears. Ethan chimed in on the fourth word:

> *Be near me, Lord Jesus, I ask Thee to stay*
> *Close by me forever and love me I pray*
> *Bless all the dear children in Thy tender care*
> *And take us to heaven to live with Thee there.*

"Yes," Kieran said softly. "That's the one. Can you sing it again?"

So Luke began it again, Ethan joined him, and so did Kieran, and by the time they got to "Bless all the dear children," Norah had joined in, too.

"'Bye, Tommy," Kieran said, and he reached down and took a handful of earth and tossed it over the box. He turned to Luke and asked for the shovel. Luke gave it to him. Kieran put the rest of the dirt over the box with the shovel and carefully replaced the first layer of sod that Luke had dug out over the top.

He stood.

A few minutes later the four of them walked back down the little hill to the parking lot and left.

They went back into town where all around them were the noises of saws and forklifts and hammers as wrong things were put to right.

⚬⚭⚬

The summer months passed as the summer months had in years past, but Luke felt there was a peculiar finality about them. They were the last summer months he would spend as a high-school student. Next May he would graduate. He would head off to college and the rest of his life. He was impatient for both.

It was different having Norah and Kieran in school and knowing they were actually going to be staying the whole year. At least that was the plan. Norah joined Luke on the stage crew for the fall musical, which made her a bona fide member of the drama clique and kept their afternoons and evenings busy.

With a little persuading, Luke's father convinced Nell to let him help Norah with her behind-the-wheel practice so that in October she passed her driving test and got her license. She was happy to have it even though she didn't have a car of her own to drive.

In November, Luke's South Dakota grandparents drove down for Thanksgiving and, as in years past, MaryAnn invited the Janviks to join them. To Luke's surprise, Nell accepted the invitation. She was quiet during the meal, and did not stay long afterward but it appeared to Luke that Nell was almost content with the way things were. Almost. Nell still seemed to regard Norah as a pariah of sorts—like someone who reminded her of all that was wrong with her life.

A major snowstorm kept most of Iowa blanketed in their homes the week of Christmas. The Foxbournes, along with most of Halcyon, stayed home. And while MaryAnn invited the Janviks to Christmas dinner, Norah declined for them, saying that Nell planned to roast a turkey.

In February, Nell fell on a patch of ice on her driveway and broke both wrists. At first it appeared to be just another stroke of really bad luck for Nell Janvik, but as Luke watched Norah care for her it turned out to be best thing that could have happened; at least for Norah. Nell could do nothing for herself. She couldn't work or drive or cook or even light her own cigarettes for several weeks. Norah did everything for her. And though Luke never went over to Nell's house, he could see how Norah cared for Nell by the silent images he saw in the Janvik windows. He could see—even when the sheers were pulled and his view somewhat obscured— that Nell had slowly began to see Norah as something other than a reminder of her losses.

By March, Luke had decided to attend the University of Iowa, even though it hadn't been on his list of "far away" colleges. It had a great writing program and was close enough to home to keep his mother happy. Plus he was offered a good financial aid package as an Iowa resident. New York or Hollywood would come later—he was sure of that.

He didn't go into the tree house much anymore, but every now and then the branches outside his window would beckon him and he would make his way into the aged wooden refuge. Sometimes

Norah joined him. It was in the tree house that he told her he'd be moving to Iowa City in August to attend college and that he was hoping to get an apartment and a job so that he didn't have to come home during the summer months.

"Why don't you want to come home in the summer?" she had asked.

"There just isn't anything here for me," he said, before he had time to consider how that sounded.

"Your family is here," she said softly, and he could tell there was deeper meaning behind the words.

"Yes," Luke said, looking down at her hands, remembering how on three occasions she had touched him; once at Goose Pond and once there in the tree house when she begged him not to tell his parents about Tommy, and the third time in his mother's canning closet when the world above them was being wrenched apart by twisted winds. "But my family will be my family no matter where I am. No address is going to change that."

"But being away will change other things."

She didn't elaborate and he did not ask her to.

It was also in the tree house that Luke told Norah he was taking Patti to his senior prom.

She had nodded. But it was a nod of contradictions. Her eyes betrayed her confusion.

"So, why are you telling me this?" she said when he told her.

"Because I wanted you to know that Patti and I are just friends," he replied.

"Just friends," Norah said absently, like she was tasting the words.

"It's not like I am dating her, 'cause I'm not."

"Okay."

"Patti thinks maybe I should have asked *you*, but I didn't think Nell would let you go since you're just a sophomore and Nell, well, Nell—"

"It's okay," Norah interrupted him. She had an odd look of satisfaction on her face; like she had just found out she had been right all along about something. "I understand. I don't think she would have let me go either."

"It's kind of dumb anyway," Luke said. "None of the guys like getting all dressed up like that and parading around in front of our parents at the Grand March."

"Mmm," Norah said.

After a few seconds of silence, Luke decided he was finished talking about the prom. "Heard from your mom lately?" he asked.

Norah shook her head. "It's been awhile. I don't think she has anything new to say. That's why she waits so long in between letters. But it's okay. When she does write, she tells Kieran and me all the things we'll do when she gets out."

It had been a long time since Luke had seen Belinda. It was hard to imagine her in jail. It was harder to imagine her showing up on Nell's doorstep in a year or two to collect her children.

On the day of the prom, Norah didn't come to the Foxbournes' house while Luke and Patti had their pictures taken, though she had been invited to come over, nor did she show up at the Grand March. In fact, neither she nor Kieran appeared for Sunday dinner the next day though they had been invited the week before. Luke purposely went into the tree house at ten o'clock that night with a small bag in his hand, hoping Norah would show up. He had something for her.

Luke waited until ten-fifteen and was about to climb back into his bedroom when he heard the sound of movement on the garage roof next to him. A few seconds later, Norah climbed inside.

"I saw your lantern was on," she said, taking a seat just on the other side of him.

"You didn't come to dinner," Luke said.

"Kieran had a stomachache."

"Oh?"

"I gave him some Pepto-Bismol. He's feeling better now."

"Oh."

"I guess I should have called your mom. Sorry."

"It's okay. It was an open invitation. She knows you can't come every time."

She looked at the bag Luke held in his hands. "What's that?" she asked.

Luke reached into the bag and pulled out a wrist corsage made of lilies of the valley and silvery-white ribbon. "This was Patti's corsage from last night," he said. "It still looks pretty good, considering. She wanted you to have it."

He held the corsage out to her and Norah took it, touching the tiny white flowers with her fingertips.

"She wanted me to have it?"

"Yeah, she did."

Norah pulled the corsage onto her wrist and held her arm out to admire it. "Patti's probably the only girlfriend I have ever had who treats me like I'm somebody important."

Luke paused for a moment. "Patti's an exceptional person."

"But you're not in love with her?"

Luke coughed. "No, she's a good friend, that's it."

Norah pulled her arm back to her chest and brought the tiny flowers close to her cheek. "I think she may be in love with you, though."

Luke looked away. He knew Patti was attracted to him. But he had never been able to figure out why. Nor did he know why he was not likewise attracted to her. Patti was as close to perfection as a person could get. But it surprised him that Norah picked up on this. He wondered if everyone knew.

"She deserves someone better than me," Luke said.

Norah looked up at him. "What do you mean, better than you?"

"She deserves someone who will love her back."

Norah nodded slowly. "Yes, she does."

Luke shifted his weight, pulled his legs up and leaned forward. "It will be better for her when we go our separate ways, when I go to college in Iowa City and she goes to college in Pennsylvania. Then she can meet someone who will fall head over heels in love with her."

"Is that what you are hoping will happen to you?"

Luke swallowed. "Maybe."

A few moments of stillness followed and Luke wished somehow they could change the subject. Norah's questions made him feel uneasy.

"I got a note from my mom and a package." Norah finally said, breaking the silence.

"Yeah?"

"Uh-huh. She didn't say a whole lot in her note, but she had a friend get this necklace for me. Norah leaned forward and reached to her neck. She placed a silver pendant in her palm and showed it to Luke. He leaned forward, too, to look at it.

"It's a little sand dollar dipped in silver. They are all over the beaches in Mexico," Norah said. "If you break open a sand dollar there are these little formations inside that look just like doves. They are so beautiful. Like little white birds."

Luke looked down at the pendant in Norah's hand. His face was very close to hers. He caught the fragrance of her hair. It reminded him of vanilla.

"The thing is," Norah said, "you have to break the sand dollar to get them out. So even though you have the little white birds, you don't have the sand dollar anymore. It's broken to bits. And you can't fix it."

She looked up then and her face looked sad, like she had pockets full of little white birds and the ruins of sand dollars all around her to prove they were hers. "Sometimes it just feels like it's never going to come," she whispered.

"What's never going to come?" he asked.

She looked away for a second, like she was searching for the right word.

"The day when everything's right. Everything," she said, turning her head back to face him.

When her flannel-gray eyes met his, Luke instinctively reached out and touched her cheek with his hand. It began as a gesture of compassion, but when Norah leaned into his palm and Luke felt the smoothness of her skin and the delicate shape of her jaw, a strange sensation crept over him. He felt a tug inside that compelled him to move toward her, as if the shared moments of their past had formed a magnet and that magnet had suddenly found the very thing it was attracted to. He stroked the softness of her cheek with his thumb. Without forethought, he bent down and kissed her, gently drawing her face toward his. He'd never kissed anyone in that way before. Never on the lips, and never *in that way*. It was electrifying. And powerful. Something deep within him—though perhaps it was just simple desire—stirred. The force of it astonished him. He broke away.

"I don't know why I did that," he whispered. He was glad the tree house was in semidarkness. He could feel embarrassment pulsing across his cheeks.

But Norah didn't seem to be wondering why he did it. Or maybe she was. He couldn't tell.

"Norah, I'm sorry," he began, but she reached out and placed a finger on his lips to silence him.

He was about to say something anyway, when Kieran's voice from across Nell's garage roof broke the moment. "Norah, I can't sleep. My tummy still hurts. Can you come back now?"

Norah removed her fingertips from Luke's lips and brushed them across his cheek.

"Coming, Kieran," she said, but she was looking at Luke.

Luke sat in bewildered silence as Norah made her way back across a wide limb that would take her to the garage roof and then her bedroom window. He saw her hands reach across to the branch above her to steady her body as she made her way across, and he could just make out the tiny lilies on her left wrist as she moved away from him.

He sat in the tree house for a long time after she left wondering what had just happened.

20

Luke was torn between wanting to see Norah the next day at school and not wanting to see her. He could still feel the intriguing softness of her lips on his mouth. Throughout the day he involuntarily relived the kiss, and each time, he felt his face grow warm. It wasn't that he particularly wanted to recall the kiss, it just kept returning to the forefront of his mind and he had no idea how to send it away. When he saw Norah at lunch, Luke could tell that her eyes sought him across the tables, but when she found him, she stayed where she was with a group of other sophomores. She didn't come over to him or wave to him. When their eyes met from across the cafeteria, it almost felt like he had kissed her again. It so distracted him that he had to look away.

That afternoon in study hall, he tried to study for his final exam in physics but he found himself staring out the window more than once, his thoughts far from the relationship of matter to anti-matter. He was glad when the bell signaled the end of the school day and he would not have to pretend around his friends that he was not preoccupied with a myriad of confusing thoughts.

Luke had asked for the afternoon off at the paper to prepare not only for the physics final, but one in English literature and another in civics. He couldn't wait to have his last finals behind him.

Next Friday he would graduate, and in August he would finally be out on his own. With the gift money he knew he would be getting for graduation, he would be buying his own car. He already had two thousand dollars of his own saved. Another thousand would buy a fairly decent used vehicle. Between the finals, the upcoming graduation ceremony, car-shopping, and preparing for his move to Iowa City, it was no wonder he had succumbed to what he now realized was a longstanding desire to kiss Norah. It didn't mean anything had changed for him. He was still moving to Iowa City in three months. And she was staying here. Nothing had really changed. That kiss had been just a spontaneous reaction to an emotionally charged moment. It wouldn't happen again. Norah fascinated him, she always had. But he was not in love with Norah. And he was leaving.

He rode his bike home, waving casually to Norah and Kieran as they walked home together to further convince himself that the kiss had been nothing more than a little experiment. Ethan wasn't too far behind him on his own bicycle. Luke parked his bike in the garage and went into the kitchen, dropping his book bag on one of the kitchen table chairs as he grabbed a box of Cheez-Its. He opened the fridge and reached in for a can of Pepsi. As he ate his snack, he could see through the adjoining dining room window that Norah and Kieran were walking past his house. He saw Norah glance up at his bedroom window as she passed.

Luke took his book bag into the living room where Ethan was watching TV and he sat on the couch with his brother relaxing for nearly half an hour before pulling out his books to study. Then his mom walked into the house with a box in her arms.

"Ethan, Luke, can you guys get those other two boxes out of the car? I'm starting to clear out my classroom now instead of waiting 'til the last minute," she said.

The brothers left the living room and wordlessly went outside to the Buick. As they walked over to the open trunk, a compact car slowed down in front of Nell's house and then pulled up alongside the curb. Nell was just coming out her front door to go to work. She stopped and looked at the car, too. It appeared to Luke that she looked surprised, like she wasn't expecting anybody to stop by.

He lifted one of the boxes out of the trunk and handed it to his brother. As he did, the driver opened the car door and got out. It was a woman with shoulder length dark hair. She had on sunglasses. The woman closed her car door and started to walk up Nell's driveway.

"Who's that?" Ethan whispered to him.

"Beats me," Luke said, starting to grab the other box. He wasn't watching what he was doing, though. He tipped it over, and a mass of books, papers, and magazines tumbled out onto the bottom of the trunk. Ethan turned to go into the house with the box he held. Luke sighed and had started to retrieve the items when he saw that the woman was removing her sunglasses. He looked over at her while he fiddled with the spilled contents and then nearly gasped.

It was Belinda.

Nell recognized her, too.

"What are *you* doing here?" Nell said to her, and her voice was laced with something other than the usual annoyance. Belinda stopped.

"Nice to see you again, too, Nell," Belinda said but then she took two more steps toward Nell. "Why do you *think* I'm here? I came for my kids."

Luke was aware that his heart had begun to beat a little faster. Norah and Kieran! Their mother was here! She had come for them. Just like Norah had said she would. Norah would be leaving, too, then. Before him. He didn't know what to make of what he was feeling inside. Was he jealous Norah was getting away first? Was he upset that she was leaving? And what must Nell be feeling? Nell, who had made it clear she hadn't asked to raise the kids that had been handed to her?

Luke stole a glance at Nell, trying to gauge her reaction.

"You break outta jail?" Nell said coolly.

"I was released. Early. For good behavior," Belinda said evenly, taking two more steps closer to Nell, Nell's house, and the two kids who were inside it.

"You got a lot of nerve just showing up like this," Nell said, narrowing her eyes. "What makes you think you can just waltz back into their lives like you were out shopping or something?"

"You got a lot of nerve asking, Nell. They're *my* kids, remember?"

"Too bad you didn't think about *your* kids when you were running around Mexico with drug dealers and murderers." Nell spat out the words.

"You don't know what you are talking about, so I suggest you quit showing off your ignorance and go tell my kids I've come for them."

"I know exactly what I'm talking about! You are an addict and a tramp. And you *abandoned* those children!"

Belinda closed the distance, clearly angry. Luke knew it wouldn't be long before Norah and Kieran heard the shouting. He was already afraid for them, though he pretended to be merely repacking a box in his mother's trunk, wondering if he had even been noticed by the two women.

"Well, I can see who you got your information from! I suppose your loser of a son told you all that!" Belinda yelled.

"You shut your mouth!" Nell shouted, cursing.

A second later Nell's screen door opened. Norah, wide-eyed and hopeful, appeared in the doorframe. Kieran was right behind her. "Mom?" Norah said, and her voice sounded very young.

Belinda's face relaxed and she sighed. "Yeah, baby doll, it's me!" She held out her arms and Norah ran into them, with Kieran at her heels. For a few seconds there was only the sound of joyful tears. Nell stood as still as a statue as Belinda, Norah, and Kieran embraced each other.

"Look how big you've grown!" Belinda said, as she broke away. "You're both so tall. And Norah, how beautiful you are! Such a lady!"

"I knew you'd come back! I knew you'd come back!" Kieran said, holding Belinda tight around the waist.

"Of course I came back," she replied, holding his head against her. "That's what kept me from going crazy in prison. Knowing I had you two to come back for."

"Mom," Norah said, and it seemed to Luke she said it just for the pleasure of saying the word aloud, because she said nothing else. He imagined she had waited a long time to be mothered, a long time.

It seemed for a fraction of a moment that for once everything was as it should be at the house next door, but then Nell found her voice and the moment crumbled.

"I have a court order that says I am responsible for these kids," Nell said, and Norah whipped her head around to look at Nell. Luke stared at Nell, too.

"What?" Belinda said.

"I said, I have a court order that says I am responsible for these kids," Nell repeated, focusing her eyes on Belinda only.

"Well, I don't care if you have a piece of paper signed by the Pope himself," Belinda said. "They're my kids, and I'm taking them."

"No, you're not."

Belinda moved forward a step, seeming to almost put Kieran protectively behind her as she did so.

"Yes. I am."

"You try it and I'll call the police," Nell said.

"But Grandma—" Norah began, but Belinda cut her off.

"Fine. You go call the police," Belinda yelled. "You think the police are going to side with you? You, of all people?"

"Get off my property!"

"I am taking my kids. Norah, Kieran, go get your things."

"You kids do no such thing."

Luke saw that Norah and Kieran were torn as to what to do.

Then Norah seemed to notice for the first time that Luke was there, watching all of it. She only looked at him for a second.

"Norah, Kieran, go get your things," Belinda commanded.

But Nell moved to block their way to the front door. "They will not!" Nell yelled.

"What is the matter with you!" Belinda screamed. "I know you never wanted these kids with you! You think I don't know what has gone on here? You think Norah didn't tell me how you've treated them? Sending them away! Twice! You've made it clear to them they've never been welcome here!"

Luke looked to Norah and saw she had closed her eyes in fear and shame. She had not expected her mother to use her letters to wound Nell.

Nell said nothing as she looked at Norah, wondering no doubt what exactly Norah had written in those letters to her mother.

"You've never wanted these kids!" Belinda continued, enraged. "You're only doing this now because you hate me! Well, you know what? The feeling's mutual, Nell."

"You're not taking my grandchildren," was all Nell could say in response. It almost seemed to Luke that she was on the verge of tears. He felt a twinge of compassion for her.

"Oh, yes I am!" Belinda countered. "And don't go pretending they're both yours. I know you know about Norah! There is no way I'm letting you spend another moment making her life miserable. She's mine, and you know it! There's not a drop of your stinking Janvik blood in her, thank God!"

Luke's mouth dropped open, and the box he had been unsuccessfully trying to fill fell over in the trunk. Norah wasn't a Janvik. Darrel had not been her father. It explained everything. It explained why Nell and Darrel had always been so hard on her. Why Nell seemed to favor Kieran over her. Why Norah had honey-blonde hair and those mesmerizing gray eyes while Darrel, Belinda, and Kieran were all brown-eyed brunettes. And yet no one had ever told her.

He looked at Norah, and it seemed she was about to faint. Her face was drained of color. Nell was not really her grandmother. Darrel was not her father. Her beloved Kieran was her half-brother. Luke wanted to run over to her, but he felt like his feet were nailed to the cement.

Then it got worse.

"Then take her!" Nell screamed. "But you leave that boy! I swear to God, I'll call the police if you even try to take him!"

At that moment, Luke heard his front door open. He turned and saw that his mother had come out to see what all the commotion was about.

"Get inside," she mouthed to him, but he just turned back to the horrible drama taking place just a few feet away.

"Kids, just get in the car. There's nothing inside *that* house that you need!" Belinda said.

Norah was stricken dumb, unable to respond. Kieran was crying, clearly torn.

Nell, chest heaving, stood for a second longer. Then she turned and stomped into the house.

"Is she really going to call the police?" Kieran whimpered.

"Who cares?" Belinda said. "I don't care what she does. Come on. We're leaving."

Kieran took a few tentative steps with Belinda toward the car. Belinda turned around. "Norah—come on, baby doll. Let's go."

But Norah seemed powerless to make her feet move. She looked up at Luke. Her gray eyes were wide and void of strength.

"Norah, come on, honey, let's *go*," Belinda said again and she turned and continued to walk toward her car with Kieran at her side.

Then Nell's front door opened and she stepped out. She carried something long and brown in her hands.

Darrel's hunting rifle.

Luke felt his blood run cold.

"You're not taking that boy," Nell said, raising the rifle.

The next second was wrapped in chaos. From behind him, Luke heard his mother yell at him to run in the house, he heard Belinda yell something, too. Norah also yelled something. And another voice yelled. "No!" It was his own.

"I said you're not taking that boy!" Nell said, and this time she shouted it.

"Watch me!" Belinda yelled.

Luke turned to his mother. "Call the police!" he said, and then he turned around and took a step toward Norah.

"Luke!" his mother screamed.

Nell raised the barrel higher, cocking it with her trembling hands. Kieran yelled, "Grandma!"

"You're not taking him," Nell said, her voice shaking, tears falling in a crazy pattern down her cheeks. The rifle was quivering in her hands. Luke thought she looked like a cornered animal. Like she had reached the end of all reason. She tried to steady the gun in her hands. "You're not taking him." She leveled the barrel at Belinda.

For a second, Luke pictured Darrel in a parking lot on that icy night when he died. He pictured Darrel waving the same rifle but making different threats. Different, yet the same.

Then the memory evaporated.

The sounds of Norah yelling, "No!" while she lunged for the rifle in Nell's hands, and of Kieran screaming, "Mommy!" as he dashed in front of his mother, and the deafening crack of the rifle shooting a bullet all seemed to meld into one sound. And then there was no sound at all except for the reverberation of a gunshot.

Kieran made no sound as he fell to the ground at his mother's feet. The bullet wound in his back quickly turned the grass red around Belinda's sandals.

21

Luke was given a waiver for his final exams, and it was a full week before he felt mentally able to take them. By then there were only a few days left before graduation, and the diplomas had already been made out. It was assumed he would pass them all. And he did. But just barely.

The last week of school was a blur. Later he would only remember bits and pieces of the last four days he spent as a student at Halcyon High School. But in the end he didn't really care. He didn't really care he would never be able to adequately remember his high-school graduation or his eighteenth birthday.

What he wanted to forget and simply couldn't was the image of Kieran falling at his mother's feet. Nor could he forget the pitch and tone of Norah's sobs, nor the timbre of Nell's horrific wails. He couldn't forget how the flashing lights of the ambulance and the squad cars merrily mocked the desperation of that awful afternoon. He couldn't forget how the handle of the policeman's gun poked out of its holster while he questioned Luke and how the squad car's radio kept squawking as he answered questions.

And what he wanted to forget most of all was that strange obligation he had felt since he was twelve that he was somehow destined to watch out for Norah and Kieran, that he was their strong protector, that he was meant to be a shield to them from the trouble that seemed to haunt them. He wanted to forget it because it had all been for nothing. There was no getting by the Janvik curse. It didn't really matter that Norah didn't have Janvik blood in her veins, that Belinda was already pregnant with her when she moved in with Darrel Janvik. Norah was a Janvik nonetheless and the curse had welcomed her.

It was this desire to forget that kept him from expending any energy trying to find out where Norah was, how she was coping, or even thinking about her. Concerned about his apparent numbness, his parents made several counseling appointments for him with his youth pastor. But Luke only went to one of the appointments. He didn't want to talk about what he saw. He wanted to forget it.

His father's headlines kept him semi-informed of Kieran's survival, and that he had been airlifted to a children's hospital in Des Moines but that the bullet had severed his spinal cord and he was now paralyzed from the waist down. Nell's agonizing defense at her arraignment was that she had never meant to fire the rifle; she'd only wanted to scare Belinda away with it. She'd never intended to shoot anyone, she had moaned. "It's that girl! If she hadn't tried to get the gun away from me, this never would have happened!"

That girl. Norah.

Several days later, Nell had a mental breakdown in jail and was put on a suicide watch.

Luke's mother sent a bouquet of balloons to Kieran at the hospital in Des Moines the week after the shooting, signing the card with all of their names. She did not offer to drive Luke down to Des Moines to see Norah and Kieran. Jack did, but Luke declined.

Three weeks after the shooting, Luke came home from buying a used car to the message that Norah had called and asked for him. She left a phone number but Luke did not recognize it. After pacing in his room for half an hour, he tried to call her back, though he was amazed by how much he didn't want to talk to her. But there was no answer and he decided not to try again. He didn't know what to say to her. Luke unwillingly kept replaying the shooting in his mind, over and over. Norah had grabbed for the gun to wrest it away from Nell and it was within the struggle between Norah and Nell that the gun went off, sending a bullet into Kieran's spine. What could he say to her? What could anyone say? It was a horrible accident. But he knew that Norah would feel somewhat responsible for what had happened to Kieran and he didn't want to share her anguish. Not any more. He was through with it. Through with the Janviks and their alliance with suffering. He waited to see if Norah would try to call him again. She didn't.

∽

As Luke prepared to leave for Iowa City the third week in August, the *Halcyon Herald* bore the news that Nell, who had been charged with attempted murder among other things, had been found incompetent to stand trial. She had been remanded to a psychiatric hospital in Davenport to be held until able, if ever, to participate in her own defense.

There were no more headlines after that. Nell was gone. And Belinda was apparently not coming back to get Norah and Kieran's belongings.

"I wonder where Belinda is taking Norah and Kieran," Luke quietly said to his dad the day before he left for college.

"They're going back to San Diego," Jack said. And Luke looked up from placing a duffel bag in his trunk.

"She called here today when you were out with your friends, Luke."

Luke stiffened. "She did?"

His dad nodded.

"Why didn't you tell me?"

"I'm telling you now," Jack said. "She didn't leave a number for you to call her back. Belinda's taking Norah and Kieran to Los Angeles. I guess she has a friend there. Norah said it's temporary."

"What else did she say?" Luke said, staring at the contents of his trunk but not seeing any of it.

"She didn't say hardly anything, Luke. I didn't even recognize her voice." His father sounded sad. "She left an address for you, though."

His father reached into his pants pocket and pulled out a slip of paper. On it was a San Diego address.

Luke looked at it and hesitated. He was reminded of the other times in his life he had wanted Norah's address and didn't have it. Now he wasn't sure he wanted it after all. But his father's hand was extended to him and finally he reached for the slip of paper. Luke said nothing as he took the paper from his father and shoved it inside his shirt pocket.

Later that night, in the barrenness of his bedroom, Luke sat at his nearly empty desk, staring at the piece of paper that bore Norah's address. Underneath it was a notecard and envelope that he had taken on impulse from his mother's desk downstairs.

The address was his only tie to Norah, and in that moment, it seemed the only tangible proof of their friendship. He stared at the letters and numbers, written in his dad's very recognizable hand, wondering what he should do. Wondering why it seemed like he only had two choices and that neither one seemed the right one to make. He couldn't make sense of why he had no desire to write to Norah and yet why he knew he must.

Luke pulled a pen from the middle drawer of the desk, one of just a few he had left when he packed the contents of his room. *Just say something. Say anything,* his nudging conscience whispered. Luke put the pen to the paper:

> Norah,
>
> I'm really sorry about what happened to Kieran. And to you. I wish I could change what happened. I wish I could change a lot of things. I'm glad your mom came back for you and that you are going back to California.

Tell Kieran hello from me. Tell him I am praying for him.

Luke

Luke read what he'd written. Twice. He placed the notecard in the envelope and licked it shut. It felt a little odd writing "Norah Janvik" on the outside of the envelope knowing what he now knew; knowing that she wasn't a Janvik. Not really. Luke looked at the spot where his new return address should go and paused, surprised at his desire to leave it blank. He raised his head to his bedroom window and stared for several long minutes at the dark and empty tree house on the other side of the glass. Then he stood up, tucked the slip of paper with Norah's address into his pants pocket and went downstairs. He took a postage stamp from his mother's purse and placed it on the envelope.

Luke stepped outside into the cooling night and put the envelope in his parents' mailbox, raising the flag before he walked away.

∽

The next afternoon as Luke drove away with his dreams for the future, and as his mother cried and waved, he tried to picture Norah on a sunny, San Diego beach, in front of a cozy hotel, chatting with her guests. He tried to picture Belinda sitting in a lounge chair nearby, reading a novel and drinking iced tea. He tried to picture Kieran sitting in a wheelchair at the surf's edge, breathing in the salted air and not feeling bitter about his dashed hopes of swimming with whales.

He tried to picture it.

But he could not.

He sped away from Halcyon wishing things were different. He wished Nell had gotten rid of Darrel's gun the first time it had become an invitation to disaster. He wished Norah hadn't tried to grab the rifle. He wished the bullet had hit Belinda's car or a tree or a streetlight. He wished there had been nothing between him and Norah but the simplest of times with no sorrows, no rescues, no kiss. Nothing agonizing or complicated or even breathtaking. But he knew wishes were only for children at birthday parties. This was the real world. And sometimes it was ugly. He would have to find a way to counter the ugliness. He would have to discover a way to create his own happiness, follow his own dreams, and bury the dead things of his childhood as surely as he had helped Kieran bury Tommy.

Luke felt in his pocket for the slip of paper with Norah's address. He withdrew it, keeping one hand on the steering wheel as he unfolded it and stared at the letters and numbers. What possible good could come from writing to her? Kissing her had been foolish enough; perpetuating his physical attraction to her by writing to her would be ten times worse. They had no future together. And their shared past was nothing to keep alive. It was time to end it. They would both be better off. She could move on, he could forget.

He crumpled the paper into a ball and held it out the car window. A rushing current of air tugged at the wad in his hand. At the moment he was about to let it go, he suddenly withdrew his arm, bringing his hand back in the car, the crumpled paper safe in his closed fist. He reached over to the glove compartment, opened it, and tossed the ball of paper inside. For a split-second, he glanced away from the road and stared at the wad of paper now resting on a folded road atlas of the United States—a recent graduation gift. The little ball of paper looked small, insignificant, and useless sitting there.

He turned back to the road ahead of him, slamming the compartment shut as the Halcyon city limits fell away from him.

PART III

22

Luke's hands fell away from his laptop and he leaned back against the bed pillows, closing his eyes. Téa stirred beside him.

He looked down at his wife's sleeping body, her hair against the pillow, her form curled into an "S" next to him. It was a little after one o'clock in the morning and he had been writing for three hours, unable to pull himself away from the manuscript. The memories had been tumbling out of him almost faster than he could write them. And now he had written all he could. All that he knew.

Téa turned over and cuddled next to him, draping an arm across his knees. When she and the girls arrived in Halcyon two weeks ago, he was buried deep in responsibilities; the paper, his father's recovery, and the writing of this memoir. But he was surprised at the relief and peace he felt when his family arrived the day before the Wooden Shoes Festival. Téa and the girls were exhausted from the long drive across several states, but they were as glad to see him as he was to see them. It had been a long six weeks of separation and so much had happened.

His father had made remarkable progress in rehab in that amount of time. Jack had regained some control over the right side of his body and was now walking, though unsteadily and with considerable effort, using a walker. He was able to produce sentences, though he had to squeeze the words out as if they were too large for the size of his mouth. His frustration was obvious, but so was his determination. His doctors were already discussing his release from the rehabilitation center. And with those discussions came other, less joyous talks.

Jack knew before MaryAnn that he would not be returning to the paper. When Jack and Luke sat down with her and tried to discuss putting it up for sale, she left the room in anger. When she came back an hour later she told them it was not the time to talk about it. Jack eventually convinced her, with dogged determination in his unwieldy voice, that it was time to think about what was best for Luke and his family. And at this, MaryAnn finally relented. Luke contacted a newspaper broker the next day. Four days later, the publisher of the Carrow newspaper called him. The meeting to discuss the sale had gone well. It had been held in the staff meeting room at the rehabilitation center and ended with handshakes and an intent to buy.

Once the paper was pried loose from MaryAnn's heart and head, it was surprisingly easy for her to discuss with Luke the sale of the house in Halcyon and the move to join Luke and Téa in Connecticut. Jack and MaryAnn had stayed in the guest cottage often when they visited. It was the perfect solution to the problem of Jack requiring a one-level home and MaryAnn's need for assistance with Jack at just a moment's notice. With the newspaper sold, there was no compelling need for Jack and MaryAnn to stay in Halcyon. And having her granddaughters playing on the floor by her feet while they discussed this plan also soothed the ache of having to say goodbye to so many things.

Téa and the girls had been a huge help in getting the house ready to sell and helping his mother choose what to keep and what to leave behind. And though he was nearly a month past his July 1 deadline, Luke was feeling a sense of calm for the first time in two months. The worst of his dad's troubles were behind them, he would soon be out from underneath the weight of the newspaper, he had a nearly complete manuscript to show Alan and he even had some answers to his own private questions.

But he knew the manuscript was not finished.

And he knew there were still questions that begged for answers.

Luke pressed the save button on his laptop and closed the program. He turned off the computer, clicked it shut, and set it on the bedside table next to his parents' bed. His mother had insisted he and Téa sleep in the master bedroom after she gave up the little apartment in Cedar Falls. Marissa and Noelle slept in Luke's old room and his mother had taken over Ethan's old bedroom. Luke leaned back against the pillow again, contemplating his next move. Instinctively he had reached down to caress Téa's arm across his legs. He was both surprised and relieved that she had so enthusiastically encouraged him in his current writing project. Téa knew a few things about his teenage experiences with the Janvik family, but as Luke never wished to totally relive those days, he had never said much more than a few sentences here and there.

Téa had been reading the manuscript as he printed out the pages and had told him it was a story that surely needed telling even though so much of it was sad.

"I do hope there's a happy ending in store, though," she had told him the day before when she handed back to him the latest pages. She had just read the pages about the tornado. He hadn't yet written about Kieran getting shot, but she knew it was coming. But Luke appreciated Téa's insight that the story couldn't just be about despair. It *had* to be about hope, too, or there was no point in telling it. Which is why he knew the story wasn't finished.

Luke's touch on Téa's arm awakened her and she looked up at him.

"Done for tonight?" she mumbled.

"I am as done as I can be," he whispered, stroking her hair.

"Then you're finished?" she said raising her head.

"No."

She waited for him to explain what he meant.

"I need to know how it ends, Téa," he said, moving his fingers through her hair.

She blinked as she digested his words. "You're going to try and contact her." It was not a question.

"I have to. I can't write the ending if I don't."

"I suppose you can't."

"I can't end it here, with the last little bit I know," he said. "And I want to give you that happy ending."

She smiled, but then the smile faded. "But what if there isn't one," she said, lowering her head and laying it on his chest.

"But I control the story somewhat," Luke said. "I'm in it. I can do what I can to make the ending a good one." And as Luke said this, he saw himself at eighteen, tossing Norah's address into his glove compartment, seeing it from time to time over the next few years, then oddly one day *not* seeing it—and being inwardly glad he no longer knew where it was. Losing the address had eased away the guilt over never looking at it again. Never sending Norah another letter. A wave of remorse swept over him. "I think maybe I should do what I can," he added.

Téa was silent for a moment. "But Luke, what if you can't do it? I mean, you can't change the past."

Luke stroked the back of her head. "No, I can't. But the future hasn't been touched yet. It's a blank page, to use a trite metaphor. I can have a hand in what will be written there. I think there's unfinished business between Norah and me."

"Unfinished business?" Téa said, worry lining her face.

"Things I should have told her when I had the chance."

"Like what?"

Luke stroked her back. "Like this world where we live out our days is not all there is. This is not as good as it gets. Remember a couple months ago, before all this happened and when I was stuck on my Red Herring manuscript and couldn't write anything? Re-

member I said I felt like I had lost my edge—that even though I
had everything, I still felt incomplete?"

"Yes," Téa said tentatively.

"I think that's how it is supposed to be, Téa. I'm not supposed
to find all my contentment here, in this time and place. None of us
are. We're all created to long for heaven. It's wired into us. And it's
a good thing, not a bad thing. That's what gets us through the hard
times. Knowing there's more."

"I suppose you will want to go see her," Téa said, after a long
pause. "Alone."

Luke paused before answering. "It's not that I want to go alone.
I'd much rather have you with me. But I don't know what's in store
for me. I think it would be best if you didn't come. Besides, with
the movers coming in a couple days, Mom's going to need your
help. If I wasn't so late already with this manuscript I would hold
off on going until later, but I need to finish it. I need to give Alan
something."

"I know you do," she said, looking up at him. "And I know
even more that you need to know how it ends."

He looked down at her, grateful to God for Téa's sensitivity. She
understood him completely.

"So where will you start looking for her?" she said.

"Where I left off," Luke said, turning to switch off the reading
lamp on the table next to him. "Right here. In Halcyon."

◦∞◦

Luke's mother was pulling out the contents of a kitchen cupboard when Luke came downstairs the following morning.

"I guess I won't need all this Tupperware at the cottage," she
said blandly. "Does Téa want some of this?"

Luke took a seat at the kitchen table and smiled. "She's got a
cupboard of her own filled with it, Mom."

"Oh, well," MaryAnn sighed. "I'm sure Goodwill will take them."

She reached back into the cupboard and withdrew several ice cube trays.

"Mom," Luke began, "Would you happen to know where Norah and Kieran ended up after Belinda left with them?"

MaryAnn's torso was half in and half out of the cupboard. Her body froze as the question fell from Luke's lips. She then slowly backed out and turned to look at him. She flicked away a stray gray hair from above her eyes. "What brings this up?" his mother said with a laugh. But it was a nervous laugh. She found nothing humorous in his question; that was obvious.

Luke wondered how much he should tell her. She didn't know what he was working on when he sat for hours on end at his laptop. She just knew it was his latest manuscript. And he was late with it.

"I just need to know, Mom. I've been going over in my mind all that happened here, trying to make sense of it. I feel like I just buried everything when I left Halcyon. And I'm thinking now I made a mistake."

"No, you didn't," MaryAnn said quickly.

"Mom," Luke said, ignoring her rebuttal, "I need to know where they ended up."

MaryAnn blinked and swallowed. "Why?" she whispered.

"I want to know where Norah and Kieran are. I want to try and contact them. I think I should, Mom. I think maybe I was wrong to just break off the friendship the way I did. It doesn't feel right."

MaryAnn sat back against the door of the cupboard, looking suddenly weary.

"Please just leave it be," she said, scarcely audible.

Luke stared at her, amazed. It was like he was seventeen again and she was trying to keep him from danger. Trying to protect him from getting hurt, from getting lost in the Janvik abyss.

"Mom, I just want to talk to them," he said, reassuringly. "I don't see the harm in that."

"Please just leave it be," his mother said again, louder this time.

Luke could tell she knew something that he did not.

"Mom, what is it?"

His mother looked long into his face before answering. "Luke, please just let this go. Don't go poking around in stuff that doesn't have anything to do with you anymore."

"Why not, Mom? That was ages ago. What's the big deal?"

MaryAnn rose slowly to her feet, walked the few steps over to the kitchen table and sat down across from Luke. Her eyes were communicating something to him; he could feel it, sense it. There was more to the sad story of Norah and Kieran Janvik. He was sure of it. Something had happened after Belinda took her children back to California. Something awful. And his mother knew what it was. Luke could feel something beginning to gnaw at the edge of his emotions. It was a strange mixture of dread and understanding. He waited for her to tell him.

Finally she spoke. "Luke…Kieran died last year," she said softly, not daring to look at him. Two of the five words she spoke ricocheted across Luke's mind like darts.

Kieran. Died.

Luke could not picture it. Could not fathom it.

Died.

"What?" he exclaimed.

MaryAnn shook her head, obviously unhappy with how the morning was turning out. "He drowned. In the ocean."

"Are you sure? How do you know this?"

"Because she buried him here! She—" but his mother broke off.

"She? Belinda? Belinda buried him here?"

"No, not Belinda. Norah did. Belinda's been dead for a few years. Drug overdose. All that money, and that's all she could think to do with it!"

"What money? They don't have any money!" Luke stiffened. "Mom, how do you know all this?"

"Because we got the fax at the newspaper about the interment, Luke. You didn't see it because we didn't run it. Dick Foshay from the funeral home called us and said it was sent in error. Dick said Norah told him she didn't want to run the death notice. She just wanted a private burial. Here. In Halcyon. And as for the money, well that was all over the newspapers!"

"What newspapers? What money?"

His mother brought a hand up to her forehead and rubbed it. "The *San Diego Union Tribune,* other California papers, even Carrow got a hold of it. Dad didn't run the story, Luke."

"*What* story?" Luke said.

"The police initially suspected that Norah had killed her brother. That she had gotten him onto that boat and then pushed him overboard because Kieran had half of Belinda's estate."

"Estate? Belinda had an *estate?*"

"Belinda married again when they got back to San Diego. Some man with an export business in Mexico. The papers said he was involved with a drug cartel in Colombia. I don't know if that is true. But he was rich, Luke. He put something like three or four million dollars in the bank in Belinda's name when they married. The papers said he just disappeared one night a few years ago; there were rumors that a hit man was involved. I don't know if that's true either. But I do know Belinda died of a drug overdose a few months after her husband disappeared. Belinda's estate went to Norah and Kieran. And Norah was the sole beneficiary of Kieran's half of that money if something should happen to him. There was just the two of them after Belinda died."

"But how could anyone think that Norah…" Luke couldn't finish the sentence.

"I don't know, Luke. I don't want to know."

Luke stared at the table, his thoughts reeling. "Why didn't you *tell* me?"

"Because I didn't want to have this conversation, Luke!" MaryAnn said, her eyes growing misty. "Your dad wanted to tell you, but I begged him not to."

Several long seconds of tense silence followed before Luke found his voice again. "Did you see her, Mom? Did you see her when she came?"

"No one saw her. She was only here for an hour, Luke. There was no one at the cemetery except her and Dick and the grounds-keeper who placed the memorial."

"Memorial?" Luke asked.

"Kieran's body was never recovered. I don't know why she wanted to place a grave marker *here* for him. After all that happened here."

"Where is she now, Mom?" Luke said, and it was almost like a command.

"Luke..."

"Where is she?"

"I don't know. Maybe Dick knows. I honestly don't know, Luke."

Luke thought of his unfinished manuscript stored away on his laptop, awaiting its ending.

This could not be it.

Luke rose from the table and grabbed the Halcyon phonebook from the basket by his mother's phone.

"Who are you calling?" his mother asked.

"Dick Foshay."

Late afternoon sunlight filtered through the leaves of the towering cottonwood as Luke made his way to the Janvik plot at Halcyon's cemetery. His steps were slow and measured. He felt compelled to pay his respects before heading out to Denver to-morrow. Dick Foshay had reluctantly told Luke he sent Norah's bill for the interment to an address in Beavercreek, Colorado. But that was a year and a half ago. He didn't know if it was still current. An Internet search had revealed nothing except news accounts of Kieran's death.

He had read the accounts on his laptop in his father's office, attempting to keep an odd kind of professional distance between himself and the words on the screen. But each sentence seem to bore into him. He had printed out one of the articles and now carried it in his pocket. He pulled it out now as he walked and re-read it:

> SAN DIEGO—Law enforcement officials have concluded that the drowning last month of Pacific Beach resident, Kieran Janvik, was in fact a suicide, after handwriting experts declared a suicide note found in Janvik's house was genuine. No charges are expected to be filed against the deceased's sister, Norah Janvik, 33, also of Pacific Beach, who was on board the ship with Kieran. Janvik when the 26-year-old apparently intentionally fell into ocean waters off the coast of San Diego.
>
> The brother and sister were an hour into a whale-watching trip on March 15 when another passenger on the ship noticed Mr. Janvik in the water, several yards away from the stern, and flailing his arms. Witnesses said that when Mr. Janvik was spotted in the water, Ms. Janvik was seen at the rail weeping and shouting her brother's name. A rescue attempt was made, but Mr. Janvik drowned before help could reach him. His body was not recovered.
>
> Police began to suspect foul play when they learned Mr. Janvik was a paraplegic, paralyzed from the waist down, and that his net worth was in excess of $2 million, with Ms. Janvik being the sole beneficiary. Investigators told the *Union Tribune* yesterday that they are no longer considering that Mr. Janvik's death might have been a homicide.
>
> "The handwriting experts concur that Kieran Janvik

wrote the note," said a spokesman for the district attor-
ney's office. "It would appear it was Mr. Janvik's intent
to end his life."

Ms. Janvik declined to comment when contacted by
the *Union-Tribune*.

Luke held the fluttering newspaper article in his hand as he
looked down on the gravestones that now lay at his feet. He read
the names on the slabs of granite one by one. *Kenneth Rodney
Janvik.* Nell Janvik's firstborn. The good son. The hero. Killed
in Vietnam in 1971 at the age of 25. *Darrel Winston Janvik.* Nell's
second-born. The wayward one. The troublemaker. Killed in a fight
in a bar parking lot. *Penelope Jane Janvik.* Dead of a heart attack—
or a broken heart—the year Luke had moved to Boston. Then the
last marker, the most recent one. *Kieran River Janvik.* Dead at 26
by drowning. A drowning in the company of the whales he had
loved as a child.

Luke stood for a few minutes longer. He turned to go and
folded the newspaper article as he walked away. He placed it
back in his pocket to rest between his flight itinerary and a slip of
blue stationery that bore words of long-ago hope—a poem about
whales. Memories of that night in the tree house reading Norah's
poem swept over Luke.

If nothing else, he would return the poem to its rightful
owner.

23

Luke eased the rental car out of the parking lot as planes ascended and descended overhead in the sky above Denver's airport. He took out of his briefcase the directions he had printed off the Internet using the address Dick Foshay had given him. In his pocket he carried Norah's poem. It would take him a couple hours to get to Beavercreek, traffic permitting. A couple hours to prepare himself to see her.

The last time he'd seen her she'd collapsed onto the grass by her wounded brother. He'd tried to say something meaningful in those horrible moments before the ambulance came and took Kieran, but only useless words had come. He'd just knelt beside her and said the thing people say when they're dazed by circumstances and can think of nothing else: "It'll be okay, it'll be okay."

But it had not been okay.

And he had not spoken to her since.

He prayed as he drove that the right words would come this time.

All the right words.

He found without any trouble the quiet, wooded county road that would take him to her house. He was nervous as he drove up the winding hill. There was every possibility she wouldn't be home and he would have to come again tomorrow. Or the next day. Or the next. Or that maybe this was no longer her house.

His breath caught in his throat as he neared a wooden mailbox that bore the name "Janvik" in peel-off letters. He wondered for the first time if she had ever thought of changing her last name.

He drove up a driveway lined with firs and aspens, and the house came into view. It was made of logs burnished brown, and the walls looked warm and strong in the late-afternoon sun. The multipaned windows were trimmed in dark green. A half-barrel full of pansies nodded their purple, yellow, and white heads as he pulled up, stopped the car, and got out.

A light was on in the house, visible from the porch, but there was no sound. No barking of a dog, no music, no voices. Nothing to indicate someone was inside. He stood by his car for a moment before walking up to the heavy wooden door and raising the knocker. He was a little annoyed that his heart seemed to be beating too fast. *Okay, God. This doesn't have to be a big deal, right?* he whispered as the knocker fell. *We're just two old friends getting reacquainted. Happens all the times at class reunions. It's no big deal.*

But when the door opened and he saw Norah standing there, he involuntarily sucked in a breath in surprise. For a moment there was nothing but the continuation of the seventeen years of silence between them. She looked older, of course. Her face and skin were tanned and etched with tiny lines, and her honey-blonde hair was even lighter, owing to little splashes of sun-induced highlights. Her eyes were the same, yet different. The same shade of gray, but less luminous than he'd remembered. They looked…faded. She was wearing washed-out jeans and an oversized khaki man's shirt. He wondered for a split-second if she was indeed alone in the house. But he dismissed the thought as quickly as it had come. He somehow got the impression from the way she was looking at him that she'd been alone for a long time.

"Norah," he said.

She blinked. Surprise at seeing him was evident in her dull eyes, but as he waited for her to respond, the shock seemed to melt away.

"You're a little late," she finally said.

He waited for her to crack a smile or say his name or step aside to let him in. She did none of these things.

"Late?" he said lamely, wondering if he knew what it was he was late for. He didn't want to consider it.

She looked past him to see if he was alone, if there was anyone in the car with him. If there were any more surprises in store.

"You just happened to be in the neighborhood?" There was no inflection in her voice.

"No. Yes. I mean, I came here to see you."

"Why?" she said in the same impassive voice.

"Because I wanted to see you."

She hesitated, and Luke thought perhaps he wasn't going to be invited in after all. He hadn't exactly expected her to burst into tears of joy at seeing him, but he hadn't expected this response either. She seemed hostile.

"I suppose you'd like to come in and talk about old times, huh, old friend?" she said in a flat tone. Her face was expressionless.

"May I?" he said, not responding to the mockery.

She motioned him inside, and he followed her into a large room with tall windows on one side, an open kitchen on another, and a sitting area on another. The whole area was cluttered with newspapers, magazines, and CDs. An open laptop lay on the sofa. Several Mexican blankets were thrown over its back and sides as well. The fireplace at the far wall was made of huge stones. The firebox inside was dark and empty, though, and only one small lamp burned in the corner of the room. The rest of the room lay in a relaxing, dusky shade of late afternoon auburn.

Luke was trying to see from the surroundings what Norah had made of her life. But the house and its contents communicated nothing to him. It looked like a quiet place where not a whole lot happened. *A great place to write,* he thought. But there was nothing to indicate what she liked, what she valued, aside from her privacy. He felt like an intruder.

"Would you like some tea?" she said quietly, walking into the kitchen.

Well, that's a start, he thought. "Sure. I'd love some."

She took two mugs out of her dishwasher and set them down on the counter next to the stove. Luke was glad the water was already hot, that she'd already been in the middle of making tea when he'd knocked on her door. Waiting for a teakettle to boil would have been uncomfortable. Norah said nothing as she slipped a tea bag into each cup and poured the water. While the tea steeped and Norah maintained her silence, he looked at the titles on her bookshelves, hoping to gain a little understanding into the person she'd become.

Books on the ocean, the desert, and the solar system filled one shelf; a row of poetry anthologies filled another. Then on another shelf sat a small stack of books that were all the same. The volumes lay flat, one on top of the other. He bent to see the title, wondering why she would keep six copies of the same book. The spine read "*'Shallow Water' and other Poems*—Andromeda Hickler."

Andromeda Hickler.

Hickler was Belinda's last name. Andromeda was Norah's middle name. He picked up one of the copies and turned to the inside flap. A tiny thumbnail photo of the author revealed the profile of Norah Janvik. Norah had written the book.

"This…this book of poetry," he said, holding the book up and looking at her. "It's yours?"

She looked up and blinked. Was she mad or embarrassed that he'd found her book and figured out she was the author? He couldn't tell. She didn't appear to be glad.

"Yes," she said, lifting out a tea bag and wrapping it tightly around the curved edge of a spoon.

"That's wonderful, Norah. I mean, really great."

She shrugged and turned her attention to the second tea bag.

Luke wanted to tell her he was a writer, too. That they still had this wonderful thing in common. But it didn't seem like the right moment to talk about himself. He didn't get the impression she'd be all that interested in what he had done with his life. Besides, that wasn't the reason he'd come to see her. He stepped away from the books and pulled in a deep breath.

"Norah, I was so sad to hear of Kieran's death. I'm so sorry for your loss," he said. His voice sounded strange in his ears. She looked up at the mention of Kieran's name but quickly went back to the tea bag, saying nothing.

"And I heard you recently lost your mother, too," he continued. He felt like he was babbling. But he had to fill the silence. "I'm so sorry."

She looked up again, and the expression on her face seemed to be one of amusement.

"So where exactly are you suddenly getting all this information, Luke?"

She'd said his name for the first time.

"What?" he said, still getting over the sound of her saying his name.

"I *said*, where exactly are you suddenly getting all this information?"

"I've…been home, in Halcyon, for the last few weeks. My dad had a stroke. A bad one. I've been keeping the paper in print for my parents until we could decide what to do."

"Luke to the rescue," she said, but it was almost like she was saying it to someone else. Or maybe to no one. "And for your information, my mother died seven years ago," she continued, pouring milk into one of the mugs. "I wouldn't exactly call that 'recently.'" She looked up at him with the milk carton poised above the other mug. It took him a second to figure out she was asking him wordlessly if he wanted milk in his tea.

"No...thank you. My...I thought it had only been a few years ago. I'm sorry. I didn't know."

"Well, of course you didn't know. How could you?" She picked up the spoon and stirred her tea.

He waited for a moment to see if she'd ask about his dad's condition or make even the smallest gesture of concern for him. But she just stirred her tea.

"I was surprised to hear you were in Colorado," he said, deciding to change the subject. "When I heard you'd moved to California I thought you would stay there for good."

She stopped stirring, raised the spoon, and let the drips fall into the mug. "Well," she said quietly, "where I live is really no one's business but my own."

"Well, of course, I only meant—"

"I know what you meant, Luke. But did you really think I would stay where my brother drowned?"

She put the spoon in the sink. Her words swirled around in his head.

"Sorry, Norah. I don't know what I was thinking."

She said nothing as she brought the tea over to the coffee table. He took a seat in a chair across from the sofa and reached for his mug.

"So, you like Colorado?"

"It's fine."

"Keeping busy?"

"I manage to find a reason to get up each day."

He took a sip of his tea. It was blistering hot. He again waited for her to ask about his life. She didn't.

"I live in Connecticut now. Married and have two little girls. I am a writer, too, actually. Mystery novels. You ever heard of the Red Herring series?"

She sipped her tea. "I don't read much besides poetry and biographies. Getting caught up in genre fiction is rather a waste of time, in my opinion. I don't see there's much purpose in reading about people who don't exist."

Luke was surprised into silence. He wondered if it would be rude to ask for some aspirin. He was getting quite a headache.

He took another tentative sip. She set her mug down and looked at him. Waited for him to say something else. Challenged him without words to say something else. *Fine,* he thought. *Small talk doesn't interest you, so no more small talk. Let's just get right to the heart of it, and I'll get out of your house.*

"You put up a grave marker for Kieran in Iowa," he said. It was not spoken like a question, but they both knew it was one.

She took her time answering. She casually cocked her head as if to communicate that what she had done was unremarkable. "He needed to have a memorial somewhere. It would have been kind of hard to put up a grave marker in the Pacific Ocean."

He stiffened. Sarcasm just didn't fit her. At least, it hadn't when he'd known her.

"But why Halcyon? After all that happened there?" he said, pretending he hadn't been bothered by her comment.

She took a sip and stared at him over the rim of the mug. Her eyes communicated that surely he knew the answer to that.

Maybe she'd been trying to make peace with the Janvik family by placing a memorial to Kieran between the graves of their father and their hero uncle. It would make sense then.

"Because that's where Tommy is," she said tonelessly. But in his head Luke heard, *Because that's where Tommy is, you idiot!*

Of course. How could he have forgotten? The shoebox, the begonias, the afternoon sun, the words spoken, the song of farewell to a good friend—it all suddenly came back. Norah had done one last, brave thing for her brother. She'd placed a witness to his existence near the remains of his innocent childhood and the best friend who'd shared it with him.

"Why didn't you write to me?" The tone in Norah's voice surprised Luke as much as the question did. He raised his head to look at her, and the images of the cemetery, the shoebox, and Kieran fled. She sounded young again, as if the expanse of seventeen years had collapsed and the two of them were back where it had all started. He felt young as well when he answered.

"What?" he said, though he had heard her.

"Why didn't you write me?" she repeated, but this time she sounded aged with cares and woes. He felt a prickle of fear crawl up his neck. She sounded like she'd been cheated out of something very precious. She was angry. He wanted to believe he didn't understand why, but…When Belinda had come back and Kieran got shot and Nell went to jail—when Norah's entire world got thrown off kilter—she'd wanted him to come to her rescue. And he hadn't even tried.

"I didn't know what to say, Norah. I didn't know what to do." He remembered how much he'd wanted to forget everything. "I was only seventeen."

Something dark and fiery veiled her eyes. He didn't realize until after he'd said it that he'd said the wrong thing.

"And I was sixteen!" Her eyes were bright with anger. "I was sixteen, and I was alone, afraid—and in love!"

The words shot out of her mouth like darts. He could not keep himself from trying to back away. He felt the chair back against him and stiffened. Hot tea spilled onto his fingers. The words he least expected to hear from her churned in his head. *In love. In love. In love.*

"How could you have done that to me?" She continued in a softer voice, but the sting in her accusation was no less. He felt it and flinched. He knew she meant, how could he have given up on her? But he was wondering how he could not have seen she'd fallen for him. He'd known she was alone and afraid. And he *had* wanted to help her but didn't know how without sinking deeper himself.

But he'd never wanted to consider that while he had managed to avoid falling in love with her, she had been unable to do that with him. And he'd eventually willed himself to forget her—a little more each day—because that was what he figured made the most sense. It had never occurred to him she would do the exact opposite. That she would spend every day—for who knows how long—waiting for him to come to her rescue, while he spent every day waiting for the memory of her to fade. An image of Téa came to mind, and he suddenly realized when his waiting had ended. He wondered for just a split second when Norah had stopped waiting.

"How could you have done that to me?" she said again.

"Norah, I didn't know what to do," he repeated.

"Is that really the best you can offer?" she said wearily, like she'd already heard this excuse many times before and it meant nothing.

"I'm sorry," he said, shaking his head. The silence that followed screamed at him. "Norah, did you ever try to call me after... after..." He didn't know how to finish the sentence. *After what? After he forgot about her?*

"I called Matt."

She said the three words expressionlessly. They fell about his ears like stones.

"When?" he said quietly, trying to picture the conversation in his head.

"The summer you turned twenty, Luke. The summer you brought your girlfriend Amy home to meet your parents. I called him to see where you were. He told me."

Luke slumped back in his chair. He put the mug he held on the table next to him. "Why didn't you just call *me?*" he said, looking up at her.

"All those years I spent protecting myself from falling for you," Norah said quietly, as if she were not addressing him at all. Then she fixed her gaze—and her voice—on him. "I gave your father *my address!* Wasn't it obvious I expected you to write me? You just sent that one pitiful note that said nothing. I shouldn't have had to call you, Luke. I shouldn't have had to chase you down. *You* kissed *me,* remember?"

"Norah, I—"

"I never expected that you, of all people, would just turn and walk away from me. Especially then."

The unbidden memory of running over to Nell's house while the civil-defense siren wailed and ushering Norah and Kieran safely into his basement filled Luke's mind. He had come after her then and led her to shelter. The tornado had whirled above their heads, sucking roofs off houses, but she'd been safe with him. But after that horrible day nearly a year later, everything had changed. He couldn't charge in on his white horse and save the day. He hadn't known where to begin. He hadn't been sure he wanted to.

"I'm sorry! I didn't know!" he countered, his voice quivering.

"You didn't know because you didn't want to!" she said, angrily, but very much in control. Luke felt his own anger enveloping him and became aware he was shaking. Norah was not.

"You stopped caring about me," she added, clearly enunciating every word.

"That's not true, I..." he started to say, but stopped in mid-sentence. It *was* true. He *had* stopped caring. He had made himself stop.

Luke eased back down in his chair. But he didn't look at her. "If I had known..."

"If you had known *what?*" She folded her arms across her chest. "That I was afraid? That I was mired in grief for what had happened to my brother? That my mother went right back to her drugs? That I wanted you to come for me? You didn't already *know* these things?"

"I didn't know you were in love with me!" he exclaimed, raising his eyes to look at her. At least that much was true. To a point. He hadn't known how deeply she'd fallen. He'd thought she'd be able to walk away from it as easily as he had.

She held his gaze, as if challenging him to withdraw his last comment. When he didn't, she spoke.

"How could you *not* have known?" she said, simply.

He had an unexplainable sense that Norah suddenly pitied

him. That she pitied someone who couldn't see love when it was right in front of him.

Had he really missed it? Had he really been that dense? He searched his mind for glimpses of the person he was when Norah was taken from him. He was suddenly aware of two truths. He'd been afraid. Afraid of two things. He'd been afraid for her, and he'd been afraid *of* her. He'd been afraid of her need for a savior because he knew he couldn't save her from anything. And he hadn't known how to point her heavenward. No, it wasn't that he hadn't known how. He'd just given up trying. It had been easier to give up. It had been easier to forget.

"I'm so sorry, Norah. I should never have kissed you that day in the tree house."

She seemed to recoil when he said this. As if she'd been struck. And then she laughed sadly. "Why did you, then?" she whispered. "That was the only moment in my life when I felt like I really mattered to someone." She had turned her face away, as if she were speaking to no one.

"You've mattered to a lot of people, Norah. Kieran loved you. Your mother loved you. And despite all of her rough edges, I think Nell loved you, too."

"Ha!" Norah said, laughing again, but clearly in pain.

"The second time you went to your aunt's house in Minnesota, Nell cried outside on her back porch, Norah. I was in the tree house. It was the saddest thing I'd ever heard. I could hardly bear to listen to her. That was the day you and Kieran left."

"You heard her that day on the driveway, Luke," she countered. "When I found out I wasn't really her granddaughter—"

"That was fear talking," he interrupted. "She was desperate at that point. When Belinda first came up the driveway, Nell told her she wasn't taking her grandchildren. She yelled it. Don't you remember how angry and afraid she was, Norah? She never wanted to have to choose between the two of you."

More seconds of silence fell between them.

"Why did you come here?"

He looked up at her, wondering which answer he should give her.

"I wanted to see you," he finally said. "I wanted to see how you were doing. I know how close you were to Kieran. I know you probably miss him very much."

She watched him for a few seconds in silence. "That's it?" she said, incredulous. "You disappear from my life for seventeen years, and then you just suddenly decide you want to see me? You came all this way *to see how I'm doing?*"

Something told him he should say, *No, there's more,* but he just swallowed and said, "Yes. I came to see how you were."

"Well, as you can see, I am just fine, Luke."

She started to walk past him, like she was heading to her front door, ready to send him on his way. He reached out and stopped her. His hold on her arm was tender but firm.

"Norah, please."

She looked down at his hand on her arm and then eased herself out of his grip.

"What do you want from me?" she said bitterly, searching his eyes for an explanation.

He hesitated a moment, afraid to reveal his selfish reason for wanting to see her. But he knew he owed her an honest answer.

"I want to know how it *ends,*" he said quietly.

She could only look back at him in confused silence.

"I want to know what happened in San Diego, Norah. I need to know what really happened to Kieran."

24

Norah studied his face, surely searching for a motive. Luke made no attempt to disguise his reasons for wanting to know the truth about Kieran. Amid all the miscalculations he had made about Norah, he needed to be assured he was right about one thing—that she couldn't possibly have killed for money. His mind provided an image of Eden Damaris, wearing the green dress and sitting in a windowsill signing the words, *A woman like Clarice Wilburt doesn't kill for money. She kills for love.*

"You surely read all about it in the newspapers," Norah finally said. "I killed Kieran for his half of the money. Everyone knows that."

"That's not true," he didn't take his eyes off hers. "I refuse to believe it."

"So what? Who cares what you believe?"

"That note was real, wasn't it?" he continued, ignoring the insult. "Kieran wrote that suicide note, didn't he? He just couldn't take it anymore, could he? He didn't want to go on living without the use of his legs. Even the money couldn't make him happy. He was tired of pretending he didn't mourn the death of his dreams. It wasn't just an ordinary whale-watching trip, was it? He didn't just hurl himself overboard when you weren't watching, did he?"

Norah's eyes were wide and unmoving. She said nothing.

"Kieran probably needed help," Luke continued. "He couldn't do it alone. Not the way he wanted to go. You had to help him."

He paused for a moment to hopefully let this fresh revelation calm her into trusting him.

"It wasn't about the money at all, was it?" he added a few seconds later.

For the first time since he'd arrived, she looked weak. She felt for the sofa arm behind her and sank into the cushions. Luke resumed his seat across from her.

"It never was about the money, was it, Norah?" he said softly.

She closed her eyes and took several long breaths. Then she opened her eyes and looked at him.

"I don't have to explain anything to anyone."

He waited.

"I did what I did because I loved my brother," she said after a moment. "He deserved to have what he wanted. He should never have suffered the way he did. He just wanted to swim with the whales. That's all he ever wanted. So I let him."

She fell silent as two tears escaped her eyes and glided down her cheeks. She was looking past him to the long panes of glass in the living room, but he knew she wasn't really looking outside. She was looking at a frothy ocean, choppy from March winds, broken here and there by occasional flukes and barnacle-covered sides. Below her was a man in the water, desperately trying to swim without the use of his legs. He was heaving himself toward the rolling beasts, smiling.

"Tell me what happened, Norah."

At first she looked as if she had not heard him. But then she opened her mouth to speak, her eyes glassy and unfocused as the words came.

"He tried to do it by himself. But he just wasn't strong enough. He tried to do it when I wasn't looking. But I heard him struggling to get himself over the railing. We were at the back of the ship. All the schoolchildren were in the front. We were alone."

The words tumbled from Norah's mouth in rambling fragments. Luke sensed she'd spoken of this to no one. He said nothing.

"I turned and saw he was out of his wheelchair and half over the railing. I ran over and tried to pull him back, and when I did, he said my name in the saddest way. That's when I knew he *wanted* to go over. He wanted it. 'Kieran, don't!' I said. And he just said my name again in that sad way. 'Norah, let me go,' he said. 'I'm so close. I can see them.' And I looked out over the water, and I saw two whales breaching, filling the air above them with spray. And then I helped him get his legs over the sides. He held onto the railing. And I held onto him."

Norah paused for a bit, poised at the moment of recollection. Her cheeks were wet and shiny.

"Then he told me again to let go. And at first I couldn't. I was crying into his hair and shaking and I wanted so badly to pull him back over. 'Let me go, Norah,' he said again. He said it so gently. I tried and I couldn't. I kept saying his name over and over. And he kept saying, 'Let me go, Norah. Let me go.' "

She paused for a moment. Luke could see she was reliving the horrible moment when she did what Kieran had asked of her.

"I took my hands off him and stepped away from the railing. And he just hung there by his arms for a few seconds. Then...he let go. I ran to the railing and looked out and he was trying so hard to swim. He was digging his arms into the water like he was digging for treasure, trying to get as close to the whales as he could. And I was crying. I wanted to be happy for him, but I couldn't. Then someone from the other side of the boat saw him, just before he...slipped under. People were running over to my side of the ship and I was standing there, sobbing and shouting Kieran's name."

Luke was vaguely aware that tears had begun to form in his eyes and were slipping down his cheeks.

"There was a siren, or horn. It was so loud, and it scared all the children. Someone threw in a life preserver. Then a lifeboat went into the water. But he was already gone. The Coast Guard came. I don't remember much else. I don't know when we got to shore. The next thing I remember is sitting by an ambulance. The Coast Guard wanted to take me to a hospital. I hadn't been able to tell them anything. I just kept calling his name."

She stopped. She was still so instantly that he feared she'd withdrawn into some distant place in her mind where she wouldn't hear him anymore. He started to reach across to her to try to bring her back. But she turned slowly toward him as he leaned forward, and he could see in her face that a portal had closed. She had retreated behind the wall of her bitterness. It seemed there would be no more honest moments between them. Not today.

"Norah, I—" he began, but she didn't want to hear whatever it was he was going to say.

"I'd like for you to go now, please," she said flatly.

"Norah, I don't want to leave you like this," he began, not realizing the deadly irony of his words. But she began to laugh.

"Oh, that's good, Luke! You don't want to leave me like this? Like *this*? *Like this*? This is nothing compared to how you left me before." She stopped laughing, but she was looking at him with a hard grin on her face. "Besides, I have Kieran's half of the money, remember? I am *rich*. I have this nice house. A new Jeep in the garage. Acres of privacy. I've got it all. So go ahead, Luke. Leave me. Leave me like this!"

Her words hit him hard. But he tried to shake them off. He couldn't leave her there alone and in misery *again*. He had to get her away from her wretched place of isolation, if only for a little while. If he could somehow convince her to come back to Connecticut with him...She could stay in The Lab while he and Téa figured out a way to help her. *God, help me,* he pleaded in his heart. *Help me reach her.*

"Norah, I don't want you living the rest of your life alone and bitter like this. It's not how we're meant to live!"

She sat back on the sofa, seemingly untouched by what he said. She narrowed her eyes and the focus of her voice.

"This isn't about what *you* want, Luke. And who are you to say I'm bitter? You know *nothing* about me anymore. And what makes you think I'm alone? You think I'm still pining away after you? I've had lovers, Luke. Plenty of them."

He knew she meant for her words to cut him to the heart. He tried not to recoil.

"Norah, I'm not talking about having money and someone to share your bed. I'm talking about having *peace*. And having people to share your *life*."

She sat unmoving on the sofa, studying him, saying nothing. He wondered if maybe she was on the brink of surrender.

"You live a fairy-tale life, Luke," she said, without anger or malice. "You always have. It's just like Nell always said about you and your family when Kieran and I lived with her. We lived next door to Paradise. That's where you lived. That's where you've always lived. You don't have the faintest clue about what it's like to truly suffer. You go ahead and live happily ever after. Go ahead."

He could only stare as her words fell on him. *"God,"* he whispered. He didn't know what else to do.

"Please come with me, Norah. It's not a fairy tale—it's the real thing. Please come with me. Téa and I have room at our house—"

She interrupted him with a laugh. "Téa and *you?* You *are* naïve, Luke."

He ignored the comment. "Please, come with me," he tried again.

She blinked but held his gaze. A few moments of loaded silence hung between them.

"No."

He suddenly knew it was fruitless to try and convince her. It would not happen today. He couldn't picture it happening at all, but he would not do what he'd done seventeen years ago. He would not forget her. He rose slowly, ready to go, and sad from the knowledge of how it ended. At least for now. Then he suddenly thought of what lay in his pocket—the poem Norah had once written about creatures that cannot see the world of light and air above them. He reached into his pocket and pulled out the folded piece of paper, wondering if through her own words she would see what he could see.

"I found this in my old room," he said, handing it to her. "I thought you might want it back."

Her first reaction was reluctant curiosity. She stood up, took the paper, and unfolded it, seeming only casually interested in what he'd brought from their shared past. But when she saw the faded ink and the tender words of a young girl who seemed to have understood so much, the tightness left her face. But she did not appear to be at ease. On the contrary, the words of the poem seemed to involuntarily subdue her. She looked defenseless and afraid.

Luke followed her eyes across the page. He saw her take in every word.

> Underneath the rocking sea
> In the shadows of the deep
> The mighty kings in silent rule
> Swim the lengths of the salty pool
> Blast of steam, plume of spray
> Tails and fins like pennants wave
> But barely touch the world of man
> Content to stay where time began
> No show of force to change or scorn
> Nature's way, Earth's slow turn
> Unconcerned or unaware
> That a world of light and air
> Is not far; just there it lies
> Just above their hooded eyes.

"You kept this," she said quietly, with no inflection in her voice.

"Yes," he said. "I love this poem. I loved it from the moment I first read it."

She said nothing as she fingered the page, not taking her eyes off the piece of paper in her hand.

For a moment, she looked as if she might give way to tears. Whether tears of regret or tears of desperation, he wasn't sure, but he imagined either would be a beginning of healing for her. But the moment passed. She folded the paper and tossed it onto her coffee table like it was yesterday's grocery list. There didn't appear to be anything more he could do or say today to change anything.

"May I call or write you from time to time?" he asked.

She laughed.

"You can do whatever you want, Luke. Just keep in mind you're a married man."

He winced. He'd meant nothing improper by his request. He started to walk toward the door, and she followed. He was inches from the door. Inches from leaving her—and he hadn't told her everything. He turned back.

"Norah, I'm writing a book, a memoir really, about what I… what *we* went through as kids. I think there's something to be learned from what happened to us. I—"

She interrupted him with a laugh. "Something to be *learned?* Just what you do you think we have *learned,* Luke? I am very curious. Tell me!"

Her gaze was steel. It reminded him of Nell. He shook the image from his head and tried to gaze back into those hardened eyes.

"I've learned that this life isn't all there is, Norah."

For a moment he thought she was actually picturing to herself something endless and beautiful, but the glimmer in her eyes lasted but a second.

"Congratulations, Luke. You'll be valedictorian for sure."

He swept aside her cynical comment and waited for the right words. There had to be a better way to say what he wanted to say. He thought of his father, then, sitting with him in the tree house on a cold Thanksgiving afternoon. He remembered that when they had climbed back into his bedroom the savory, blended aromas of sage, onion, and celery had enveloped them. He could almost smell it. The fragrance of heaven.

It was within reach. Not so far away. Just next door.

Paradise.

"You've been in the deepest of deep places," he said softly. "But it's still just above you, Norah. It's right above you. It always has been."

"What?" she demanded angrily. "*What* is right above me?"

"Everything you have ever longed for."

She said nothing for a few seconds.

"How do you know what I long for?" she said softly, but clearly challenging him to supply the answer.

He remembered back to the day he'd kissed her, to the moment *before* he'd kissed her, to the moment when she'd told him she ached for the day when everything would be right but didn't think it would ever come. His mind took him back to the moment when he'd had a chance to show her the way to God and wasted it.

"Because I want the same things," he replied, matching her tone. "We all do."

She said nothing…only waited.

"We all want to be in a place where, finally, everything is as it should be." Regret made his voice sound thick in his ears. "We all want a place where we can have the beautiful sand dollar *and* the little white birds. A place where we can have them both."

Norah's hand instinctively went to her neck, as if she meant to finger a long-ago necklace. But her neck was bare, and her fingers met only skin.

"There is no place like that…" she whispered.

"Yes, there is."

"Not for me."

"Especially for you."

She swallowed, as if a question had been poised on her lips and she'd pulled it away, sending it back to the deep places inside her.

"Goodbye, Luke." She didn't meet his eyes.

"Don't turn your back on God forever, Norah."

"Goodbye," she said again, eyes raised. And this time there was no hostility in her stare, only sadness.

"I will write you," he said, touching her arm. She looked at him and slowly pulled her arm away.

He wanted to hug her goodbye, but he knew she would not welcome it. A kiss on the cheek would not be welcome either. Nor appropriate. Shaking hands—like two business associates—would be laughable. He stood on the threshold, half in and half out of her house. She stood just to his right, waiting for him to leave, arms folded across her chest. Twilight was dappling the porch with spent sunlight.

"If you change your mind about coming to see us in Connecticut—" he began, but she cut him off.

"Goodbye, Luke."

He hesitated just a second longer.

"Good night, Norah."

He turned and walked to his car. After he got in and started the engine, he looked up and was surprised to see that Norah was still standing in her doorway, watching him. In that final moment he noticed that directly in front of his car stood a giant elm, just like the one that grew between their houses when they were children. He turned his head back to her and, on impulse, pointed upwards—their old sign for "meet you in the tree house after dark."

Elm tree, he mouthed to her through the car window. He saw her raise her eyes to the tree shading her house. When she looked back down he thought perhaps he saw a glimmer of hope in her face. It was difficult to tell in the failing light.

And he was suddenly struck by the knowledge that he was also pointing to the sky, to the expanse above them, beyond which lay so much.

∾

Luke spent the night in a Denver hotel that offered an early-morning shuttle service to the airport. It took him only a couple hours to write the last pages of his manuscript in the quietness of his room—the words on the screen were echoes of the words shared at Norah's house. As he typed the last few sentences, he sensed no regrets about coming to see Norah, though his emotions felt raw and exposed from the encounter. He knew now how the memoir ended...but he also knew it wasn't truly the end. He had Norah's address safely in his pocket. He would never again be without it.

The last sentence reverberated in his mind long after he'd turned the computer off.

The outstretched branches of Norah's elm tree filled my rearview mirror as I drove away, as if reaching in anticipation for what waits above the sky...

EPILOGUE

A September sun was starting to inch its way down to the Connecticut horizon as Luke clicked his cell phone off and placed it on his copy of *Shallow Water*, which was resting on the patio table.

Téa poked her head out of the door to the kitchen. "Was that Alan?"

"Yep."

"And?"

"And he doesn't like it."

His wife stepped out into the twilight. "Why not?"

"It's too personal, too spiritual, too not Red Herring," he said, squinting up at her.

"Well, of course it's not a Red Herring book," she said, angrily. "It's not meant to be. And what's wrong with writing something spiritual?"

"It's not what my readers want." He was repeating what his editor had told him.

"How does he know what *your* readers want?"

"He gets paid to know, Téa," he said, leaning forward in the chair. "Maybe he's right."

"He's *not* right. What else did he say?"

"That people don't want to read this kind of stuff after a long day at work. They want to be entertained. They like Red Herring books because the bad guy never gets away with anything. Good always wins out. It makes them feel better about their world."

He looked up. "They want the happy ending," he added and winked.

"Did he use those exact words?" she said, narrowing her eyes.

He grinned. "He did."

"Well, that's just laughable. Happily-ever-after books are so overrated."

Luke couldn't help but chuckle.

"You don't seem very upset," she continued.

"I'm not. I don't regret writing it, Téa. It's the smartest thing I've ever done. Maybe it was meant just for me. Maybe there *is* no audience for it right now."

"That's silly. Of course there is!"

"Well, we'll see. I'll give it to Carmen and see what she can do with it."

"So what about Alan?"

Luke looked up at her. "We've set a new deadline. I still have those ten chapters. I only need ten more. I have until October 31 to finish it—I think I can make it."

"So, you know where to go with the story then?"

"I think so," he said, nodding. "I've decided Eden was right about Clarice Wilburt. She killed for love, not for money."

"So does that still make her the bad guy?"

He shook his head. "Not really. It makes her someone readers can still care about. Readers will like her, they'll sympathize with her. I'll dream up someone else to be her accomplice. Someone who doesn't love. Someone readers can loathe."

"And that's what readers want?" Téa chuckled.

"Yeah, I think they do. They want good to prevail. They want the ending to make them feel good. Hopeful."

She came up behind him to rub his shoulders. "I guess I can understand that."

Talking about hope brought Norah to his mind as Téa's touch soothed him. He'd written her three times in the past two months but had heard nothing from her until two days ago. At his request, she'd sent him a copy of *Shallow Water*. She'd signed the title page with nothing but her name. But the capital "N" was large and flowing—it didn't look like the signature of a woman who has no hope. He'd also been noticing that while some of the poems in *Shallow Water* were dark and bleak, others were fragrant with expectation. Norah had not completely forgotten how to dream.

It was not too late.

In his last letter he had asked her to join their family for Thanksgiving. The note she'd included with the book said she was considering it, "If I can get away." He pictured her unhurried, quiet life in Colorado and was confident there was nothing to keep her from coming except lack of persistence on his part. *That* was not going to be a problem. He would not let her down again. Somehow he would convince her to come.

"We'd better start getting ready to go, don't you think?" Téa said, interrupting his thoughts. "Traffic might be a problem with the weather being so nice. People will be out tonight."

"I just want to sit here a little longer," he said, patting her hand on his shoulder, feeling no hurry to get ready for the Connecticut Literary Awards banquet. "It's so peaceful here."

"Okay, I'll take my shower first, then." She squeezed his shoulder and turned to walk away. "By the way, the woman in green you saw at the last dinner—the one that looks like Eden Damaris? She won't be there."

He spun his head around. "*What?* How do you know that?"

His wife patted him on the head as she walked away. "'Cause I know who she is."

"You do not!"

"Do so."

"You're toying with me," he said, grinning and turning back around.

"Am not," she replied, coming back to the table. "When we got this invitation and you said we'd be going, I asked around."

"Yeah, right!"

"I did! I know who to ask when I need to know something. So I know who she is. I know her name. Want to know?"

He turned back toward his wife, who was smiling broadly with the knowledge she possessed. He smiled back, remembering how troubled he'd been that night he'd seen the woman in green. How complicated his life had seemed on that spring evening five months ago. How the image of the woman in green had been the catalyst to move him into a new stage of his life as a writer, as a father and husband, as a believer. It was almost like a divine apparition from a world apart had set things in motion for the fresh enthusiasm he now had for writing and for living. He didn't want to ruin the effect with a mortal name. He suddenly had no desire to know who the woman was.

"No, I don't," he said.

"Liar!" Téa said playfully.

"I really don't! If I find out who she is, then it will remove the mystery—you know, the pleasure and intrigue of not yet knowing what I really long to know. It will make her mortal."

She looked back at him, open-mouthed. "Are you nuts? She's just the daughter of—"

"I don't want to know whose daughter she is!" he yelled, putting his hands over his ears.

Téa stepped in front of him and looked down at his face. She pulled his hands away from his head. "You're serious."

"I'm serious."

"You really don't want to know."

"You're right—I don't."

She stood up and put her hands on her hips. "Not knowing would drive me absolutely crazy!"

He grinned and looked past her at the grove of birch trees beyond The Lab. "I think it drives me forward."

"What? *What* drives you forward?" She was laughing.

"The lovely lure of the Not Yet," he said, smiling up at her.

She shook her head. "Writers," she muttered and turned toward the back door again.

Just then the door to the guest cottage burst open and Marissa and Noelle came running out of it in leotards and fairy costumes.

"What have they got on?" Luke asked, smiling.

"Oh, they wanted to show Grandma and Grandpa their fairy costumes for the ballet recital next weekend."

Their daughters sprinted up the path to the patio.

"Look, Daddy!" Noelle called out. "We can fly!"

The girls sailed onto the patio.

"This part's coming off on mine," Marissa said, showing Téa a place on the skirt where the material was separating from the waistband.

"Oh, dear. Let's go inside and pin it right now before it gets any bigger. Come on, sweetie."

Téa and Marissa went into the house as Noelle twirled about on the patio, watching her skirt ripple through the air. "Are my wings moving?" she asked him.

He smiled, looking at the glittered-covered wings hanging a bit lopsided on her back.

"They look great. You look just like an angel."

"Except I'm a fairy. Angels are in heaven."

He leaned back in his chair, watching her twirl. "Yes, they are."

"I don't think there are any fairies in heaven."

"Probably not."

Arthur the cat sauntered onto the patio then, and Noelle stopped twirling and scooped him up.

"Will there be cats in heaven?"

Luke looked at his daughter, standing in a patch of fading sunlight and stroking the cat. He had met Norah when she was just about the same age. And when she was almost as innocent of the sometimes-weary weight of the world as his own child.

"I think everything that makes us truly happy will be there," he said.

"All the best things."

"Yes, all the best things."

He stood and reached for his cell phone and his copy of *Shallow Water*, tucking the book under his arm. He watched, smiling, as his daughter jumped off the patio onto the grass, twirling with her arms stretched toward the heavens, the amber glow of spent sunlight glinting off her glittering, transparent wings.

A Note to Readers

One of the first gospel songs I remember hearing after I surrendered my heart to Jesus was the one with this chorus:

> *This world is not my home; I'm just passing through*
> *My treasures are laid up somewhere beyond the blue*
> *The angels beckon me from heaven's open door*
> *And I can't feel at home in this world anymore.*

It thrills me to know that I was created to long for heaven, that someday it will be home to me. Home *for* me. And it thrills me to know that I am being beckoned, and that there is an open door to that beautiful place. I trust you sensed the pull of your own heart toward heaven as you read *In All Deep Places*. It was my prayer as I wrote it, and is still as you read it.

Discussion questions for *In All Deep Places*, as well as questions for my other books, are available on my Web site at www.susanmeissner.com under the "For Book Clubs" link. There is also an e-mail link for you to contact me if you so desire. I would love to chat about heaven with you!

Yours in Christ,
Susan Meissner

Susan Meissner is an award-winning newspaper columnist, pastor's wife, high-school journalism instructor, and the author of three previous novels. She lives in rural Minnesota with her husband, Bob, and their four children. If you enjoyed *In All Deep Places*, you'll want to read her other novels...

Why the Sky Is Blue...What options does a Christian woman have after she's been brutally assaulted by a stranger...and becomes pregnant? Happily married and the mother of two, Claire Holland must learn to trust God "in all things."

A Window to the World...Here is the story of two girls—inseparable until one is abducted as the other watches helplessly. Years later the mystery is solved—and the truth confirmed that God works all things together for good.

The Remedy for Regret...Tess Longren is twenty-eight, single, and at a crossroads in her life. She finally has a job she enjoys as well as a proposal of marriage from a man she loves, but she can't seem to take hold of a future filled with promise and hope. Her mother's long ago death remains a constant though subtle ache that Tess can't seem to move past. When her childhood friend Blair Holbrook asks her to accompany her to their childhood home to resolve a situation left unsettled fifteen years ago, Tess falsely imagines that by helping her friend find peace, she will find contentment for herself.

Here is a masterful novel about finding the courage to change a painful situation and bearing what cannot be changed...about understanding the limitations of an imperfect world and the vast resources of a perfect God.

Other Good
Harvest House Reading

AFTER ANNE
Roxanne Henke

Newcomer Anne and aloof Olivia's unlikely friendship blossoms in the midst of misunderstandings, illness, and new life. Will Olivia, drawn to Anne's deep faith, turn to God when her life is threatened?

THE GATE SELDOM FOUND
Raymond Reid

The Gate Seldom Found weaves the threads of true stories drawn from a little-known Christian fellowship that flowered late in the 19th century. Its origin and setting have been imaginatively recast among the farms and villages of historic Ontario.

THE EDGE OF THE WORLD
Phil Callaway

Adventure worthy of a Mark Twain novel, a cast of colorful characters, and a mysterious illness await Terry as he tries to hide his guilt and control his fear of the consequences his actions might bring. A yearning for forgiveness and the hope of restoration lead him to even more amazing discoveries in a town called Grace.

INKLINGS
Melanie Jeschke

It's 1964, and young American Kate Hughes anticipates finding knowledge—and perhaps love—at Oxford University. Kate's heart is torn between two men, and her convictions are challenged as her vulnerability draws her to a rendezvous she may regret.

HARVEST HOUSE
PUBLISHERS

Fans of Susan Meissner also enjoy the fiction of Roxanne Henke's wonderful Coming Home to Brewster series....

HERE'S WHAT THEY SAY ABOUT *AFTER ANNE*

From California: "A dear dear friend gave me *After Anne* several weeks ago... Your book was awesome and should be sold with a box of Kleenex!"

From North Carolina: "I felt as though the characters were my best friends. The last time I cried this much was when I read James Patterson's *Suzanne's Diary for Nicholas.*"

From Oregon: "I could hardly put the book down. Oprah should know about this!"

From Christianbooks.com: "*After Anne* is probably my favorite [book of the year]. This moving story of an unlikely friendship between two women will have you laughing and crying and longing for a relationship like theirs."

From an Amazon.com reader: "I don't know how I got this copy of *After Anne* but however I got it, I am so glad I read it! It's just beautifully written—and so true...It is one of the must-reads for the coming year if not tomorrow."

From North Dakota: "We read *After Anne* for our book club in our MOPS (Mothers of Preschoolers) group in Fargo and all fell in love with it. We all kept saying even if you can not make it to book club this is a book you have to read."

AND BOOK NUMBER TWO, *FINDING RUTH*

From Virginia: "I read *Finding Ruth* after I finished *After Anne* and I thought this book couldn't be as good...but sure enough you did it again! You are my favorite author."

From California: "I just finished reading the last page of *Finding Ruth*....the tears went down my cheeks as I read it...But what kept me so on the edge.... was your showing me Brewster town. I could see everyone, even their laugh lines."

From Kentucky: "Your book couldn't have come to me at a better time. I struggle with contentment or lack of. Thank you for a touching story that fit quite nicely into my life. I was moved by it...If I had my way, your book would be topping all the best-seller lists."

From Indiana: "I chose your book from the new fiction section at our public library without realizing it was a Christian book...I could hardly bear to put it down."

Via e-mail: "I love your characters, all of them, even the broken ones. Even the selfish ones. Even the unlovable ones. I can't remember the last time a book has made me feel such empathy for a fictitious person, first with Anne and Libby and now with Ruth's friends and family. I feel like I know them personally."

AND BOOK NUMBER THREE, *BECOMING OLIVIA*

From Indiana: "I've been burning up the e-mail lines telling anyone who will listen that your books are required reading. Please hurry with number 4!!!!"

From North Carolina: "Just finished *Becoming Olivia* and loved it! ...Your Christian insight and faith shine through as realistic and practical without coming off 'preachy.'"

From South Dakota: "I could not put it down! I could relate to so many of the things Olivia went through, especially the struggle with depression and anxiety...*Becoming Olivia* was the first of your books that I have read, and I look forward to reading the others. Thank you!"

From Ohio: I've just read *Becoming Olivia* and am so moved. There are many words to describe the book, but none seem adequate enough."

Via e-mail... "I am a voracious reader and many authors have touched me, moved me and changed me but you are the first one I've written to. I needed you to know how important your writing is to people like me. Thank you."

"I just finished *Becoming Olivia* and *had* to write and tell you how much I loved it. I have read all 3 of your books...but *Becoming Olivia* especially spoke to me...I know that this had to have been a difficult book for you to write, but you did a superb job, as always."

"[*Becoming Olivia*] is amazing for its healing powers...I'm going to use the book in my clinical practice to give to patients who know they don't feel right but don't think it's bad enough to be classified as depression. Thanks for telling the story so beautifully."

"I cried and laughed through the whole book, finishing it in under two days!! This was the very first Christian fiction book I have read and I want more! I cannot wait to find your other two books so I can read them."

AND ABOUT BOOK FOUR, *ALWAYS JAN*

From "Dorothy": "I just finished reading *Always Jan*, and, like your other books, I loved it...God has truly given you a beautiful talent...one which I pray you will continue to use so that we can share in His goodness and mercy through your stories."

From "Ellen": "I just finished *Always Jan* and hated leaving Brewster as I read the last page...I absolutely loved this series...I want to go to Brewster and see these wonderful people. I want to go to Pumpkin Fest. I want to visit Aunt Ida. I wanted to buy her house. I want my life to be transformed like Jan's and Kenny's and I want to be a friend like Libby."

From "Nancy": "I just finished your book, and man! This is your best work yet!"

From "a housewife and mother in Indiana": "I just finished reading the fourth book in the Brewster series. Wow! What a read...Life can sure be difficult at times and a good uplifting honest book is a treasure."

And just released: the final volume in the Coming Home to Brewster Series, *With Love, Libby.*